VENGEANCE FROM THE DEEP

BLOOD OF THE NECALA

~ BOOK 2 ~

RUSS ELLIOTT

*This book is dedicated to my wife Danielle
and to my mother for always being there.*

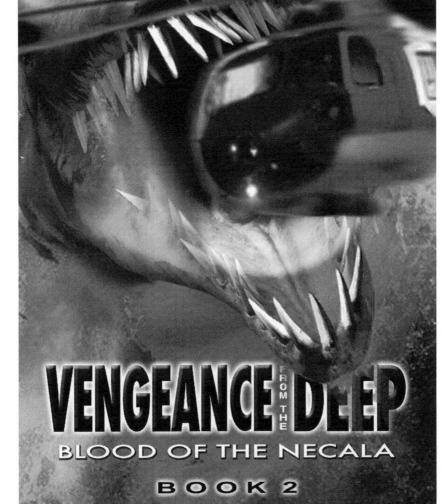

VENGEANCE FROM THE DEEP

BLOOD OF THE NECALA

BOOK 2

Chapter 1
THE SIGNAL

Archeologist John Paxton sat silently in the passenger's seat of the vintage Atlas Oryx military helicopter. The old craft was loud and drafty. Beside him, he could just make out his pilot, Kate, her headset and wavy black hair silhouetted against the evening sky. A glance to the right showed the hazy Indian Ocean flashing below. The light from the helicopter glided eerily over the mist. Every breath was like a punch in the face, a pungent reminder of the concoction of rotten meat and blood stowed in the cargo bay. John's mouth was perpetually dry from stress. He was exhausted, yet his mind spun faster than the thumping rotor blades.

Peering into the horizon, he pondered their destination, a state-of-the-art research ship, the *Nauticus II.*

Will it be the break we need? In an attempt to film the elusive giant squid, the ship had been tracking four sperm whales equipped with cameras and transmitters. Knowing that whales feed on squid, the crew hoped that the whales would lead them to the object of their study. But early that morning, when two of the whales were butchered, and one of the transmitters ended up wedged in a giant pliosaur's jaw, the expedition took a new direction. John prayed that the transmitter inside the creature was holding up.

It has to be, he thought. Otherwise, he knew that an ambush predator, which could lay in wait on the seafloor for up to two hours, would be nearly impossible to find.

John looked down at the tightness in his left forearm. In the fading light, he studied the myriad of scars running from his elbow to his wrist, souvenirs from his expedition to the island.

The island, the inauguration of this cursed nightmare.

In his mind's eye, he went back to that hellhole three hundred miles off Port Elizabeth. He still felt the ropes around his wrists as torches and half-painted faces flashed before him. The drumbeat still seemed to pulse through his veins. He remembered how he miraculously escaped with his life, only to spend two days adrift at sea before making it back to South Africa.

And that's when the real battle began.

He recalled turning on the news only to learn that he hadn't come back alone. The creature's swath of destruction flooded his mind, all the missing boats, the bloody footage. The face of every victim was etched into his brain. A familiar sense of guilt crept over him. But as always, the unrelenting guilt slowly manifested into the rage that now drove him. Lost in these thoughts, John stared downward at the sea.

Still, it troubled him deeply that the ship hadn't picked up a signal in nearly twenty-four hours. While he and Kate had spent the better part of the day prepping her backup chopper, rounding up chum, depth charges and such, the Navy had been searching. Nothing. Not even a whale carcass had turned up within fifty miles of the creatures last known position. *Maybe Admiral Henderson was right,* John feared. *Maybe the transmitter is no longer in the creature at all.*

Kate's voice crackled in his headset. "Wakie, wakie, we're only about fifteen minutes from the ship."

"And only a day late," John added. "Guess it's better late than never."

"We came pretty close to never," Kate scoffed. "I can wait to be trapped in the water with that bloody thing again."

~~~

A hypnotic blue hue radiated inside the *Nauticus II*'s surveillance cabin while Nemo and Nathan huddled over the tracking monitors. Their eyes were fixed on a red dot on monitor two.

"Still eight miles out, Captain," Nathan said. "Too far to pick up a scent."

The red dot disappeared from the screen, and Nathan picked up the mike.

Nemo grabbed Nathan's hand. "What are you doing?"

"I was going to relay the pliosaur's coordinates to the chopper that's on the way, like we promised them."

"Let's not be too hasty," muttered Nemo. He took the mike from Nathan's hand. "Yesterday, this Paxton was working with the Navy to destroy the creature. So we can't be too careful."

Nathan had finally heard enough. "This is insane," he demanded. "Since the last signal we relayed to Paxton yesterday, we've picked up five new signals from the transmitter in the creature. You can't just sit on this. You can't let the Navy search blindly for twenty-four hours when we know the creature's coordinates."

"The Navy doesn't have our best interest in mind," growled Nemo. "Besides, the beast has been staying about six to eight miles northeast of the ship. But soon, it will come close enough to pick up a scent. It has to…I can feel it."

"Our best interest." Nathan's lips curled in disgust. "There's a bigger picture here than our best interest. You're risking countless lives just so you can get footage. This is wrong. If it kills, while we withheld information that could have had it destroyed—that blood is on our hands."

It was as if Nathan had said nothing. Nemo thought for a long moment, staring at the gridded screen. "There's not much daylight left." He flashed a crooked smile "Originally, I only needed this Paxton character to bring us bait...but he could be of further use." He winked and keyed the mike. "We still may get footage of this beast before nightfall."

~~~

The helicopter glided low over the water while John stared anxiously out to sea. He was pumped. They were just ten minutes from the ship. Beside him, Kate had her headset off, while struggling to work a rubber band around her hair to create a ponytail with her free hand.

"Need some help with that?" John asked. But without her headset, Kate couldn't hear a word he said in the noisy cockpit. John went rigid when his earphones crackled. "Do you read? This is the *Nauticus II*. Over." John looked at Kate who was oblivious to the call, then pressed the headset more tightly to his ears. "We're here, Captain. Did you pick up a signal?" he asked excitedly.

"That depends," said Nemo.

John picked up on the reluctance in Nemo's voice. "What are you getting at, Captain?"

"Earlier, you said you were searching with the Navy...do you have any explosives on board?"

John glanced back at the crate of depth charges in the cargo bay. He laughed. "Captain, I'm just an archeologist. I'm afraid the Navy isn't big on issuing explosive devices to civilians. We were just tagging along as spotters. But we *are* loaded with chum." John bit his lip, hoping the captain would buy the fib. He looked at Kate again, who was finished with her ponytail. When she finally did notice that John was on the air, she mouthed the question: *Nemo?* John nodded, and she slid her headset back on to listen in. John remained silent, awaiting Nemo's answer. Finally, he heard, "All right, but do you have a camcorder onboard?"

"Sure do," John said with exaggerated enthusiasm. "Loaded and ready to go."

Kate looked at John, puzzled. She frowned and shook her head in an attempt to correct him. John held his finger to his lips: *Shhh.*

"Okay," said Nemo, still with hesitancy in his tone. "We just picked up a signal about eight miles northeast of the ship. But be sure to use the chum to lure the beast up first; I want good clear footage of it. Understand?"

Kate did a fist pump in the air. "All right," she roared into her headset. "Now we can drop the depth charges and blast that thing back to the Jurassic!"

John's shoulders slumped, and he rolled his eyes.

"Blast it!" Nemo growled. "Paxton, you lying—! You said you weren't armed. No one's blasting anything until I get it on film. I forbid it. This is the greatest zoological find of all time."

Kate was on the verge of ballistic. "Zoology my—"

John grabbed the cord to her headset and yanked her headset off, nearly taking her head with it. Her hair tousled about her face, she looked at him in disbelief.

John spoke frantically into his headset. "That's just the pilot. She's wound too tight emotionally. Needs some rest. Listen, Captain, I'm a scientist. I understand how you feel. Just give me the exact coordinates, and I'll get all the film you want—"

Kate's jaw dropped. She couldn't believe her ears.

When John realized Nemo had ended the transmission, he lowered his mike. "All the film you want of its carcass, that is," he added.

He looked at Kate who was still giving him the eye. "Your timing is impeccable. Relax. We're gonna blow that thing to oblivion. I was *trying* to make Nemo think we're on the same team; otherwise, I knew he wouldn't give me the coordinates, which he didn't, but he did say eight miles northeast of the ship. At least that'll get us close."

Kate grinned suddenly. "I'm impressed with your street smarts, cowboy," she said as his intentions became clear. "Uhhh, but would you kindly return my headset?"

Chapter 2
NEED FOR SPEED

Two miles east of Pearly Beach a young boy with curly, red hair, gazed through his bedroom window. Being on the second floor, he had a clear view of the ocean, twinkling against a beautiful sunset. "What a great evening to be on the water!"

With his shoes in his left hand, Mat carefully walked down the staircase, keeping his weight close to the wall to prevent the old, wooden stairs from creaking. At the bottom of the stairs, he peered around the corner into the kitchen.

The late sun streamed through the window as the open curtains lifted from the light ocean breeze. In front of the window, his mother hovered over the sink, preparing a late dinner for his little sister. The little blonde sat at the table, struggling to open a box of cereal.

"Don't open that. I've already fixed you something," said their mom.

"But I want cereal."

"Not for supper. Besides, that one's not good for you. It's loaded with sugar."

"But how come you buy it for us then?"

"I didn't. That's the cereal your father bought for you. He knows I hate for you to eat that sweet stuff!"

The little girl pleaded, "But Mom, it has fruit in it. It's got to be good for you."

"What are you talking about?"

The five-year-old pointed to the multicolored balls of cereal on the front of the box, "See? Look, it has munch berries!"

"Nice try, Christy." Her mom placed a bowl of soup on the table and took the box from the little girl's hands.

Peering from behind the corner at the foot of the stairs, Mat looked away from where Christy sat. His eyes drifted to the window on the door beside the kitchen, where he spotted his prized possession tied to their private dock. He watched the setting sun twinkle along the red metallic finish of the speedboat. It had been a gift he received last August on his fourteenth birthday.

When they were looking for just the right boat, his dad had insisted he didn't get one too powerful or fast. They'd finally decided on a small inboard engine.

A smile slowly formed on Mat's face. *But I've found ways around that!*

Finally, he saw the signal when Greg's hand waved outside the window. *It's about time*, Mat thought as he tiptoed across the kitchen behind his mother's back. Just as he touched the door handle, his mother's voice echoed behind him, "Ma-a-at! Where are you going?"

Mat grimaced as he opened the door. "Me and Greg are going for a quick spin before dark."

"You mean, Greg and I!" replied his mom.

"Yeah, sure, Mom. You can go too if you want!"

"You know what I mean!"

"Just kidding," laughed Mat, stepping into the doorway.

Her voice grew louder. "Well, this time you'd better not break anything on that boat! Because if you do, your father's not going to pay for it. He's spending a fortune trying to keep that thing on the water. If it breaks one more time, you're going to get a job and pay for fixing it your—"

"Okay, okay!" Mat quickly closed the door behind him.

Outside, Greg laughed. "I heard that. You haven't broken anything on the boat; what's with the lie?"

"So they'll give me money."

"To fix the boat that doesn't need fixing? Oh man. That's so wrong." Greg chuckled and shook his head. "Yeah, I told her I ran across some coral and had to get the hull repaired," Mat said as they walked further along the dock.

"So, what did you *really* get?"

Mat grinned. "A bigger carburetor and new intake."

"Why don't you just ask her for the money straight up? Your folks got plenty . . . I mean, your old man is a *doctor*!"

"She won't just give it to me without a good reason. You gotta know my parents." Mat stepped onto the red speedboat, mimicking his mother's voice, '*No! That boat's too fast already!*' So last month the windshield cracked, the prop broke, and of course, the hull had to be repaired and refinished from the . . . uh . . . coral incident."

Greg snickered. "Doesn't she get suspicious about your boat's bad string of luck?"

Mat sat down sideways in the driver's seat and wedged his feet into sneakers that hadn't been untied in months. "Nah, but I've got the engine about the way I want it. So I'll lighten up."

"You'd better before she makes you get a job."

"Yeah, no doubt." Mat shuddered dramatically, and they broke into hysterical laughter. With a press of the start button, the engine roared to life.

"So, does the new carb make a difference? Can you really feel it?"

asked Greg as he untied the bowline and hopped in.

"You tell me!" Mat slammed the throttle down causing a twenty-foot rooster tail as the boat rocketed away from the dock.

~~~

Staring ahead through the helicopter's windshield, John watched the sun slip lower into the open sea. Would there be enough daylight? The familiar tingling sensation rose in his stomach. Soon, he would again be face-to-face with the pliosaur, but this was a different round. He wasn't trapped on the seabed completely helpless. No, this time he was prepared; he had a way to kill it.

He'd better get ready.

Rising from his seat, he made his way into the cargo area and to the crate of depth charges. Searching around the floor, he picked up a crowbar. He called back to Kate, "Guess I should open these up, make sure we're good to go!"

Kate looked back. "Remember, before you drop one of those, if the target's shallow, give a three-second count first, or it'll detonate too deep!"

John looked at her, perplexed. "You sure? How do you know that?"

"Says so on the crate." Kate turned back to the windshield and shouted loud enough for John to hear: "Men! Do they *ever* read the directions on *anything*?"

~~~

Mat cruised across the water at about half speed, waiting for just the right moment to show Greg the boat's full power. He saw his opportunity when another speedboat appeared in the distance. He accelerated the boat just enough to pull close.

"Aaahhh, it's Dr. Phillips and his young girlfriend. He thinks that boat's so fast!" Mat pulled up closer until both boats were side by side.

Greg cupped his hands beside his mouth. *"Leeet's get ready to RUUUMBLLLE!"* he howled.

The older man glanced over, acting as if he was ignoring the two boys, but Mat knew better. He could see the doctor's hand slowly reaching toward the throttle. The strawberry blonde, obviously far younger than her counterpart, glanced over with a smile. Dr. Phillips' hand then rammed down the throttle. The bow rose from the water, and the black speedboat lunged forward. Mat eased into the throttle just enough to stay side by side. He saw the girl excitedly yelling at the older man, her words muted by the roaring engines. Mat could read her lips. *Faster! Faster!*

Mat shouted to Greg, "Hey, blow her a kiss!"

Greg lifted his rear end to the side of the boat and lowered the back of his shorts.

Mat laughed wickedly, yelling, "*See ya!*" and hit the throttle full bore. Greg fell to the deck, lily-white keister to the sky, as the speedboat became a shiny, red blur, passing the doctor's boat. Ten feet . . . twenty feet . . . their lead continued to grow until the doctor finally veered his boat off to the right, knowing he didn't have a chance. Mat looked back as the black boat headed in the opposite direction, but still he could see the young girlfriend laughing uncontrollably. He glanced at the instrument cluster and pulled back on the throttle. The roaring engine stopped, and the eighteen-foot speedboat slowly drifted in front of a brilliant sunset.

"Whoa, bro! This thing pulls like your old man's Porsche." Laughing, Greg yanked up his swim trunks.

"Yeah, the new carb did the trick," Mat agreed. "But look at the temperature gage. That's all it took to make it overheat. We'd better take it easy until I get the cooling system upgraded." He squinted into the horizon, then picked up a set of binoculars and focused them in the same direction.

"So, when do you think you'll have the bucks for the upgrade?"

Ignoring the question, Mat continued to stare out to sea. "Doesn't look like a freighter . . . more like a research ship. Cool! I'll bet that's the *Nauticus II*. Saw them on the news the other night. They're out here searching for the giant squid."

"Giant squid? Errr . . . And I was considering making a dive."

"Relax. Usually, those squid are way out where it's deep, really deep—over three thousand feet. Wonder why the ship is in so close? We're only around a hundred feet, practically in the shallows."

Mat tossed the binoculars onto the console. "So, you ready to head back—" He froze. Forty yards off port he saw something project from the water. The tip of an enormous fin rose higher then slapped the surface. "Whoa! You see that?"

"Yeah, the huge splash!" Greg pointed. "Come on, bro. We've gotta catch it. I've always wanted to dive with a whale shark!"

Easing into the throttle, Mat adjusted his course until they reached the spot where they saw the splash.

"This is the spot. Wow! Look at the size of the thing," Greg said excitedly, staring at the obscure shadow beneath the boat. He quickly slid on his dive fins.

As Greg grabbed his snorkel, Mat turned around in his seat. "Just make it quick. I didn't have supper yet, and I'm starting to get a little hungry."

"Yeah, yeah . . . you and your appetite." Greg slid the snorkel into his mouth and dropped backward from the stern.

~~~

Beneath the surface, Greg turned around and found himself less than two yards above a gray mass that completely filled his field of view. He marveled, *Wow, these things are a lot bigger than they look on TV!*

Then he noticed something that disturbed him to the core. *No spots.*

What set his heart to beating uncontrollably, however, was the lack of a dorsal fin. In its place, a jagged frill ran atop an armor-plated hide. Raising his gaze, Greg looked down along the huge wide back that led to the thick head.

As if sensing his presence, the creature turned its head. A red eye glared up at him. Slowly, the gigantic muscles behind the eye sockets rippled, and the mouth fell agape. The fading light in the water glittered across the bottom row of enormous spiked teeth.

Greg sprang from the water and landed on the deck, still swimming.

Mat sat with his feet propped on the steering console. "Bro, I said I was hungry. But you could have taken longer than that!"

"Get. Out. of. Here. Now," Greg gasped from the deck. His eyes were wild as he lay sprawled across the fiberglass.

"What the h—"

"It's NOT a whale shark down there!" Greg's voice reached increasingly higher pitches. "It's something else, and we need to get moving *now*!"

"How do you know tha . . . " Mat stopped midsentence when he saw a gigantic upper jaw rise above the stern. The boat fell dark in its shadow. Mat grabbed the throttle just as the jaws began to close. The boat lunged forward, but the creature's upper row of teeth caught on the transom causing the boat to point straight up in the air. Finally, the fiberglass gave way to teeth, and the boat shot forward, speeding across the surface at a forty-five-degree angle. Eventually, the bow dropped down, gently kissing the surface.

Mat glanced over his shoulder and saw that a large, semicircular section of the transom was missing— along with Greg.

"God no, Greg . . ." Mat was breathing rapidly, panic rolling through his body.

"Hey, man! Slow it down!"

Again, Mat looked back. This time, he saw Greg hanging through the half-moon hole in the back of the boat, his body skimming across the surface. Mat closed his eyes briefly and gave a silent thanks.

The moment was short-lived.

Before he could say a word in response to Greg, a jagged frill rose twenty yards behind the transom. From the front, it looked like a mound of gray, pebbled flesh that tapered up to a point as it plowed through the sea.

One of Greg's dive fins came off from the force of the water and skipped across the top of the massive head.

Slow down so Greg can get on the boat? Or go faster to get away from the freak beast? Mat was in full panic mode.

Suddenly, the frill dropped back. *Is it getting tired?* Mat wasn't so sure, but he eased back on the throttle, slowing the boat enough for Greg to slide his body through the hole and onto the deck. After pulling up his trunks which were miraculously still attached to his skinny white legs, he quickly fell across the passenger seat. Neither said a word; instead, they looked across the water behind them. The frill was slowly closing in.

This time, Mat did not hesitate. "See ya later!" He slammed the throttle wide open and held it there as the frill became a remote fleck in the water.

"Bro, that was close!" gasped Greg, trying to catch his breath, shivering. He seemed on the verge of going into shock. "What do you think that thing was?"

"Oh God." Mat said another silent prayer as he pointed at the jagged frill which was now beside the boat.

Greg refused to look, clearly knowing what Mat was pointing at.

Greg whimpered now. "Mat, open this sucker UP. Get us out of here. Please, man. Oh man. Oh God."

"We're at top speed!" Mat shouted, not taking his eyes from the frill which gradually began to fall back behind them again. He watched over his shoulder with relief as the frill continued to get smaller. "I knew after a while that thing would have to tire."

Greg nervously replied, "Just don't slow down before we get to shore!"

The engine sputtered.

The frill was about forty-five yards behind them, closing in rapidly now, as if they weren't moving at all. It wasn't Mat's imagination; the boat was definitely slowing.

The boat jumped, lunging forward, just as the massive frill pushed into the stern, bumping them to a speed beyond that of the boat's ability. Mat struggled to control the wheel.

Mat looked over the edge to see a massive shadow, the rocky head.

"Look over on your side, Greg. What do you see?"

Greg hesitated, then looked. "You don't want to know!"

Mat gave a wide-eyed nod.

There was silence as the boaters tried to come to terms with their predicament. Suddenly, Greg jumped up and grabbed Mat's shoulders.

"Outmaneuver the sucker, bro! No way it can follow you in a series of turns. It's too big!"

Matt nodded and cut the boat hard to starboard.

Greg fell, catching himself on the gunwale as the massive shadow shot past them. "Nice move. But tell me when you're gonna do it next time!"

"Like I give a crap, Greg. No time for public service announcements, bro," Mat said, looking for the frill.

His mouth dropped open, eyes wide.

Greg grabbed his arm. "Bro! What?" Then he saw what Mat saw, and he cursed under his breath.

The creature had quickly adjusted its course and dropped back in behind them. Again, it showed a sudden burst of speed, pulling its frill up to the stern of the small boat as if to make a point. The water surrounding the boat turned dark. Then the creature plunged beneath the surface, and the massive shadow and the frill were gone.

Mat kept heading straight at full speed, his knuckles white on the throttle. The engine was sputtering and skipping.

Greg looked at him and shouted, "Bro, you're going *farther* out to sea. We're going the wrong way!"

Mat's curly hair was blown straight back from the wind. "No, we're not! The wrong way is wherever that thing is!"

"Yeah, but I think it's gone. We gotta start heading back."

Mat slowed the boat down. He glanced at Greg while easing into a turn. "We need to let the engine cool off, man. With all the modifications, I can't push it like that for long. It's overheating bad. I just pray that . . . *thing* finally tired out."

"I don't know . . ." Greg nervously scanned the surface. "I got the feeling that thing could have taken us out any time it wanted, ya know? Like it was playing with us or something." He looked back at the half-moon bite mark in the transom, which went down to the waterline. "But one thing's for certain."

"What's that?"

"I'm sure glad you got an inboard!"

~~~

Kate guided the helicopter over a darkening sea while John searched through binoculars. Visibility was fading with the setting sun.

"This is the general vicinity," Kate said. "If my calculations are correct, we should be about eight miles northeast of the *Nauticus II*."

"But the creature's most likely moved on. It's been a half an hour since we got the ship's call." John's frustration grew with every passing minute. "If only Nemo would give us the new coordinates." He looked at

Kate, who raised an eyebrow. "Yeah," he said, "I'm not holding my breath."

Kate said, "Think we should drop some chum? Lay down a scent to try and lure it back?"

"No," John focused his binoculars through the side window, "better not waste it."

After searching the glimmering waters for a few more minutes, John lowered the binoculars. He flipped a switch on the instrument cluster and raised the mike on his headset. "Guess all I can do is give Nemo another try."

~~~

Mat pressed the start button, and the powerful speedboat roared to life. "It's been about twenty minutes," he said. "The engine should have cooled off enough." He proceeded toward the coast at about half speed. Greg continued to stand watch, carefully scanning the surface in all directions.

After a few minutes, Greg pointed off starboard. "What was that?"

"Oh no! You've GOT to be kidding me, man."

"No, no, it's not that," replied Greg. "It looks like . . . I know this sounds crazy, but . . . there is someone out there. We gotta go back and check it out."

"I . . . I don't know! That thing could be anywhere!"

"But if it is someone, they won't have a chance, Mat. There's no one out here other than us!"

"*Okayyy,*" Mat replied, his tone hesitant. "We'll check it out, but you keep your flippin' eyes wide open. I'm not going through that again if I can help it."

"You're preaching to the choir, dude." After turning around and backtracking about forty yards, Greg said, "It was around here somewhere. I know I saw it. It was black!"

"Maybe it was a seal."

"No. It looked kinda square, like a box . . . wait a minute. There it is, there." Greg pointed. Veering the speedboat around, Mat saw the black fiberglass strewn across the surface. Drawing closer, he saw a piece of debris—the only piece of debris that was identifiable in a slew of other smaller pieces.

A boat.

A rectangular section of the transom was bobbing in the water.

Greg gasped. "That's Dr. Phillips' boat!"

Mat slowly pulled alongside the wreckage. Greg's eyes carefully scanned the surface. A patch of blood surrounded the section of transom. Then he noticed all the shadows—the water was alive. Nearly a half dozen bull sharks were writhing in and out of the debris. The section of transom slowly turned in the fray. And that's when Mat and Greg could see the frail hand clinging to it. Then the young woman's pale arm and back came into view. Eyes clamped shut and shivering, she clung to the wreckage.

"She's still alive!" Greg shouted.

Matt quickly pulled the speedboat behind the trembling girl.

"I've never seen so many sharks in one spot!" Greg said, picking up an oar.

"Hope all of that blood's not coming from her!" Mat rose from the driver's seat just as a ten-foot bull shark lunged for the girl's side. Greg pushed the shark's head down with the oar, veering the creature away from the girl. Missing the naked flesh, the jaws slammed the hull, rocking the boat. Regaining his balance, Mat swooped down and pulled the girl up to the gunwale. "Her leg!" he shouted. Greg yanked her left leg up from the surface just as another shark's open mouth glided beneath it.

The woman's body shook as it lay across the deck. The ends of her strawberry blond hair were stained a deeper shade from the bloody water. She began to cry hysterically.

Mat examined her, and asked Greg, "Where is it? I can't find where she's bleeding."

Greg's eyes followed a red trail from the side of the boat to a long cut across the back of her right thigh. "Yeah, yeah . . . it's her leg! Think all the blood's coming from there. Doesn't look like a shark bite, though. Maybe it's from a jagged edge of the wreckage." Her blood began to pool beneath her and trail toward the back of the boat where the bite mark met the water. The small boat jolted. Tilted. The frenzied sharks were nudging the fragile hull.

"Go go go go go go," Greg yelled. "They're starting to come after the boat!"

Suddenly, an eight-foot bull shark shot through the bite mark at the stern, its white underbelly sliding across the bloody deck, its open mouth swaying beside the girl. Mat pulled her to him as the shark thrashed wildly behind her. She screamed as the shark's cold skin brushed her back. Frantically, Greg beat the paddle against the shark's gills while Mat continued to pull the girl to safety at the front of the small boat. The shark jerked sideways, trying to draw its open mouth closer to bare flesh. *Wham!* Greg slammed the paddle end of the oar into the shark's mouth and pushed the creature until it dropped back through the hole and into the water. He looked over the side of the boat and noticed there were more fins than before. Another shark nudged its nose through the opening in the stern until Greg cracked the paddle between its eyes.

"What are you waiting for!" he shouted, his voice a frantic whine now. "Get us outta here, NOW!"

Mat raced to the cockpit. With his hand on the throttle, he looked back. "Get her away from the hole first. I don't want to shoot her out the back."

"I heard that!" Greg said. He quickly reached down and pulled her legs away from the jagged opening. He kneeled on the deck and tried to console her. "It's okay. You're safe now. It's all over. We're gonna get you to a hospital."

The rocking subsided.

Mat reached for the throttle as he noticed the sharks starting to disperse the wreckage area. Several fins streaked through the water– away from the boat.

The girl lifted her head and muttered, "It's not over."

They all followed her gaze through the bite mark in the boat's stern. The frill had returned.

~~~

Young Erick slowly ascended the stairwell leading to the main deck of the *Nauticus II*. He was careful to keep Rex behind him. Nearing the top step, he froze at the sound of Nemo's voice. Carefully peering over the top step, he saw Nathan and Nemo beside the stack of crates. The reddish-orange sunset seemed to ignite the waters behind them. It seemed the two were taking a break from the hours spent watching the monitor.

The men were having a heated conversation. As the argument escalated, Erick grew more concerned. He had never seen his easygoing Uncle Nathan so upset.

"But you have no idea how dangerous this creature is. It must be stopped now."

Nemo withdrew his pipe. "I'm not saying we don't destroy the pliosaur. They can blow it to oblivion for all I care, but *not* before I get it on film." He leaned closer to Nathan. "Once the beast is dead, do you have any idea how *valuable* the *only* LIVE footage will be?"

Nathan looked at Nemo completely dumbfounded. "I've said all I can say. If it kills the blood is on *your* hands."

Erick ducked back behind the stairs when Nemo glanced in his direction. "Come on, boy," he whispered to Rex. "Don't want the captain seeing us." Guiding the dog by the collar, the boy crept back down the stairwell.

~~~

"I repeat. *Sky Hawk* to *Nauticus II*, do you read? Over." John flipped a switch on the instrument cluster in frustration and collapsed back in the seat. "That's it. Nemo's definitely gone dark on us."

"What do you want to do?" asked Kate, working the stick.

"It'll be dark soon. May as well head to the ship."

Working the pedals, Kate veered the chopper around and headed west.

John stared at the darkening horizon. Once at the ship, he wondered how things would play out with Nemo. Would it be a civil argument or break out into an all-out brawl? At this point, John was in favor of the second option. He glanced across the instrument cluster. "How we looking on fuel?"

"We have enough to—" Kate paused, listening. She tilted her head.

Suddenly, a voice came over the radio. It was a child's voice in little more than a whisper. "Guys. Can you hear me?"

John and Kate shared a look.

John spoke into his headset, "Who is this?"

"Erick."

"Erick, how old are you?"

"I'm eleven . . . eleven and a half. I'll be twelve in April. I'm on the ship, Nemo's ship. Just wanted to let you guys know . . . they picked up another signal on the creature about ten minutes ago, but Nemo won't let anyone call you. They stepped away from the control room for a minute. I don't know how to read this stuff, but I heard Nemo say six miles off Cape Agulhas." Erick paused. "Uh-oh, someone's coming. Gotta go!"

And he was gone.

John looked at Kate in disbelief.

Kate gave John the thumbs-up. "I'm on it." She twisted the throttle, and the chopper peeled back around, heading for the coast.

Chapter 3
WOUNDED PREY

"Hurry! I think she's going into shock!" Greg kneeled beside the trembling girl, trying to keep her stabilized on the slippery deck.

Mat looked back at the approaching frill. "She's not the only one. Gotta get this thing to go faster."

The massive frill closed in.

Mat yelled to Greg, "Tell me when it's within ten yards."

Greg yelled back, "Now!"

Mat cut the boat hard right. Greg fell onto his side, still clinging to the girl. The frill glided past their port side. For a split second they looked up at a pebbled, gray mass slicing through the sea. Then the towering structure slowed as if to adjust its course. The boat pulled away about forty yards.

"Good move!" Greg shouted.

Mat replied without looking back, "Tell me when it catches back up!"

The frill accelerated quickly, but this time as it drew nearer the stern it slowed, inching its way closer. Greg yelled again, "Now!"

Mat cut the boat to port. The frill shot past their starboard side and then slowed down slightly, same as before. Mat saw they hadn't gained as much distance this time. *It's hopeless,* he thought. The creature was too smart for this zigzagging to get them all the way back to shore, even if the boat's small engine could maintain this rate of speed without overheating, which was questionable.

Leaving the girl lying behind the passenger's seat, Greg ran up to Mat and picked up the radio mike. "I'm gonna call ahead and try to have an ambulance waiting for her!"

Mat nodded his head without looking over, knowing the loss of hope would be evident in his eyes.

~~~

The jagged-toothed helicopter soared over the glimmering waters, heading farther southeast. John peered into the distance, wondering if the new plan would finally bring the nightmare to an end. He looked at Kate. "How far away are we?"

"We're about three miles from the site," said Kate, "but we're losing daylight."

John glanced at his watch. "I can't believe it isn't dark already. It's eight thirty-five."

"We're fortunate," Kate said. "December is our high summer; the longest days of the year. Sometimes the sun doesn't set until nine p.m."

John leaned back to relax for the remaining few minutes before they'd reach the site. He needed to get his head right, focus on the task at hand. Just as he closed his eyes, a frantic voice came over the helicopter's radio.

"SOS! Mayday or whatever! We have a woman on board who's been in a boating accident. She's going into shock. We need an ambulance to meet us on shore."

John sprang to the edge of his seat. "Do you think that was the pliosaur?"

"I don't know." Kate replied. "It could have been just an accident, but I've got enough fuel to check it out!"

The frantic voice returned. ". . . and there's a dinosaur chasing us the size of Moby Dick!"

Kate flipped a switch on the console. "What's your location?"

"About four miles South of Pearly Beach."

"Okay, hang tight! We're only a couple of minutes away!" Kate eased back on the stick and adjusted the helicopter's course. John picked up a pair of binoculars and scanned the waters east of the chopper.

With each passing minute, John's stomach tingled. The binoculars felt moist from his hands.

"Keep looking east," Kate said. "You should be able to pick up a visual by now."

Suddenly, a shiny red speedboat ripped into John's field of view. Not far behind the boat, he spotted the enormous frill. The tingling in John's stomach rose to his heart, making it flutter wildly.

"I've got 'em in sight."

"Where? Where?"

"Eleven o'clock. And that frill is moving. Your friend Steve wasn't kidding about the creature's agility."

"Okay, I see them now." Kate turned toward the boat. As they drew closer, a massive shadow appeared beneath the frill and Kate's face went pale.

John looked at her. "You okay with this?"

She nodded. "As long as we're seeing it from up here rather than in the water, I'm good." She gasped. "I still can't believe the size of that thing. Its head is wider than the poor boat. What are we supposed to do now?"

"Just get me behind the boat and keep it steady." John ripped off his headset and ran back to the cargo bay.

"What are you doing?" Kate yelled.

John slid the cargo door open. The sound of the main rotor filled the cargo bay as the wind pushed back at him. Pulling a depth charger from the crate, he carried the awkward object to the doorway. Thirty feet below he saw the spray shooting up behind the speedboat's props.

Kate shouted back, "Remember to give a—"

"I know, I know . . . give a three-second count first. It says so on the crate!" He held steady, aiming just behind the boat. He estimated that the chopper had about a fifteen-yard lead on the creature. Activating the depth charge, he gave a three-count, and let it go.

KABOOM!

A plume of water erupted about twenty yards behind the pliosaur. *No way,* John thought. *It's not gonna work. The creature's moving too fast to use the depth charges. I'll never time it right.* Thinking fast, he ran back to the chum barrels.

"Now what?" Kate shouted, brow tense with worry as her eyes flickered between John and the creature and the speedboat.

John unhooked the strap from around the first barrel. "Our only chance is to draw it away from the boat. Get about forty yards ahead of them and lower the chopper!"

Kate shouted back, "We're going nearly thirty-five knots just to keep up. That beast is flying!"

Sliding the barrel to the doorway, John looked down at the speedboat. He saw a young woman lying on the deck. A boy knelt beside her. Just behind them was an enormous bite mark in the stern. The driver looked straight up at John and then back over his shoulder to the giant shadow. Even from the air, John could see the horror in the driver's eyes.

Furious, John grabbed the barrel. "There's no way I'm gonna see these three faces added to the tally on tonight's news!" he muttered to himself.

The helicopter sped up until it was in front of the boat. John threw the soup ladle aside and poured the chum straight from the barrel. He looked back at Kate and shouted, "Zigzag the chopper from left to right . . . but slow!" He poured more chum from the barrel. "Yeah, yeah . . . that's it! Now pull the chopper to the right."

Kate slowly veered off to the right while John continued to pour the red trail leading away from the boat's path.

The frill sped through the bloody trail, never veering from the boat's wake. The giant paddle fins pumped even harder, keeping the giant on pace with its quarry.

"We've got to try again," John shouted. "It didn't pick up the scent."

Kate nodded. She veered the helicopter back around and flew over the boat. John waved to get the driver's attention then motioned for him to pick up the radio mike. Just as the boy picked up the mike, the beast dove. The boy looked back to the stern and yelled into the mike. John couldn't hear a word, but he could read his lips. *Where . . . where did it go?*

John saw the creature's shadow soften as it dove farther beneath the waves. In a split second, the shadow lightened as it arced straight back up toward the surface, transforming into an open set of jaws beneath the boat's port side. John yelled to Kate, "Tell him to cut starboard. NOW!"

Kate relayed the message.

The driver cut to the right just as the massive head broke the surface. The upper row of teeth scraped against the hull, lifting the side of the boat from the water. The boy fought the steering wheel as the boat skimmed across the surface on its starboard side, out of control.

~~~

The speedboat's hull miraculously dropped back down to the surface, picking up the greatest distance thus far from the beast. Gaining control of the boat, Mat looked past the stern and found the frill already back on track. His heart sank. By the sound of the engine, he could tell that it was already overheating—and still there was no trace of the shoreline.

~~~

From the doorway of the helicopter, John watched helplessly as the frill again closed in on the boat. The barrel in his hands was half full. There was one barrel left, but he knew that by the time he unstrapped it and pried the lid off, this would be over. This was his last shot.

John looked down at the boat—both boys were looking at him now, mouths open, eyes wide with fright, the girl lifeless on the deck floor. He again motioned to the driver to pick up the radio mike, and then said to Kate, "Tell him when you say 'NOW' to cut the boat as hard as he can."

"Which way?"

"It doesn't matter—just hurry!" After Kate relayed the instructions, the boy looked up at John and nodded, then glanced back to check his distance from the speeding giant. The helicopter darted ahead of the boat.

John hand signaled for Kate to start zigzagging while he began to pour a thick stream of chum from the barrel. Then, as the creature entered the red trail, he shouted, "Now!"

"Now!" Kate echoed.

The second John saw the boy turn the steering wheel, he pushed the entire barrel out the side door. As the boat turned hard to the right, the barrel hit the surface in an explosion of blood. Red-stained water shot up behind the chopper. John watched, holding his breath . . . until it finally happened.

The pliosaur slowed and adjusted its course for the barrel. The boy who'd been kneeling beside the girl ran up to the cockpit and high-fived the driver. They both looked up and gave John the thumbs-up sign, and the speedboat pulled far away from the massive shadow.

"You did it!" Kate shouted. "Looks like it took the bait!"

"Yeah, but let's keep an eye on them until they reach the coast. Just in case."

As they flew behind the speeding boat, John looked ahead to the coastline and saw dozens of flashing ambulance and police car lights pulling into the beach parking lot. He looked down at the driver and waved.

He looked to Kate who was grinning wide. He flashed a half-smile of his own, wiping the sweat off his face with his shirtsleeve. "Looks like they're gonna be okay. Let's get back on *our* course now. With the creature slowing its pace some, I'd like to take another crack at the depth charges."

As the helicopter slowly turned around, John watched the receding lights along the coastline and said, "Any bets on what tomorrow's headlines will say?"

Kate looked down at her watch. "Better make that the evening news!"

~~~

Beneath the bloodstained waters where three young lives had nearly become human chum, the enormous silhouette of the sea beast glided through the red haze. Its colossal mouth opened and closed searching for prey. Sensing the glare of the light from the chopper, it rose to the surface in greeting, breaking the red with its gray tiger-striped skin.

Kate shook her head. "No matter how many times I see it, I still can't believe the size of that bloody thing."

John carried another depth charge to the doorway. Wind from the main rotor pounded his shirt. "Okay, this is it," he shouted to Kate over the roaring rotor blades. "Drop down, and stay over it . . . close!"

"You want close, you got it, baby!" Kate lowered the chopper, and the frill turned on its side, slipping into the sea. The entire right side of the colossal head appeared in the light, keeping pace with the chopper.

Wow, I didn't mean to land on it. Hope she didn't forget Devil's Claw.

Now hovering about fifteen feet above the creature, its sheer size took John's breath away. He stood at the edge of the doorway, hypnotized by the giant eye staring up at him.

Mindless killer? John thought. *No way. That thing is thinking.* It was almost as if the creature knew it had been tricked. He could see the wheels turning. It seemed to be sizing him up, and plotting its next deadly move. All the while, John's thumb searched for the detonation button. He found it . . . *okay, now!* But as he went to activate the depth charge, his sweaty thumb slipped off the button, instead pressing it in. He cursed and regrouped, ready to try again. As if reading his mind, the monster's head rolled into the sea. An explosion of water reached up to the chopper's doorway, showering John as a kicking paddle fin propelled the pliosaur far beneath the waves.

Dripping with seawater, John couldn't believe his eyes. He collapsed back onto his knees, the depth charge clanking against the floor as he slowly pulled his shaking thumb off the detonation button. He stared down at the frothy water. *That didn't just happen.* He'd missed his only shot. The creature was gone.

Sliding the depth charge away from the doorway, John slowly made his way back to the cockpit. He wiped his wet hair from his eyes and took a seat.

"What happened?" Kate asked. "I was dead on top it. You didn't get a shot?"

He had no answer.

~~~

The binoculars had been pressed against John's eyes for the better part of an hour. He stood at the cargo bay, straining to see something, anything, but there was clearly nothing. Visibility was almost nil with just a hint of light rippling across a lead-gray sea. Still, he couldn't look away. The creature had to be out there somewhere.

Kate shouted back from the cockpit, "John, we've been searching for an hour or more now. At this point, we're just wasting petrol."

John walked back to the cockpit nodding his agreement and paused beside Kate. Resting a hand on the back of the pilot's seat, he stared blankly through the windshield.

Kate followed his gaze to the silhouetted mountaintops in the distance. "Since we're so close to shore, we may as well make a fuel stop before heading out to the ship. On the outskirts of Simon's Town there's a small airport. I share an office there with one of my late husband's old military mates. I use it when I'm up here flying charters during the tourist season, so the stop shouldn't take long."

John again nodded his agreement, too frustrated to speak.

Kate nudged him with her shoulder. "I know how you feel. We didn't get the creature, but we saved three lives; even in your book, that should count for something."

John gave her a forced smile and took his seat. In spite of his unrelenting guilt, he knew she had a point.

~~~

John rinsed his face in the cramped restroom of Kate's office at Simon's Town airport. As much as he splashed his face, the cool water did little to calm his nerves. He caught his reflection in the small, dirty mirror. In the dim light his cheeks were hollow, and his face looked drawn. *No surprise*, he thought. He hadn't had more than three hours of sleep since he'd left the island, and it showed. Yet he wasn't even tired; pure adrenaline kept him going.

He struggled to wrap his mind around the pliosaur. After witnessing the beast up close, it was easy to see why the islanders worshiped it as a deity or an avenging spirit spawned from the abyss. Its power and size— even its intelligence—seemed almost supernatural.

Drying himself with a towel, he headed back into the small office and eased down onto a firm leather couch. Across from him was a wall-mounted, flat-screen TV. Behind it, an oscillating fan hummed on an office desk. To the right of the desk was a small kitchenette. The room felt sterile compared to Kate's office in the Eastern Cape. No photos on the walls. No exercise equipment or workout clothes strewn about. In fact, nothing in the office felt like Kate.

She hadn't returned from fueling the chopper, so he still had a few minutes to check the news. John found the remote and turned on the TV, scanning the channels even as his mind's eye wouldn't leave the chopper. He could still see the foreboding head trailing below, the red, glowing eye looking up at him, taunting him. He had to stand, finding it impossible to stay seated. Every thought of the creature rekindled his fury. *How could I have blown the perfect shot?* An adrenaline-charged rage pulsed through his veins. He felt like a warrior in the midst of battle—he couldn't come down from the rush.

At least the night had proven one thing—the transmitter inside the creature still worked.

Now to get Nemo's cooperation. He flipped to another channel and paused. There it was beside a female reporter—the red speedboat parked haphazardly at the shoreline. In the background, several policemen struggled to hold back anxious onlookers as they tried to get closer to the boat. The camera zoomed in on the bloody deck and followed the red trail to the bite mark in the stern.

"Well, that didn't take long." John sat back down to the couch, elbows on knees, leaning forward in anticipation of the news he already knew.

The camera panned to a curly-haired teenager standing by the jagged opening. John immediately recognized him as the driver of the speedboat. A constant flurry of flashbulbs illuminated the night shoreline in the background. As the boy spoke to the reporter and the crowd, John was struck by how different the kid looked now—his face no longer contorted in fear. ". . . uh, like my bro Greg said. . . uh, man, we were lucky we had an inboard; otherwise, that thing would have taken the motor right off." The boy pointed to the vessel's ravaged stern. "I mean it was unbelievable, like a sci-fi creature . . . I mean, its head was way wider than the boat. *Waaay*. It had to be a hundred feet long. And. . . and. . . yeah, it started bumping us and all. I mean, basically, I thought we were history, okay?

"Then, this helicopter came out of nowhere, and some guy poured some bloody gore into the water to distract the creature. Lucky for us, it worked. I mean, we wouldn't be here telling this story if he hadn't done that. Man, we owe that dude big time. I mean, yeah, sure we pulled the girl from the water and kinda saved her too, but the guy in the chopper, he . . . well, he's the one you ought to be interviewing. He's the one that saved us all."

The camera returned to the reporter as she summarized the story for her TV public.

For the first time in a while, John's guilt was shoved aside. They had made a difference. A smile came to his face as he thought about what the kid just said, what Kate had said earlier in the copter. Three lives saved is good. But his joy was short-lived when he looked back at the TV. One by one, four photographs of black men of various ages appeared on screen. The reporter said, "And these are the faces of four other people who weren't as fortunate as our survivors on the speedboat. Many men are still reported missing from the Motanza Fishing Festival. Details are still sketchy on how these four men met their fates two days ago in the waters at that festival. But already many are linking the incident to the same creature that attacked this boat behind me. Now we're going to take you live, to Ron Albertine, who is with one of the fishermen who'd participated in the festival."

The image on screen switched to a male reporter interviewing an old black fisherman. Several overturned dinghies were collected along the dark shoreline in the background. The old man shook his head adamantly while using a stick to draw something in the sand. All the while, he spoke rapidly in Afrikaans. Once finished, the old man pointed to what he'd drawn. The camera closed on a twelve-foot-long paddle fin etched in the damp sand.

The reporter interpreted. "And there you have it: another eyewitness who claims to have seen an unusual sea creature under the net and insists what he saw was no whale, but a beast that swam with enormous paddle fins—a beast that matches up disturbingly well with the speedboat attack this evening."

The office door swung open. "The chopper's topped off." Kate entered the office with a duffle bag. "Ready to head out to Nemo's ship?"

"*Ohhh* yeah," John said, a trace of disdain in his voice. "I can't wait to have a little chat with the good captain."

"Well, I suggest you cool your jets. Just because the bugger wouldn't relay us the beast's coordinates doesn't mean you can punch his lights out. We still need their cooperation." She winked. "But after we destroy the beastie . . . I suppose you could still have your *little chat*."

"Fair enough." John said with a grin.

Kate glanced at the TV. "Anything show up on the news yet?"

"*You bet*," John said. "And I knew it was coming. Just caught part of an interview with our friends from the speedboat, then something about the Motanza. The media's starting to piece it all together, Kate." He aimed the remote at the TV to click it off. "We've got to stop this thing tonight."

Chapter 4
DEAD OF NIGHT

Erick tiptoed down the dark hallway and carefully approached the light coming from the ship's surveillance cabin. Rex was at his heels. Reaching the doorway, the boy held out his arm to keep the anxious dog from passing. He peered in through the window next to the door and watched Nathan and Nemo. They were at each other's throats again.

Grownups were starting to make less sense to Erick. After weeks of being depressed because they couldn't find the giant squid, the crew had come upon something even greater: a living pliosaur. That at least should have made everyone happy, he thought, crouching lower behind the window. But he couldn't have been more wrong. To Erick, ever since they'd discovered the creature, all anyone did was argue about it.

Mid-rant, Nemo looked at the gridded monitor. "I know we'll get better footage in the daylight. Any fool knows that . . . but by then, the beast could be long gone!" Nemo picked up the radio mike and pointed it at Nathan. "And you're sure you didn't call anyone earlier?" he growled. "You swear you didn't relay the new coordinates to Paxton?"

Nathan bellowed, "NO, for the last time . . . NO!" Nemo slammed the mike back down. "If you didn't call anyone, then explain to me why, when I walked back into the cabin, the mike was dangling by the cord."

"I have no idea, Captain. It wasn't me," said Nathan. "I was with *you*, if you recall. I returned to the cabin just ahead of you. The mike had to be like that already."

Nemo's face reddened. "Well, if you didn't use it, then who did?" He paused, and looked toward the doorway, his eyes narrowing. "Where's that kid?"

"You mean Erick?"

"Yeah. Let's see what he has to say about this."

Crouched behind the window to the control room, Erick whispered to Rex, "Uh-oh, time to go, boy." When Nemo was looking the other way, he tiptoed past the doorway with his dog close behind him.

Erick crept along the dark hallway. The ship swayed and creaked around him as if it were somehow alive. Cautiously, he ascended the stairwell leading to the main deck. When he reached the top step, an eerie sensation gripped him as lightning filled the night sky. The moment the white flash disappeared, there was almost total darkness due to the smoke-like clouds that shrouded the moon.

Erick pressed on into the pitch, guided only by the faint reflection of moisture on the deck and across the top of the port rail. He could barely make out the stern and the silhouette of the crane's long arm which bent down to the water. He whispered to Rex, "Wow. I've never been on the ocean when it was this dark before!" Another jagged streak of lightning tore through the night sky. The deck appeared before him as if it were in broad daylight, then quickly disappeared to black again.

Rex stopped with a whimper. Erick reached down and rubbed the dog's head. "Don't worry, boy. It's just an electrical storm."

Reluctantly, the dog continued to follow Erick until they came to the stack of crates tied off along the ship's starboard rail. Climbing up the first layer of crates, he saw lightning reflect from a shiny, red, metal box. "Looks like Nathan left his toolbox out here. I'll bring it in for him when we go back. Don't want it to rust."

Reaching the top of the crates, Erick stood tall, face lifted toward the darkness of sky, and closed his eyes. He felt the sway of the ocean beneath his feet as he balanced on the crates. The cool ocean breeze swirled around him and up the back of his loose-fitting shirt. Slowly, Erick opened his eyes. The view was almost the same except for a slight reflection of light on the distant waves. Suddenly, another streak of lightning danced across the sky, and a haunting groan echoed from the sea.

Erick froze. He stood atop the crates, paralyzed in fear, while the eerie sounds continued. He slowly realized they were the same sounds that he and Nathan had listened to three days ago in the Atlantic.

It's only the mating calls of distant sperm whales, stupid.

Stepping across to another crate, he tried to rationalize the creepy surroundings. The lightning was only an electrical storm, and the weird sounds were only whales, but the combination of the two was nearly enough to send him running back to the cabin.

Another flash of lightning showed him the familiar opening between the crates—his secret hiding place. Erick climbed down into the comforting space and called, "Here, boy!" Rex shot through the small opening between the crates in front of him. The dog's eyes glowed in the light of the flashlight Erick had just clicked on.

The boy slid the back of his flashlight into a knothole in the crate behind him and opened his science fiction paperback to the folded page. As he began to read, another haunting call from the whales evoked a whimper from Rex. Erick scratched the dog's neck. "Don't worry, boy, it's just whales . . . but it's still kind of spooky, huh?"

After only a few pages, the bright light began to tire his eyes. He leaned his head back against the crate and allowed his eyes to focus through the narrow opening between the crates in front of him. Suddenly, a strange speck of light floated across his view. He closed his eyes then reopened them, but the mysterious light was still there.

Quickly, Erick scurried up to the top of the crates for a closer look. "Wow . . . what is that?" he whispered, trying to distinguish what he was seeing.

Slowly, the strange, white shape floated closer. Then another one appeared from behind it and drifted across the deck toward the bow. Erick dropped back to his hiding spot and turned off the flashlight. He quietly climbed back up. The mysterious light was now close enough for him to see that it wasn't an actual light but rather a swath of some type of luminous, white paint. As the object drew nearer, Erick could see it was in the shape of a long triangle. A glint of metal dangled below it.

Suddenly, a flash of lightning revealed a muscular black torso beneath the glowing triangle. A white streak reflected from a long machete blade. Adorned only in a pair of khaki shorts, the massive figure approached.

Erick dropped back into his hiding spot. He tucked into a fetal position in the shadows of the crates, Rex right beside him, growling low. "This can't be real, boy. It must be a dream, right?" He hugged the dog with all his might. He squeezed his eyes shut to make it all go away. The haunting calls of the whales continued to supply background music to the perfect nightmare.

Thomp . . . thomp . . . thomp!

Heavy footsteps stopped just on the other side of the crates. Then the crates above Erick creaked. Someone was climbing up to the opening! Rex growled more loudly, the lightning reflecting off the dog's glossy coat.

"Dead dog!" Erick whispered urgently, and Rex plopped down motionless on the deck.

The footsteps stopped directly above the opening. Erick lay motionless, not daring to take a breath. He peered upward from the shadows.

The powerful figure was looking down in his direction, into the dark space between the crates. He turned his attention to the ship's port side just as another bolt of lightning illuminated the small space, exposing Erick as he lay shivering beside Rex. Holding his breath, Erick prayed that the dark figure hadn't been looking in his direction just then. His eyes clamped shut, he held his breath, and clung tightly to Rex.

Eventually, the footsteps headed toward the outside edge of the crates again. Erick heard the man jump to the deck with a deep thud. Time seemed to stand still. Then, the eerie calls of the whales were interrupted by a curious noise from the opposite side of the ship—a dull thud followed by a loud splash.

~~~

Inside the surveillance cabin, Nathan reached over to adjust the tint on the monitor covering an underwater camera attached to the hull. Suddenly he saw something crash through the surface in a haze of bubbles.

"What is th . . . ?"

Nathan froze as the mass of bubbles dissipated, revealing a thrashing man—the chef! He was gripping his throat, blood gushing through his fingers. The blue hue from the monitor turned pink.

"Oh no . . . Nemo's finally snapped!" he shouted and jumped from his chair.

He hit full speed along the dark hallway and stumbled up the stairs until he reached the main deck. Blindly, he stepped forward as his eyes struggled to adjust to the darkness.

He walked toward port when a flash of lightning revealed a shiny, dark puddle which continued around the corner. Nathan cautiously approached, keeping his back to the wall, then stepped out onto the open deck that ran along the side rail. He stopped when he saw a glowing white spike, a glint of steel.

Swooosh! A searing pain crossed his chest.

Nathan fell back against the rail as a bloody blade rose above him. He looked at the black hand and long, muscular arm that raised the machete and then into the smoldering eyes behind the white spike—eyes burning with rage. Again, the blade whistled through the air and sliced across his chest, sending him backward over the rail. Plummeting thirty feet, he splashed into the black water below.

~~~

Kota gave a satisfied glance over the rail. He turned back to the ship in time to see a thin man with a camera round the corner. Their eyes met.

Freddie's eyes widened as the dark figure stepped toward him. Lightning reflected from the long blood-streaked blade.

"I . . . I didn't see nothing. Hey, guys, I'm just the photographer," pleaded Freddie, stepping backward. "Take anything you like! We have more gas if you need it. Hey, take the ship! I don't ca—"

Suddenly, Freddie's chest bowed outward and his elbows strained back as the point of a blade protruded from his chest. His scream pierced the night as he was lifted to the tips of his toes, Kolegwa guiding him from behind toward the side rail. Then, in a single motion, Kolegwa thrust him over the rail, gripping the machete at the proper angle so it would exit the body as it dropped away.

Freddie's high-pitched scream ended with a loud splash.

For a moment, Kolegwa watched the body writhing beneath the

surface, then he looked up and pointed his machete behind where Kota stood.

Footsteps were clanking up the stairwell.

~~~

Reaching the main deck, Nemo shouted at the darkness. "Nathan, where in the blazes are you?" Enraged, the captain headed toward port, murmuring, "How dare he go on break and leave no one covering the . . . "

Nemo stopped when he noticed the enormous bloodstain beneath his feet, looking at it curiously. When the lightning flashed across the sky as it had been doing all night, he looked up and saw two dark figures before him: half-painted faces, demonic grins, blood-soaked blades rising into the pitch.

Nemo grabbed his heart and stepped back, slipping on the blood and tumbling onto the deck. He quickly rolled over and scrambled across the bloodstained area. Racing in the darkness to port side, he reached the large stack of crates. Looking over his shoulder, he could see the first man was closer than he'd expected, and Nemo pushed one of the empty crates toward him.

Effortlessly, Kota knocked the crate aside with his machete while Nemo scurried up the crates. The captain reached for the metal toolbox and tried to throw it at the charging tribesman, but it only flew a few feet because of its weight. Another crate came crashing down causing Kota to stumble slightly. He quickly regained his footing and began a slow, menacing climb toward Nemo.

Straining and grunting, Nemo pulled himself onto the top layer of crates. He ran across them precariously, passing Erick's secret hiding place. Then, just when he reached the other side of the crates and started to climb down, Kolegwa's face, glowing with its painted triangle, rose in front of him. The warrior smiled, machete cocked. A glint of steel whipped through the air. Nemo dove from the top of the crates, narrowly missing the slashing blade, and tumbled hard onto the deck. When he got up to run, he felt his ankle collapse beneath him.

~~~

Inside the stack of crates, Erick remained silent, motionless, listening to the brutal struggle less than ten feet away. He felt the vibration of the crashing crates and could hear Nemo grunting as he tried to claw his way up the pile in a last ditch effort to get away. Then Erick heard the whistle of a blade, a defeated moan, a thud, then more thuds as the dying body of Captain Nemo tumbled back down the crates.

Through the a narrow opening between the crates, Erick could see the captain's face as he lay on the deck just in front of the side rail, and he could see that the captain saw him. The seaman's intimidating demeanor was gone as he looked toward Erick, desperately reaching through the opening with his left hand. Erick quietly pushed himself back against the crate and away from the opening. He watched Nemo being pulled away, his hand still reaching out. Their eye contact never broke until Nemo's face disappeared into the shadows.

A moment later, the anticipated splash. Trying to inch farther back into the hiding space, Erick inadvertently pinched Rex's paw with his elbow. The dog yelped, the sound seeming to echo like a foghorn in the night. Erick froze.

Maybe they didn't hear it, maybe they didn't hear it, maybe they didn't hear it . . . A glowing white triangle appeared in the small crevice.

"Let's get out of here!" yelled Erick as he scurried up through the hole, out of his no-longer-secret hiding spot, and across the smattering of crates. Rex darted through the mess to the other side of the crates, meeting Erick at the exact same time the boy hit the deck.

Boy and dog ran to the stairwell, nearly falling down the steps in their panic. Blinded by the darkness, they raced to the surveillance cabin, jumped through the doorway and turned off the overhead light. Still, the blue hues from the monitors offered just enough of a hint as to what was inside the room: a terrified boy and his faithful companion, panting in unison. A quick glance down the dark hallway showed a pair of white spikes and steel blades floating down the stairs. Slowly so as not to cause a sound, Erick backed farther into the surveillance cabin, taking Rex with him.

A pink haze coming from monitor three caught his eye. The chef floated by.

Erick barely flinched at the gory scene. His mind was on his own survival. He tiptoed into the adjacent sound room, Rex at his side. He walked through the pitch-black room, careful not to turn over any of the mike stands and sound equipment. He stopped beside the far door which led back into the hallway.

From across the sound room, he could see the shadowy figures stop in front of the surveillance cabin and open the door. The machetes glimmered in the blue hue of the room. When the men entered the surveillance room, Erick threw open the back door of the sound room and raced down the hallway, taking him back to the stairwell. Reaching the top of the stairs, he stopped briefly to look behind him. There were no white triangles, no machetes, and no Rex.

~~~

Kota lunged through the surveillance cabin and then entered the sound room, slashing at and knocking over equipment on his way toward the far door. When he stepped into the hallway, something furry tripped him, causing him to lose his balance and fall, hitting the floor hard with his rear end. The dog growled, snapping at shadows until a few sweeps of Kota's blade sent him running toward the stairwell.

When Kota reached the top of the stairs, he saw the boy already climbing the left side of the stacked crates.

He motioned for Kolegwa to go around to the opposite side of the crates, so they could corner their prey. The moment they reached the crates, there was a loud splash. They raced to the side of the ship where they saw the dog with its nose beneath the bottom rail, whimpering at the sea. The frantic dog then pressed its body beneath the rail and plummeted thirty feet into the black water below.

The tribesmen looked at one another, gave one impassive look over the side of the ship, and shrugged their massive shoulders.

They headed back to the surveillance cabin.

Inside the blue room, Kota flipped on the overhead fluorescent lights. He sneered at the wall monitors, and with four powerful blows, bashed in the screens with his machete handle and then sliced all the cables with a sweep of his blade.

On the opposite side of the cabin, Kolegwa violently kicked the four monitors which tracked the homing devices, sending them crashing to the floor. He picked up the monitor closest to him and held it overhead, pulling cables from the wall, and hurled it down on top of the others. Broken glass spewed across the floor and into the hallway.

Kota looked around then nodded approvingly at their handiwork. "Like to see them find Kuta-keb-la now!" he said in their native tongue.

He motioned for Kolegwa to follow him back to the stairwell which they saturated with gasoline. Kota then opened another can of gas, laid it on the deck, and kicked it over, gas spewing from the opening. After he scanned the deck one last time to make sure all bodies had been thrown overboard, he raised his machete above his head.

"Behold!" he shouted as lightning filled the night sky. "It is as the prophecy foretold: all who interfere shall be delivered into our hands!"

Kolegwa howled with delight, whirling his machete and jumping from the ship's stern to their small fishing boat. Kota untied the boat's bowline and quickly followed.

As they sped away from the ship, Kota raised a flare gun. Carefully, he took aim at the mini-sub laying sideways on the ship's stern. *Poof!* A red arc reached through the darkness, and the burning ship illuminated the night sea. He slowly turned the boat around and headed in the direction of the African Coast.

He felt no remorse, only intense satisfaction.

Chapter 5
GHOST SHIP

"Well, there she is." Kate peered through the helicopter's windshield at the night sea. A distant ship appeared on the horizon, and its long silhouette slowly became more detailed. She worked the stick, descending toward the huge vessel. "Didn't expect a welcoming committee, but it doesn't look like there's a soul on deck. Of course, it's really foggy out there."

John watched as the *Nauticus II* came into view, its bulk rising sharply from the dark sea. Through the haze, he could just make out the crane, its long arm bent down toward the water. "Look at the crane," he said. "Just like Nemo described. Before setting her down, let's take a closer look."

Kate lowered altitude and approached the ship's portside. Gliding just above the waterline, they followed the massive hull. When the chopper's light reached midship, their eyes widened. Below the mangled side rail was a huge indentation in the hull that ran all the way down to the waterline. Light glistened from jagged streaks of bare metal where the paint was scraped away.

"Wow!" Kate gasped. "They're lucky this thing's still floating."

His eyes fixed on the huge indentation, John motioned for her to land. Pulling up, the helicopter slowly rose above the mangled side rail. And that's when smoke blew through the chopper's light.

"That's not fog—it's smoke!" John exclaimed, his eyes scanning the massive main deck. "The stern . . . looks like there was some kind of fire."

"Yeah, over there too. Portside and around the stairwell, it's all black," said Kate. "What in hell did we miss?" She began to lower the helicopter toward the ship's small landing pad which appeared undamaged.

Moments later, John stepped from the side door of the helicopter. From the towering perch of the landing pad, he could see the entire main deck. The damage was far worse than it looked from the air. Large charred patches of debris and soot were scattered everywhere as smoke still rose from the wreckage, curling into the wind.

Descending the narrow stairwell from the landing pad to the main deck, John could feel the grit beneath his boots; could hear the crunching sound. But the ship was otherwise silent. No engine noise, nothing, except for an occasional moan of metal echoing from deep within her hull. Another step, and John stopped cold.

There was a large, dark puddle of liquid beside a stack of wooden crates. At first glance, he pegged it as oil, but there was something odd about the way the puddle's coagulated surface ripped with the wind. Stepping closer, he saw smears of the same substance across the crates and the top of the side rail.

Blood.

"This place looks like a battlefield," Kate said as she stepped next to John. Kneeling down, John examined the bloody mess. He pointed to the bloody paw prints which seemed to go in every direction. "Definitely a battle of some sort," John murmured.

A rattling noise came from behind the crates, and John quickly stood in front of Kate, protecting her with his arms. They gasped as a tan-colored dog leaped toward them, tail wagging playfully. "Awww, looks like there's still someone on board," Kate said, kneeling down to eye level with the dog. "Looks like a Weimaraner maybe." She scratched behind its ears and noticed its bloody paws. Looking up at John with wide eyes, she gasped. "Oh! Oh no! What about Erick, the boy who called us?"

John ran his hands through his brown hair and blew out a long exhale, thinking. "Let's go check out the rest of the ship, see if we can piece this thing together."

A voice spoke from behind them. "It was two men from a boat."

John and Kate spun around, startled. Erick stood rigid on the charred deck. His black-framed glasses, which were cockeyed on his small nose, magnified the terror in his eyes. "Two black men with machetes came just after dark. They killed everyone."

Kate ran over, knelt in front of Erick, and hugged him close to her. "Thank God, we thought you were—"

John interrupted, "Who came? Why'd they do this?"

"I don't know. They were, like, tribal people—they had these weird, glowing triangles painted on their faces."

John stared in stunned silence, his mind reeling at the impossibility of what he just heard. "Kota!" he whispered loudly, then to Erick, he said, "Tell me all you remember; can you, Erick?" Kate sat back on her haunches to hear his answer. Clearly not wanting to let the shaking boy go, she held one of his hands with both of hers. The boy was nodding repeatedly but didn't begin until the dog came over and lay at his feet. As if gaining courage from the canine's presence, Erick found his voice and began to describe the horrific events. "They came yesterday evening on a small boat. Said they needed gas. Nathan let them on board and gave them something to drink and some gas. Then they left. Tonight they came back . . . and killed everyone." The boy's gaze dropped to the deck, his tone lower, "Even Uncle Nathan."

John rested a hand on the boy's shoulder. "Erick, I'm so sorry."

Kate's eyes had filled with tears, but she said nothing, still holding Erick's hand, rubbing it comfortingly.

John said, "Those men won't be back, Erick. You'll be okay now. But tell me, how did you manage to—?"

"Stay alive?"

John nodded.

"When they were chasing me, I was so scared, and I ran and hid behind these crates, and then I threw Nathan's toolbox overboard so they would hear the splash and think it was me." He said this all in one breath, quickly. His chest rose and fell quickly, as if he'd just finished a marathon, which John figured was pretty close. Erick then broke Kate's grip so he could kneel down and rub the back of the dog's head. "Even fooled you, too, huh, old boy?" He looked up at John and Kate. "This is Rex. He dove in after me. After that, the two guys poured gas in the hallway and around the mini-sub and lit it on fire."

"Did you put the fire out by yourself?" Kate asked.

Erick nodded. "I put the fire out in the stairwell with the fire extinguisher from the galley. Then I used the crane to knock the submarine overboard."

"That's pretty quick thinking, Erick," John said. "I'm proud of you. And Rex, too, but . . ." He scratched the top of the dog's head. "How did you manage to get Rex back on board?"

"I tied one of the life rafts to the crane's cable and lowered it over the stern. Had to let most of the air out of it first so Rex could climb on top of it. Then I pulled it up."

Kate raised her eyebrows. "You know how to operate the crane?"

"Yeah, it's easy. Uncle Nathan showed me . . ." Erick again lowered his head then wiped quickly at his eyes.

Kate and John looked at each other, sadness mixing with a moment of silence for the lost lives here. Kate put her arms around Erick, and that's when they heard it.

A sound, a voice, faint.

No one moved for a second, and then all three turned around, scanning the deck. Nothing.

Then they ran to port and looked over the rail.

Far below, they could see someone in the water, hugging the anchor chain and waving.

~~~

Nathan leaned back against the portside rail while Kate examined the long wound beneath his torn shirt. Erick was overjoyed at the happy turn of events, yammering on in a one-sided, rapid-fire conversation as his uncle listened.

Kate said, "You're lucky this wasn't any deeper."

"I'm lucky you guys showed up," corrected Nathan. "A white tip was starting to take interest, getting a bit too close for comfort."

Erick quickly turned to John, his eyes flared with revelation. "Hey, you guys never told me what happened out there. Did my call help you find the dinosaur?"

Kate gasped and arced her eyebrows.

John crouched down on one knee, eye level with Erick. "That was a brave thing you did, little buddy, calling us—and it saved three lives. If it hadn't been for your call getting us to the general area, we would have never reached these boaters in time. They were being tracked by that . . . dinosaur, as you call it. Without that call to us . . ." He let the thought trail off as he tightened his grip on the tiny shoulder, compassion in his eyes. "You helped save three lives, son. And you shouldn't take that lightly . . . you can trust me on that one."

And just that quickly, John's eyes turned to rage. He turned to Nathan and jacked him up against the side rail, ready to throw him over. "And he did it all in spite of you!" shouted John, pushing Nathan back farther. "Give me one good reason I shouldn't put you back where we just found you!"

"No, no, you don't understand," Nathan pleaded. "Nemo wouldn't let me near the mike! I swear it!"

Erick grabbed John by the leg, begging. "He's not lying. My uncle's not that kind of guy. Let him go!" Spurred on by Erick's frantic pleas, Rex barked frantically, nipping at John.

"*John!*" Kate shouted. "Stop."

John paused when he saw the boy's tears. He reluctantly lowered Nathan until his feet touched the deck again. Before releasing his grip, however, he gave him the eye. "If it happens again, you'll wish Kota had finished you off."

"You've got to believe me when I say that I'm with you on this one. I've seen this creature," Nathan said, catching his breath. "I'm with you," he said again, more softly. Then his eyes lit up. "Oh no . . . what about the surveillance cabin?"

~~~

"Ow! They did a number on this place," said Kate as they followed Nathan into the surveillance cabin. "The lads were thorough."

John scanned the room. The remaining ceiling light offered poor visibility, but the damage was clear. Glass and overturned monitors were everywhere with so many cables and wires coiled around the floor that it looked like a snake pit. "Looks like they didn't miss anything."

Nathan looked behind the wall that still contained two of the large video monitors. "Afraid everything's been cut back here too."

John sat down on one of the chairs in front of the console. Glass crackled beneath the wheels of the chair as he scooted closer to the monitors. "Well, it doesn't look like we'll be tracking anything with this equipment."

Kate sighed. "So much for a plan A."

Nathan glanced around the room, "Maybe I can fix it."

"Fix it," John said, his tone laced with doubt. "Fix this?"

Nathan walked over to one of the monitors with gridded screens. He pointed to monitor two and at its smashed-in screen. "This is the one we were tracking the pliosaur on."

John shook his head. "Well, I don't think you could pick up snow on that thing now."

Brushing the glass away from the floor with his foot, Nathan knelt down and examined the black casing beneath the smashed tracking monitors. He came to his feet. "It's doable. They smashed the monitor and cut the power cord, but the receiver beneath it looks okay. We keep a backup supply of monitors in storage. If I hook one up, and if the transmitter in the creature is still sending a signal, this just might work."

"Definitely worth a shot," John said, getting up from the chair. "Otherwise, we're out of options. Let's get started."

~~~

While Nathan worked on the monitor, John and Kate stepped out onto the main deck of the *Nauticus II*. It was nearly pitch black with the exception of a partial moon that reflected faintly on the waves. Most of the ship's electricity had shorted out as a result of the fire. Only an occasional light flickered here or there. Soot still hung in the wind, invading their noses and mouths.

Kate glanced at her watch. "Well, it's exactly midnight. Nathan's been at it for nearly an hour now."

John approached starboard. He stopped beside the bent side rail, which was above the massive indentation in the hull. He stared out to sea, his mind reeling. Kate joined him at the rail. "What is it? I can tell there's something on that mind of yours."

John finally broke his silence. "Nemo. It's not like we'd be exchanging Christmas cards, but no one deserved to die like that. And Kota . . . how could he have possibly known what was going on here? Now, our only way to track the creature is . . . destroyed." He paused, staring blankly, "No matter what I do, it's almost like fate wants to keep that thing alive."

"I don't know how, but I assure you there's a logical explanation." Kate rested a hand on his shoulder. "Come, you can't let it eat at you like this. I mean, moments ago you almost threw an injured man overboard." She squinted, "That's not your normal MO . . . is it?"

Kate was right. It was as if John didn't know himself anymore. He recalled the rage he felt when he had Nathan pinned against the side rail. It had completely possessed him. But in the back of John's mind, he knew his fury wasn't aimed at Nathan but at himself for missing his shot at the creature. He noticed Kate was still looking at him, waiting for an answer. "What? Have I ever threatened someone's life before?"

Kate nodded.

"No. Well, not really . . . you can't count in-laws."

Kate snickered just as they heard someone emerge from the stairwell. They turned to see Nathan, with his lanky silhouette and long hair blowing in the wind, jogging toward them. "Well, we're hunky-dory on our end; the receiver is up and running!" he proudly announced, smile beaming. "The new monitor and power cord did the trick. Providing the transmitter in the creature is still functional, there should be no reason we can't pick up a signal." Nathan wiped his hands with a rag from his pocket. "Also rigged up a backup generator to run power to the surveillance equipment. If we pick up a signal, we definitely don't want it going out on our end."

"Bravo!" Kate shouted, high-fiving Nathan. "Excellent work." She turned to John. "I'm going to check on Erick . . . errr, is it safe to leave you two alone?" She winked at John who gave her a sardonic look. He then turned his attention to Nathan. "This is great news, Nathan, really. Some *good* news for a change." He reached out to Nathan, and they shook hands. "Look," John nervously lowered his gaze. "What happened earlier . . . I guess I got a little carried—"

"Hey, man, there's no need to even speak of it," Nathan insisted. "I completely understand where you're coming from. I practically begged the captain to let me relay you coordinates." Nathan gave a genuine smile. "Let's just say we got off on the wrong foot and move on from here . . . to better things."

John leaned in for another handshake. "Works for me." The men gazed over the sea for a moment, and then John added, "I wasn't really going to throw you over."

"You certainly had me fooled."

"Yeah, I lost my head for a minute . . . forgot that without you we wouldn't have anyone to give us the creature's coordinates."

John turned his head so Nathan couldn't see his grin, but Nathan shoved him playfully anyway. Then they both burst into a brief fit of laughter until John glanced at the bent side railing. It felt like a sobering slap in the face as he gazed down the huge indentation in the hull. Nathan seemed to pick up John's change in demeanor.

"Oh man ... how can we even be laughing right now?" said Nathan, wiping his eyes. "Anyway, I just finished inspecting the rest of the ship. Those friends of yours were quite thorough. The engine room is in worse shape than the surveillance cabin. We're not going anywhere."

"That's all right." John stared at the distant waves. "We know the pliosaur is in the area. We don't have to be mobile to track it."

Nathan rested his elbows on the rail. "But what if it's gone? What if it has already passed the Cape and continues going west? For all we know, the creature could be halfway to Namibia."

"I don't think so."

"Why?"

"Admiral Henderson," John said, turning to lean with his back on the rail, arms crossed. "When we were searching with the Navy earlier, the admiral didn't think it would go into the Atlantic. Didn't think the pliosaur would like the temperature change."

"Ahhh, yes," Nathan said with an emphatic nod. "The Cape of Good Hope ... a perfect feeding ground."

"Feeding ground?"

Nathan explained, "In Cape Town, right in front of Table Mountain, there's a long stretch of land that reaches out to a spot called Cape Point. Past Cape Point is a very interesting area referred to as the Cape of Good Hope. This is where the Atlantic and Indian Oceans meet and create an instant twenty-degree temperature drop in the water. On some days, you can see a distinct line where the blue, cooler waters of the Atlantic collide with the green, warmer waters of the Indian Ocean. It's amazing.

"So the admiral's probably onto something. If the pliosaur ventured past Cape Point, it would be like running into an icy wall of water. No doubt, it'll turn right back around and head this way."

John liked what he was hearing. He scratched his chin thoughtfully, then said, "You said something about feeding ground."

"Yes. This is also where the southern right whales migrate annually from the cold Atlantic. They come here to breed in the Cape's warm waters, then feed on the rich plankton to put on extra blubber for the long trip back home." Nathan enumerated with his hand. "One, temperate waters ... two, rich food supply. The pliosaur will find everything it needs right here ... the perfect feeding ground."

John's heart raced with the possibility that he may be given another fighting chance at this monster. "Earlier, you mentioned seeing it?"

"Oh yes!" Nathan's eyes went wide, his voice excited now. "Up close and personal. Saw three sperm whales have a go at the thing yesterday. Sure got more than they bargained for. The sheer brutality was incredible, the way it slaughtered those whales. But the third attack was rather peculiar."

"Peculiar?"

"The third attack wasn't in self-defense. That whale had been running away and *still* the pliosaur ran it down . . . as if for the sheer pleasure of killing it."

~~~

In an office at Simons Town Naval Headquarters, Tom Hayman ducked when a chair tumbled by him and rolled to a stop.

"This is absurd!" roared Admiral Henderson. "Six of our choppers searching half the day for naught . . . and now this." They were watching a small TV on a bookshelf. It showed a female reporter beside a red speedboat as the camera closed in on the unbelievable bite mark in the stern.

"This story's already broken wide," grumbled the admiral, "and we don't even know where the bloody thing is." Through the large window before him, the still rotors of numerous helicopters shone tauntingly in the dark naval yard.

Tom dared to repeat his question. "But what should we tell the media?"

The admiral was deep in thought, and then snapped his fingers. "I know!" He turned to Tom. "We'll tell them it was a hoax. The witnesses were just kids after all, so that might work. That'll put off the media, bide us more time to get a handle on this. Now we know the general area where this creature may be. At the crack of dawn, we'll scour every inch of it. There's still enough time to eradicate this beast before the media pieces it all together."

~~~

At four forty-five a.m., John Paxton stepped from the surveillance cabin and into the dark hallway. He was haunted by the fact that there hadn't been a signal since they boarded the ship nearly six hours ago. *What if the transmitter in the creature wasn't working?* he wondered. *What then?* He passed the room that housed the generator powering the tracking equipment. Even with the door closed, the lawnmower-like sound echoed into the hallway.

He reached the next cabin that served as a place to rest. With the ship's communication system down, it was the only room within earshot of the surveillance cabin. Inside, he saw Kate sitting on the room's single bed reading one of Erick's paperbacks. The boy and his dog were curled up beside her.

Just before John stepped in the room, he heard Erick ask, "Is John your boyfriend?"

John eased back behind the doorway. He had to hear this.

"No."

"Ever kiss him?"

"No . . . what makes you ask such a thing?"

"Guess it's the way you look at him sometimes. It's kinda the way my mom looks at my dad before they smooch."

John grinned wide from behind the doorway. Erick continued, "But anyway, I didn't think he was your boyfriend."

"Why's that?"

"He's too old for you."

John's grin faded, and Kate burst out laughing. "Oh, is that right?" she said.

Erick said, "But ya know what? My uncle Nathan is single. He's more your age. He does all kinds of cool stuff like..."

Kate interrupted Erick. "Enough. I think it's time someone gets some sleep."

John waited for a moment then approached the cabin in plain view. Once inside, he eased down onto the floor and leaned back against the side of the bed.

Kate rose from the bed. "Ah, just the man I wanted to see." She tossed the paperback onto the table and picked up a plate of food, handing it to John. "Threw this together for you in the galley. Come now, we must keep our strength up."

John eyed the warm tuna sandwich but didn't take the plate. "I'm really just kinda thirsty."

Kate shoved the plate closer.

"How about after this headache eases up . . . okay?"

With a clank, she returned the plate to the table and picked up a bottle of water. "Very well then, enjoy your supper."

After a few long, satisfying gulps of the water, John eased his head back against the bed. He closed his eyes, listening to the generator thumping in the next room. *Okay, just five minutes to ease this headache,* John thought. *Then I'll go cover the monitor for Nathan.*

~~~

John rolled over in his sleep and squinted. "Someone turn off that light," he mumbled. *Wait,* he thought. *With no electricity, how can there be any light?* Opening his eyes fully, he discovered the cabin filled with daylight. Stranger still, he was lying on the bed and under the covers. Sitting up, he saw his boots beside the bed. "What is this?"

Wiping the sleep from his eyes, he stumbled through the door and into the bright hallway.

"I see someone's back with us." Kate stepped from the surveillance cabin, Erick and Rex trailing.

John was disoriented, "How long was I . . . what time is it?"

Kate glanced at her watch. "Two thirty-five p.m."

"*Two thirty-five!*" John gasped. "What . . . that can't be." He looked through a porthole and saw the sun perched high in the African sky. "Why didn't someone wake me?" he demanded. "I've slept away half the day!"

"You needed your sleep, so Erick and I tucked you in. And I must say you snore profusely."

Erick gave an exaggerated nod.

"Sleep? Who needs sleep with this thing—"

Kate put both hands on his shoulders, looked him in the eye. "There hasn't been a signal since you fell asleep. I would have woken you. Also, just an hour ago I used the radio in the chopper to contact Tom with the Shark's Board. He and the naval squadron have been scouring the last attack since sunrise, and they haven't seen a thing." She grinned. "Tom said Admiral Hot Head is quite miffed about it."

John looked through the porthole again. He still couldn't believe he'd slept this long.

"Also, said our boys from the speedboat have become quite famous. But the admiral's attempting to hush it by claiming it was a hoax. Other than that, Tom said nothing else has shown up on the news. So calm yourself. Other than the stale salami sandwiches we had for lunch, you've missed absolutely nothing."

John nodded, but the feeling in the pit of his stomach suggested otherwise. They were definitely missing something.

~~~

Darkness fell over a lonely beach in Hermanus as a young black couple approached the crashing waves. There wasn't another soul in sight. The woman stopped when her feet touched the wet sand. "No way, Kabir. This is as far as I go!"

"Come on, woman." Kabir slipped his hands around her hips and tugged at the side of her string bikini bottom. "It's our honeymoon . . . and what could be more romantic than a moonlight skinny dip?" He paused, listening to the roaring surf. "Can't you hear the ocean calling your name? *Moooriiisaaahhhh.*"

Morissa pulled his hands off of her hips. "No can do. I'm not going in there—with or without my clothes!" She raised his hands above her head and twirled seductively. "How about a moonlight dance on the beach instead?"

Kabir winked and tugged the back of her bikini bottom. "Okay, but after a quick swim out to those rocks."

Morissa looked out at the rocky mound about thirty yards from shore. "How many fools did your mama raise? You know sharks feed at night!"

"Look, woman, that feeding at night is just an old wives' tale." He walked backward toward the water, beckoning to her with his pointer finger. "Come on. There's nothing to be afraid of. I'll show you!" Kabir's feet were now in the waves. "I'll swim out to the rocks first, and then you can swim out to meet me . . . okay?"

Suddenly, Morissa gasped and pointed behind him.

Kabir laughed aloud. "No, no, woman. You can't fool me with your spooky face." Another step back. "Woman, please!" When he turned around to dive, he stopped frozen, teetering on the edges of his toes. The rocky formation that he was about to swim to rose before his eyes, doubling in length as it started gliding through the sea. The jagged mound headed farther west and slowly submerged, leaving a white froth waving on the black water.

~~~

Stretching his legs after a three-hour shift in front of the monitor, John headed along a dark hallway. He paused at one of the open portholes and took a breath of crisp sea air. His gaze drifted up to the smoke-like clouds. *Nine hours of sleep, and I still feel exhausted. Has to be the stress.* It was ten p.m., and they still hadn't picked up a signal. Turning away from the night sea, he continued to make his way toward the blue hue emitted from the distant doorway.

Reaching the surveillance cabin, he saw Kate and Erick snuggled up on the floor in front of the monitor. She gently stroked the boy's hair,] as he lay curled up beside her with his head in her lap, sleeping soundly. Above the faint hum of the equipment, he could hear Kate humming a lullaby. John paused in the doorway. He'd never seen this warm, tender side of Kate. It seemed so natural. Losing himself, he imagined his head lying in Kate's lap as she stroked his hair and gazed lovingly into his eyes.

She turned and caught him looking at her. "What?" she said, perplexed. "Why are you staring at me like that?"

Embarrassed, he turned his attention to the monitor. "Anything show up yet?"

"No." Kate wrinkled her nose. "We've been staring at this thing for nearly a day. Nathan said it was fixed, but I question if the bloody thing's even working!"

And just like that, the spell was broken.

"Okay," John said, smiling to himself. "I'll take over for a while."

Gently waking Erick, Kate came to her feet. "I'll put him to bed, then I'll come back."

~~~

A silver crescent moon carved its way into the night sky. Its pale reflection danced across the waves between the old wooden rails of a pier. Sprawled out on a lounge chair at the end of Pier 18, an elderly man struggled to stay awake. Again, the glittering waters faded as his eyes closed. Cracking an eyelid, he checked to make sure his trusty fishing rod was still leaned against the rail.

Suddenly, the bottom of the rod started to dance. His hand quickly slapped the top of the rail, but it was too late. He just missed his rod as it shot over the end of the pier.

"Aaagh! That's the second time that's happened this season," he grumbled, opening his eyes fully. Slowly, his gaze rose above the top rail, and he saw what looked like the top of a gray picket fence gliding through the waves.

"Blimey!" the old timer wheezed.

Beneath the wake from the frill, the moonlight showed a massive stretch of gray, tiger-striped skin. He watched as the frill—as long as his son's forty-foot yacht—continued to head west, slicing through the sea, the tangled fishing rod trailing behind, spraying water into the air.

~~~

Alone in the dark surveillance cabin, John and Kate sat nestled on a sleeping bag in a corner. It was a cozy arrangement, nice and close. The sole source of light was the gridded screen that bathed their faces in blue.

Kate said, "Nathan assures me the equipment's still working on this end. Even though the ship's electrical system fried, he said the generator is all we need." She eased her head back, stretching her neck. "Now if we could just pick up a signal . . . get the pliosaur's position."

John discretely gave Kate the once-over. Her face, arms, and legs were enticing shadows in the cabin's low blue light. Kate fidgeted when she noticed he was watching. He could feel the tension between them.

To end the awkward silence, John made an attempt at conversation. "I guess it's obvious how you got into this business—genetics."

"Hardly," Kate gave a weak laugh. "I used to think my parents were nuts roaming around in all of those godforsaken places. I was always more of the girly-girl type, although I didn't look like it. 'Straight Kate,' that's what they used to call me in high school. From head to toe, straight up and down, without a curve. And as timid as they come."

John gave her another long look, not hiding his admiration this time. "Clearly, something happened."

"Ted is what happened. It was through his eyes that I finally saw what lured my parents to the field of archeology. It didn't happen overnight, though. With my fear of heights, I didn't think I would ever set foot in that rickety helicopter of his."

"Ted," John said. "What happened?"

Kate paused for a long moment.

"I'm sorry." John felt like an insensitive fool, "If it's too painful, you—"

"No, no," Kate insisted, "it's okay." She gave a wink, "After all, you did spill your guts to me." She eased her head back against the wall. "Since our wedding day, Ted constantly hounded me to join him on an expedition. On our six-month anniversary, I finally relented. Nothing heavy duty, mind you; just a little jaunt to one of the uninhabited Seychelle Islands." She said boldly, "He promised me when I came back from that island, I'd be a new woman."

Staring blankly at the monitor, Kate continued. "About half a mile into the thick, Ted started complaining about a pain in his right calf. He said he thought it was a cramp, and he had been trying to walk it off for the last ten minutes. When he pulled up his pant leg, his entire calf was red. In the center, two puncture marks . . . from a black mamba. No anti-venom kit. Nothing.

"By the time I got him back to the chopper, he couldn't move his leg. No way he could work the pedals. In spite of my fear of heights, I hopped into the pilot's seat. He coached me through it, told me exactly what to do." She paused for a long moment. "After about twenty-five minutes, the instructions stopped coming. By the grace of God I made it back to Madagascar . . . on my own.

"Guess you never know what you're capable of until you have to do it. But in some strange, twisted way, Ted still made good on his promise. When I came back from that island, I was a different woman."

She lowered her gaze. "After that, I couldn't bring myself to sell the chopper. Instead, I took lessons. Six months later, I had learned to fly it. Guess I did it out of respect for him . . . whenever I'm flying it, I feel like he's still with me, guiding me." Kate stared at the screen for a long moment, pursed her lips and inhaled deeply, as if gathering up her nerve. She said shyly, "You know, in some ways you remind me of him. Not just the bad jokes and the snoring, but the way you feel for people."

She then turned to face John, who'd apparently fallen asleep. "Figures," she whispered.

Then just a heartbeat or two later, John opened his eyes. "Why don't you get some sleep? I'll watch the monitor for a while."

Kate laughed, "That's okay, Sleeping Beauty. We'd miss the signal for sure. A minute ago, I was right in the middle of a conversation with you, and when I looked up, you were fast asleep."

John yawned. "Just resting my eyes."

"Sure. Right!"

He gave a coy smile, "Well, don't keep me in suspense, Straight Kate . . . what else about me reminds you of your husband?"

Kate's jaw dropped, mortification on her face. "You . . . you heard me!"

John shh'd her and took her hand. She bit her lip with a shy smile.

He slowly pulled her closer. As their fingers interlocked, he whispered, "If they called you Straight Kate, it must have been a school for the visually impaired."

For once, Kate was at a loss for words. Their faces moved closer together, outlined by the glowing monitor. Then, just before their lips touched, the red dot came on between them, marking the pliosaur's position.

"The signal's on," Kate whispered.

Eyes closed, John murmured, "Yes, the signal's on." Then his eyes sprang open.

"THE SIGNAL'S ON!"

Chapter 6
PIER SIXTEEN

Seven miles west of Hermanus, at the end of a long pier, Lewis Jones was hard at work drowning bait. At fifty-eight, he was an excellent stockbroker, but was at a total loss on the finer points of fishing. After one more click of the reel, he lowered his fishing rod and leaned it against the rail. He watched the line arc with the night's breeze as it led down to the water.

Katherine, his fifty-seven-year-old wife, adjusted a scarf around her hair and gazed out to sea. "Look. It's so dark out there, you can barely see the horizon. And this fog . . . it seems to have appeared out of nowhere."

Turning around, the man looked at a small, wooden structure at mid-pier. It was a shop where patrons paid five dollars each for the privilege of gazing at a giant sea turtle in a tank before passing through a gate to the end of the pier. The attendant was lowering hinged sheets of plywood over the windows. Lewis looked at his wife. "Look at that, will ya. If I'd waited another fifteen minutes, I coulda saved ten bucks."

Katherine turned around. "Relax, Lewis. We're on vacation. You don't have to count every penny. Besides, you wouldn't have gotten to see the big turtle."

"Turtle, shmurtle. No one cares about the turtle; that's just an excuse for them to charge you more to come out here and fish!" Lewis glanced back at the shop as the attendant walked in the opposite direction. "Too bad they closed up. I need a bottled water or Gatorade. I'm starting to get a headache. Don't think I'm hydrated enough after all that sun today."

"Well, I haven't been getting much exercise since we've been on vacation." Katherine looked down at her watch. "I'll see if Jim and Kelly are still on the beach. If not, I think I saw a drink machine in front of that bait shop we stopped at earlier."

"Thanks, hon. By the time you get back, I'll have tomorrow's supper already filleted."

"You'll be lucky if you get a bite before I get back." Katherine said, and laughed as she walked down the pier toward shore.

~~~

Soaring over the night sea, John nodded and spoke into a walkie-talkie. "Okay Nathan, let us know if it moves again. Out." Clicking off, he looked at Kate. "According to Nathan, the signal's headed inland. Seems the generator he rigged up to the ship's receiver did the trick."

John glanced down at the walkie-talkie in his hand. "I'm glad he remembered they had these on board. With the ship's cell tower and electrical system fried, we wouldn't have had any other means of communication."

Kate smiled behind the mike on her headset. "Guess we're fortunate that you decided not to hurl him back into the sea, huh?"

Still mildly embarrassed by the incident, John raised a pair of binoculars. After a few minutes of staring at the night sea, he paused. The binoculars trained on a distant boat. "Tell me I don't see that."

"What? Do you see the creature?"

"No," John adjusted the binoculars. "That boat at four o'clock. Not sure, but it looks like they're finning sharks."

Kate was appalled. "But that's illegal."

"You might want to tell them that." John lowered the binoculars, "Take her down over top of them. Let's have a look."

Descending over a forty-two-foot Sea Ray, John peered down through the chopper's side window. The glaring light illuminated the bloodstained deck. At the stern were two men in gory jeans—one man was thick and muscular, the other thin. They both looked up with a friendly wave. A young blonde in a purple bikini was sitting atop a closed bait bin. She looked up into the glaring light, waving with the others. Even at this height, she was breathtaking. It wasn't just her shapely figure, but the way her blue eyes seemed to glow in the light. It took a conscious effort to look away. Then, beside the bait bin, John discovered the source of the blood. Two large yellowfin tuna were sprawled out on the deck, one with its head and tail severed.

"Okay, you can take her back up," John said. "Looks like they're just fishing for tuna. Boy, filleting those warm-blooded fish really makes a mess."

Kate cringed. "That's disgusting. Just the same, I'd say they're lucky the signal we picked up is eight miles from here."

Raising altitude, John gave a final glance down at the boat. Turning back around, he found Kate looking at him. She rolled her eyes.

"What?"

"I know what you were looking at . . . that purple bikini." She returned her attention to the windshield. "Like those were real!" With a twist of the throttle, the chopper dipped forward and headed for shore.

~~~

Leaning his fishing rod against the rail, Lewis watched his wife head farther along the deserted dock toward the shoreline. Eventually, her footsteps became muted by the crashing waves. After she faded into the shadows of the beach Lewis turned his attention back to the water.

He leaned his forearms against the wooden rail and felt a sudden stinging. "Ouch! Last time I'll ever fall asleep in the sun."

He stared straight down over the railing. Eighteen feet below he saw the water's glimmering surface. For a few minutes, he watched a small fish swim playfully around the submerged light that illuminated the water beneath the pier. He closed his eyes to ease the tension, hoping his headache would go away. After rubbing the bridge of his nose, he reopened his eyes to find the light had gone out. But it hadn't—it was being eclipsed by an enormous gray head. Red eyes spaced ten feet apart stared up at him from just beneath the surface. The shadows of the giant nostrils pulled even with the edge of the pier. Lewis grabbed his fishing rod and stepped back. "Wow! What kind of bait am I using?"

~~~

The black sea flashed below as John Paxton stared intently through a pair of binoculars. "According to Nathan's last signal, the pliosaur is still headed for shore."

Kate said into her headset, "But that signal went out fifteen minutes ago. Hope the creature's still in the same area. Think we should call the admiral yet?"

John lowered the binoculars, taking a look with the naked eye. "Not until we pick up a visual. He's loosing faith in this tracking process . . . can't risk giving him a false alarm. Besides, we still have depth charges and chum. That's all we need." He glanced down at the flashing waters.

No way am I going to miss again.

~~~

Lewis stepped back on the pier without breaking his gaze from the massive form. His eyes followed the glittering back. It stretched out from the end of the pier and seemed to extend all the way to the horizon. The beast slowly rose. The jagged frill along its armor-plated hide broke the waterline.

"No one's gonna believe this!" Lewis muttered. He reached down to the camera lying beside his tackle box without taking his eyes off the mammoth back.

The creature slowly glided closer until its tooth-studded jaws disappeared beneath the pier. Red glowing eyes shone just below the rail.

With a nervous right hand, Lewis picked up the camera and flipped off the lens cap. And that's when the muscles along the massive back convulsed. The head arced. With a powerful upward thrust, the giant's nose crashed through the pier behind Lewis, catapulting him into the air. Soaring thirty yards out across the water, he slapped the surface hard, his camera splashing somewhere behind him.

He broke the surface, gasping for air, groggy at first, then absolute terror settled in. Feeling nothing from his waist down, Lewis struggled to tread water with his arms, slowly turning around. He tried to kick with his legs, but his lack of buoyancy told him they weren't moving. Desperately, he swung his gaze, but could see only darkness and shifting fog.

In the distance, he spotted the glowing water at the end of the pier. At that moment, his field of view divided as the massive frill rose in front of the light. Two blazing eyes appeared behind a pressure wave, then submerged. Lewis clawed at the sky as if reaching for an invisible force to pluck him from his fate. But his fingers found only the empty sea air. Then on either side of him long, glistening white scalpels swept up from the water, and the sea collapsed beneath him.

Without a sound, the saber-like teeth interlocked, curling over pink gums as the giant maw closed and sank into the sea.

~~~

"Well, I hope he likes it. I know diet soda's not his favorite, but it's all they had. Can't be too picky at this hour." Walking past the last light on the pier, Katherine's eyes slowly adjusted to the darkness. In the distance, she saw the jagged planks where the end of the pier was supposed to be. She did not see Lewis anywhere. "Lewis? What's going on?" Her voice trembled.

Katherine stepped closer to the edge. Through the missing section of pier, she saw a red reptilian eye staring up at her from the water.

Clank. The Dr. Pepper can hit the pier, cool brown liquid disappearing between the planks. She turned around and made for the shoreline.

Half jogging, Katherine glanced past the railing and saw the creature swimming beside the pier. The luminous gray body tilted, the red eye gliding above the water. It stayed even with her every step.

Her pace increased.

The beast continued to match her pace while staying as close to the pilings as its massive paddle fins would allow.

Katherine broke into a sprint. She looked ahead. The piers entrance and the shoreline was still so far in the distance, it seemed to her. Would the water soon be too shallow for the creature to follow? She said a prayer, then glanced again to her right. The eye was still there ... watching her.

She adjusted her course and ran closer to the left side of the pier, distancing herself from the other side as much as possible, hoping to drop out of the monster's field of view. She saw the creature slowly move away from the pier and adjust its distance.

It's keeping me in its sight!

Katherine began to tire, but also knew with every stride the water below was growing more shallow. She had to stop anyway—she had reached the toll area. Her already rapid pulse quickened. She knew there was only one way past the small wooden shop: a narrow walkway that ran along the right side of the structure.

The walkway that would force her to within inches of the right side of the pier.

The pliosaur glided in closer.

For a moment, she paused in the shadow of the building, wondering if she should wait it out.

No way, she thought. *That thing could be down there for hours. I've got to get back and get help. Lewis could still be alive out there in the water.*

She knew if she could only make it past the toll area, the water would soon be too shallow for the giant to follow.

Warily, she stepped onto the narrow walkway that forced her closer to the rail. She dared a glance over the side. Eighteen feet below at the water's surface, she saw the creature's back glistening in the moonlight. The size of the gray body was much greater than she could comprehend. Her fifty-seven-year-old heart raced faster when she reached out and opened the swinging gate. The yawning of rusty springs pierced the silence. Slipping through, she closed the gate softly behind her. Once past the narrow toll area, she raced toward the center of the pier.

The great beast lunged from the water, and its lower jaw slid beneath the rail. The side of the pier bowed up in front of her then exploded beneath her feet in a surge of whitewater. Katherine was in the air, weightless. She rolled across the creature's nose. Its jagged hide tore her pants as she free fell eighteen feet into the cool black water.

Beneath the surface, Katherine bumped something and realized it was one of the pilings. The cool, slippery algae slid beneath her hands as she moved around to the opposite side of the piling and worked her way up to the surface.

Instantly, the monster had her in sight.

Kicking off her remaining shoe, Katherine swam back farther beneath the pier. The massive head closed in, broken planks sliding off its back. As the creature drew nearer, she realized the distance between the pilings was narrower than the beast's head. The creature slowly pressed its snout between the pilings. The red glowing eyes stared directly at her.

She heard the sound of a helicopter. The thumping in the sky grew closer.

Someone is coming!

She decided to make a break for the shore. On her third stroke, the colossal head thrust sideways. The pilings snapped with the sound of a gunshot, and with a horrible rumble, the pier collapsed down on top of her.

~~~

As the chopper approached the coastline, John saw the distant pier in the windshield–its crumbled end drawing nearer.

Kate worked the cyclic control, lowering altitude. "That pier . . . look at the end of it!"

"Not just the end," said John, peering through binoculars. "Past the toll area there's a huge section missing." John's stomach dropped when he saw a plume of whitewater rise behind the missing section of pier, then an enormous paddle fin slapping the sea.

"I'm on it!" Kate banked the chopper into a dive, when suddenly they saw the woman in the water.

The pliosaur lunged, twisting through the debris.

John pressed against the window, keeping the woman in sight. She was beneath the pier, on the side opposite the beast. But she wasn't moving. She was caught between two collapsed pilings.

The pliosaur thrashed madly. Pilings snapped like twigs as it charged beneath the pier after its prey.

Kate was frantic, "She's trapped! Try to use the chum to divert that thing away from her . . . so you can use the depth charges!"

John was already at the cargo door. He hurled it open, the noise of the chopping rotors blaring in. *"There's no time!"*

Kate looked back, eyes wide when she realized . . .

"What are you? *Noooo!*" she screamed as John hurled himself from the doorway and plummeted forty feet, into the black sea.

~~~

As the bubbles cleared beneath the cool water, John saw the long pilings silhouetted by the chopper's light. Surfacing, he swam like a man possessed. The thumping helicopter echoed above.

Reaching the woman, he saw the jagged frill waving beneath the pier. The pliosaur charged, twisting through the pilings. Throwing an arm over her neck and shoulder, John ripped her away from the piling, tearing off part of her shirt in the process–just as the monster's upper jaw slammed down on that same piling.

John fought to swim backward through the churning water, staring at the massive head. The jaws stretched open. The enormous maw flushed white as Kate swept down, attempting to blind the creature with the chopper's light.

A deafening roar shook the night.

It is not happy, John thought.

The creature lunged, but stopped suddenly, shaking the pier. Evidently, its sprawling paddle fins kept it from passing between the remaining pilings. More of the pier crumbled into the sea.

A glance back toward shore showed John that they were approximately sixty yards away, but in this tumult and darkness, he couldn't be sure. The monster paused beneath the mangled pier, staring in their direction. The colossal head rolled back, destroying another piling, and with an explosion of whitewater, the creature was gone.

Backstroking, John continued, the woman in tow. "Not sure if it's given up," he gasped, catching his breath, "but I don't think it can get all the way through the pier." He looked at the two rows of pilings that led to the shore. "We'll follow those in." *It's our only hope,* he thought. *Can't let it catch us out in the open water.*

Beyond the pilings, he saw the long frill rise, glowing in the light from the helicopter. "Atta girl," he muttered, knowing Kate was trying to show him the creature's position.

Keeping one eye on the illuminated back of the creature on the opposite side of the pier, John said to the woman, "Think you can swim on your own?"

Her terrified eyes locked on him through a tangle of wet hair. She nodded, her trembling lips unable to utter a word. John slowly released her, and they headed toward the shallows. Cautiously, they swam beside the pier, the twin rows of pilings supporting the east and west sides of the pier protecting them like bars on a cage.

The pliosaur moved in. With every passing column of wood, John could feel the beast's frustration growing as the eye glared at them from just above the waves. John paused, treading water. He reached down with his left foot, but still couldn't feel the sandy bottom.

Suddenly, the monster glided about five pilings ahead of them and pressed its snout between the east row of pilings on the opposite side of the pier. It was daring them to pass.

Keeping the woman behind him, John paddled farther back from their side of the pier, swimming behind the west row of pilings as he passed the massive nose. The creature inched forward until the thick pilings prevented its head from moving farther. The sound of jagged skin grinding against wood echoed beneath the pier.

John cautiously proceeded. From twenty feet away, he slowly passed the enormous snout. The lantern eyes locked on him. The grinding noise stopped. He heard only the creaking pier and the waves washing over the massive head.

Daring not to make any sudden movement, John inched his way

past the tip of the enormous nose. Then all around the colossal body, whitewater whipped through the air as all four paddle fins thrust in unison. The two pilings creaked, bowing outward until they snapped like twigs. The now-open mouth lunged forward, consuming the twenty-foot distance in a split second. With a thunderous crash, the creature's upper jaw slammed into the surface between the second row of pilings. A small section of the pier collapsed.

The enormous head twisted, its snout ripping through falling planks.

God, no! John realized his mistake. They were too close to the pilings. He back-paddled, throwing an arm around the woman's neck, pulling her back, knowing she couldn't swim fast enough to get out of the way. Again, he heard the thumping in the sky as Kate tried to use the chopper's light to distract the beast.

But this time there was no stopping it. The pliosaur plowed farther beneath the pier. The colossal head thrust upward, swaying above the surface, glowing in the light. It slammed down just in front of John, showering them with water.

Panicked, John kept back-paddling away from the pier, pulling the woman with him. He had to be twenty yards away from the pier, still he kept swimming back, not knowing if the beast could make it all the way through.

The creature's forefins slammed angrily against the pilings, shaking the pier. John's breath was coming in ragged spurts as he witnessed their good fortune. Despite the veracity of the pliosaur's attack, its enormous paddle fins still wouldn't allow it through. Just short of trapping itself, the monster swung its head sideways and rolled away from the pier. An enormous splash from all four paddle fins, and the creature soared off in the opposite direction.

It had finally given up the chase.

John slowed his movement to catch his breath, using every ounce of his strength to hold on to the woman. His arms felt like lead. They were nearing shore though, and he hoarsely whispered, "It's all right . . . almost there." He said it for the woman and for himself.

~~~

Inside the cockpit, Kate raised altitude with guarded relief. Through the windshield, she watched John tow the woman toward shore. She then looked through the side window. Her heart sank. "God, please no," she whispered.

~~~

Stroking toward shore, John noticed the helicopter dip. Again, the chopper dove toward the end of the pier and pulled up. Kate was driving erratically as if trying to tell him something. And that's when he saw the jagged frill soar around the end of the pier. And the horrific realization hit him—he had played right into the creature's plan. The pliosaur had no intention of plowing all the way through the pier. It only wanted to scare them out into the open water where it could reach them.

The creature barreled through the water with terrifying speed. The woman's catatonic eyes sprang to life. She began paddling with her hands frantically. But the creature closed on them faster than they could possibly swim,

The head burst from the water, jaws swelling before them like a canyon.

John's feet finally hit sand, and the water lowered to his waist.

WHAM!

The beach quaked, throwing John back as the pliosaur ground into the shoreline. The woman fell from his arms, and he lunged for her. The beast hurled its bulk sideways, and the huge jaws dropped closer, knocking the woman from his fingertips. The surging water hurled John backward.

Surfacing, he saw a wall of gray-striped skin. Looking higher, he saw the giant head rise above the woman.

"OVER HERE!" John shouted, splashing in the sea.

The huge eye froze.

Locating its second prey, the pliosaur turned toward John.

Wow! That worked!

The beast lunged and missed, pulling him beneath the surface with the force from its closing jaws. Brushing the sandy bottom with his body, John saw nothing but black water.

WHOOOSH!

The lower jaw flashed by in a haze of bubbles. The creature was swinging its head blindly, trying to work him through the water and into its mouth. John ducked and rolled across the seafloor, away from the thrashing water. His head broke the surface. Now in the shallows, John half ran, half crawled toward dry land. With every step, the beach shook as the enormous jaw ground into the shoreline, paddle fins splashing wildly.

John slowly rose, panting in shock. He couldn't believe he was alive. Through the corner of his eye, he saw the woman slog onto the dark shore. He looked up at the vast reptile. The creature paused, its head tilted sideways in the moonlit shallows. Enormous flanks swelled and dropped with each breath while waves crashed around its tremendous girth.

Seawater gushed out from between huge, interlocked teeth.

A red eye stared at John. *It's deciding whether to keep fighting or give up*, John thought, convinced of the pliosaur's ability to rationalize. Then the head arced, the huge forefins thrust forward, digging, and pulling its bulk farther into the shallows. One final attempt . . . in vain.

John stood frozen in terror, burning with rage. The pliosaur swung its jaws in front of him—stretched them open—and unleashed a deafening roar.

~~~

Inside a bamboo shack on the beach, a black man with long dreadlocks stopped planing a surfboard. Pulling the coils of hair back from his face, he peered through the open window of the hut.

More inland, behind a seafood restaurant, a young black boy emptying trash into a dumpster stopped abruptly. On the other side of the chain-link fence, a black couple froze on the sidewalk.

All eyes stared toward the sea.

~~~

The monster glared at John as if daring him to take another step. Its guttural growl shook the sand beneath his feet as the hot stench of its breath enveloped him.

John stood his ground. Still the huge orb remained fixed on him. It was the same chilling stare he saw after rescuing the speedboaters—a taunting gaze as if the beast was appalled that someone would dare interfere. Behind John, he heard the sound of a helicopter landing on the beach.

After a long moment, the colossal head swung sideways, and the pliosaur thrashed its way into deeper water. Froth sprayed up behind its rear paddle fins.

Finally able to look away, John turned to look for the woman. A young man ran up to him. Eyes bugging, the man pointed as if demanding an explanation of the monstrosity heading back out to sea.

John muttered in passing, "You might want to stay out of the water for the next couple of days."

Struggling across the sand, he noticed more people appearing out of the shadows of the beach. And that's when he heard the screaming. A young woman was crying hysterically in the shallows, as a man struggled to pull her back onto the beach, attempting to console her. Breaking away from the man, she ran up and latched onto John. She was the splitting image of the woman he'd just rescued, maybe twenty years younger. "Did you see an older man?" she pleaded desperately. "My father . . . he was with her . . . fishing?"

Her words fell on John like a ton of bricks. Hearing no answer, the young woman slowly slid down his body and dropped to her knees, inconsolable.

Eyes wide, John could only back away as the young man ran up to help her. The sound of the thumping rotor blades finally brought John out of his shock. Just ahead, he saw Kate's helicopter perched on the dark beach.

~~~

John slid inside the helicopter, soaking wet, a glazed look in his eye.

Kate could tell he wasn't all right. "That was the bravest thing I've ever seen in my life!" She looked at his eyes. "What's wrong, John? You *saved* her . . . she's okay."

"She wasn't alone . . . on the pier."

Kate leaned closer, her voice stern. "Listen to me. You saved her. There was nothing else you could have done. *Nothing!*"

He didn't hear a word as he frantically scanned the windows. "Where is it?" he said between breaths. "Do you still have a visual?" He turned to her, his eyes burning with fury. "Let's go . . . take 'er up. *Now!*"

Kate was taken back. She'd never seen him like this. She twisted the throttle. "I lost sight of it. Last thing I saw was the frill headed south, back out to sea." She glanced through the side window at the beach. "What about her?"

John was stunned, still taking it in. "She's okay. Still, I-I'll call an ambulance for her," he muttered in a monotone voice.

"I already did," Kate said. "I also relayed our coordinates to the admiral. The demolition squad is on the way." She glanced at him. "Don't worry . . . we'll find it."

~~~

Lifting off, he watched the woman he'd rescued embrace her daughter as more people appeared out of the shadows to help them. The way they were talking and pointing at the water told him they'd seen it all. He muttered blankly, "If we'd only gotten here sooner."

He did a double take. And it slowly sank in . . . the people were pointing . . .

It's still there. An uncontrollable shudder went through his body.

The chopper flashed over the pier, and there the creature was, its long frill gliding into view.

"Got it!" Kate said, twisting the throttle.

Drawing closer, the light swept across the frill and the massive shadow beneath. Patches of fog muddied the view. Kate swooped down closer, keeping pace above the enormous silhouette.

John hurried back to the cargo bay. He glanced through the doorway to check the beast's position. The giant head rolled to one side and a red eye broke the waterline, looking up through the mist. And there it was again, that same taunting stare. *Oh yeah. You keep looking, you piece of*

. . .

John lunged for the crate. Pulling out a depth charger, he swung the awkward object to the doorway with fury. Wind pounded in. He glanced once more below.

He saw nothing but fog.

Kate played the light over the area.

The creature was gone.

~~~

Lowering the walkie-talkie, Nathan leaned back against the doorway of the ship's surveillance cabin. Releasing a long breath, he stared out into the dark hallway.

Erick raced up to him, wide-eyed. "So what happened? Did they get the dinosaur?"

"Kate said they saw it, but it slipped away. She didn't seem to want to go into detail." Turning back to the cabin, Nathan paused, staring at the blue hue emitted from the doorway. "It's been over an hour . . . if we could just pick up another signal . . ."

Erick wandered out farther into the dark hallway. "Why's it so quiet out here?"

"What?"

The boy stopped curiously at the closed door beside the surveillance cabin. "Isn't this the room with the generator? It's usually so loud I can't sleep in the next room."

Nathan swung open the door. "Oh crap!" To his horror, he found that the generator powering the surveillance equipment had shut off. Running over to the old engine, he dropped to his knees. He waved to Erick. "Hurry, go back and get my toolbox."

Erick started to run and paused. "That's gonna be kinda hard."

"No," Nathan said. "Not the one you tossed overboard; I have a smaller one. It's in my cabin under the bed."

As the boy disappeared through the doorway, Nathan's eyes darted over every nook and cranny of the twenty-year-old engine.

Chapter 7
MASQUERADE

In the wee hours of the night, twenty-two-year-old Amy Richards lay fast asleep in the main cabin of her husband's Sea Ray. Black satin sheets bathed in moonlight from an open window outlined her shapely figure. The sound of the sea whispered to her.

A splash outside caused her to stir. She reached over groggily to her husband's side of the bed and discovered she was alone. Slowly waking, she slid out from beneath the sheets in a black teddy and a pair of panties. She noticed her purple bikini at the foot of the bed, thought of changing into it before going on deck, then decided to go as is. Adjusting her lingerie, Amy crept toward the doorway. Her long, blond hair shimmered as she passed the cabin window.

Entering the galley, the ocean breeze whipped her hair in front of her face. When she pulled it back, she noticed the red blinking light on the console. "I knew it . . . they're at it again."

She stepped through the doorway and out onto the stern. Her husband, Chris, a powerfully built man in his thirties, and cohort, Gary, were at the transom. They were peering down into the dark water. Chris turned around. His lean abdomen and denim pants were slick with blood.

"Sleeping beauty awakes!" he announced with a grin. "I haven't thanked you yet, hon . . .the way you handled things when that old chopper hovered over us, putting the top on the bait bin and sitting on it in all your loveliness, then giving your innocent little wave." He chuckled and winked at her. "A brilliant performance. You might make it as an actor yet."

Gary laughed, his orange life jacket covered in blood. "Yeah, and the "filleted tuna on the deck" bit fools 'em every time. They just think we're out here fishing for yellowfin. They don't know it's our bait fish!"

"I almost regret doing it," Amy protested. "I'm telling you, one of these nights you'll get caught."

Chris eased back against the transom. "Well, this ain't that night, hon, and they weren't the Navy. In case you didn't notice, that chopper had a set of shark jaws painted on it." He cursed the night sky with a raised fist. "Bloody activists!"

There was a sudden commotion in the water. Turning around, Chris waved excitedly to Gary.

Oh no. He's got another one. Amy stepped back to the doorway, barely able to watch.

Gary glanced at his dive watch. "Think we can beat our last time?"

"Let's go for it."

Chris's muscular back rippled as he yanked in the line while Gary reached over the stern with a meat hook. Wrestling the eight-foot hammerhead onto the deck, Gary sliced off the creature's dorsal fin and lobbed it into the bait bin.

Chris muscled the shark around until its white underbelly faced upward. Planting a boot on the squirming shark's throat, he sliced off the pectoral fins while Gary lopped off the tail. With an underhanded toss, the severed fins flew across the deck and landed in a bait bin with the others, their bloody edges glistening in the moonlight.

Next, the two pulled the finless shark up to the side of the boat. Holding the helpless creature on the gunwale, Chris plunged his knife into its underbelly and opened it up from throat to tail. Then they rolled the bloody carcass back into the sea.

Gary clicked his watch. "*Yyyes!* Beat our best time by three seconds."

Chris high-fived him. "An Indy pit crew's got nothing on us, bro."

Amy was appalled, her face contorted in disdain. "Disgusting. You've made a sport of your butchery."

Chris turned around. "Don't look at me like that was a puppy." As usual, his tone was defensive. "Besides, that shark didn't feel a thing! You saw how I sliced it open so it would die quickly. Some guys just fin 'em and toss 'em back over, letting them die from asphyxiation. At least I make it quick." Chris turned from Amy and looked over the side rail, down at his handy work.

Amy could only imagine what he was watching. She had only seen the hideous sight once, but now, in her mind's eye, she could see all too well the descending shark squirming and rolling in a cloud of its own blood. *Who does he think he's kidding?* She knew Chris could care less about any shark's suffering, but merely used the extra blood in the water to draw more sharks to the boat.

"It's just looks so cruel!" Amy said in a whisper. "The suffering."

Chris wiped his bloody hands on his pants. "Babe! How many times do we have to go over this?"

"But you said you'd quit after we got married. The honeymoon was six months ago . . . and look at you!" Amy planted her hands on her hips. "Besides, Dad's getting wise to all this. He keeps asking how an ex-lifeguard who owns a small bait shop can live the way we do."

"Lighten up," Chris gasped. "Besides, I don't kill a fraction of the sharks those Japanese tuna ships do when they pass through here. With those long lines, they land more sharks in a day than I do in six months. Look, Hong Kong alone buys seven million pounds of fins per year . . .

and hon, it ain't all coming from me!"

Gary looked up from the bait bin. He shouted to Amy, "On your way out, did you notice if the switch is on. . . the flashing red light on the console?"

"You mean your death switch? Afraid so. I saw it flashing."

"Death switch," Gary grinned. "I like that."

"No, no," Chris said, also grinning, "you mean *money* switch!"

They high-fived again. "You've got that right, bro. That underwater frequency device you rigged up really draws them to the boat. It's like a shark magnet. Check it . . . we've already got over thirty fins."

"And the frequency isn't very strong. Doesn't have to be." Chris walked proudly to the bait bin. "Hammerheads can detect an electrical field as low as a millionth of a volt." He looked down into the bin, resting his hands on the sides. "But after that last surfer attack near J-Bay, I'm starting to get a little nervous. Already the locals are talking about thinning out the shark population. If that happens, bro, we're gonna have lots of competition out here." He looked across the night sea. "So I guess we'd better get 'em while we can!"

Gary slapped him on the back. "Yeah, but those old school guys don't have technology on their side!"

Chris laughed. "Got that right; nothing like a competitive edge!"

Amy scoffed. "Listen to you two. You act like this isn't illegal!"

"That's a good point you make!" said her husband. "So get your cute little gava to the helm, and keep a lookout so we don't get caught!"

Gary nodded, his eyebrows waggling. "Cute little gava is right."

Chris noticed Gary checking out his wife in her panties. Moonlight glistened off her tanned skin beneath the short teddy. "Hey, man. What do you think you're looking at?" Chris then turned on Amy. "And you . . . what are you thinking, coming out here like that? Put some clothes on."

Amy gave a taunting smirk. "But you always liked the way your friends looked at me *before* we were married."

"Did you not hear me?"

"*Okayyyy.*" Amy scowled at her husband. She looked along the blood-smeared deck. "But all of this still doesn't feel right. It *isn't* right."

Chris's eyes narrowed. "Well, those two-carat diamond earrings, do they feel right? Driving around in the new 'vette, does that feel right? Not to mention those oh-so-perfectly-perky little enhancements you're so proud of . . . do they feel right?"

Amy knew she'd crossed the line.

Chris stepped closer, on the verge of going ballistic. "And let's not even talk about what happened to my little sister . . . that didn't feel so right, did it? She was in less than a foot of water . . . it practically beached itself to get to her!" He was yelling now, his voice going hoarse from the intensity.

"In case you've forgotten, it happened right in front of me. I was on duty that day. I could hear her screams from my tower, Amy. To this day I still have nightmares about those screams, the thrashing water. People on the beach had to pull my mother into the shallows to keep her from going after the thing. By the time I got there, all I saw was my mother coming out of the water, with her arms cradled like my sister was still in them. Her white one-piece swimsuit was completely red."

Amy took a step back, wishing she had kept her silence.

Chris had a disturbing gleam in his eyes. "People said you can't blame the shark. It's a killer. A killing machine . . . that's what it does!" He pointed to his chest, leaving a smeared red dot from his fingertip. "And now *I'm the killing machine*, and that's what I do!" He stepped forward. "I still protect the beaches, all right. Only now, instead of from a lifeguard tower, I do it from out here."

Amy looked down at the deck without a word. When she turned back around toward the bow, she saw a fog bank headed their way. "Did you guys move the boat?"

"Yeah, we did," Gary spoke up, eager to change the subject. "We're only a few miles off shore, farther east. What happened earlier with the chopper spooked us. Chris thought it would be safer to change locations just in case they had seen something and decided to report us."

The fog reached the boat. Amy stared into the silver mist, watching as it slowly curled over the gunwale and across the bloody deck. "Guys, are you about ready to head in? All of this is starting to creep me out."

~~~

John peered down through the side window as the chopper's light continued to scour the night sea.

"Are you okay?" Kate's voice rang in his earphones.

He didn't answer—just continued to stare blankly at the light cutting through the haze below.

"All I need is the right shot," he muttered, more to himself than Kate. "One shot . . . at the right speed, not too fast. I can make it all stop . . . make it right . . ."

"What did you say? I can't hear you."

"Nothing," he said, shaking his head. "Nothing." But the creature's red eyes were burning in his mind. He couldn't stop thinking about the beast's unsettling stare. He could feel its blood boiling, as if enraged that a mere human would dare to interfere. And the way it taunted him, as if reminding him that he didn't have a chance, had failed every attempt to destroy it. Nothing could stop it.

But there was something else in those red lantern eyes. At first he swore it was his imagination, but no. Now he was certain of it, and the very thought chilled him to the bone.

It remembers me.

And John understood. It was more than an animal trying to feed; it was an animal craving the death of another in an unnatural way.

It wanted vengeance.

"So what do you think?" Kate's voice again interrupted him. "Think we've gone too far out?"

Snapping out of it, John asked, "Where are we in reference to the pier?"

Kate looked at the instrument cluster. "We've been heading west. We're about two miles offshore."

"Your guess is as good as mine." John glanced at his watch. "I still can't believe the Navy hasn't shown up yet. We need more eyes out here."

"It's only been about twenty minutes since I called. Shouldn't take them too much longer to get here from Simon's Town."

After a few moments of looking at the sea, she turned to him. "I don't really mean to bring this up . . . but earlier . . . when the creature beached itself . . .well, I still can't believe the size of the thing. And the way it looked at you, its eyes. Like you could see it thinking."

She'd mirrored his thoughts—he wasn't going mad. "I know," John said with a slow nod of his head. "Should have seen it from my angle. It didn't seem too happy that I took its food away."

John headed to the cargo bay. He checked the depth charges for the third time then approached the open doorway. Looking down into the fog, he muttered, "Come on, Nathan. We need another signal."

Amy crept out onto the stern of the Sea Ray, noticing the fog had thinned out to mere sprinkled patches drifting over the black water. The mist felt cool against her bare skin. Anxious to head in, she wanted to see if Chris had pulled up the anchor.

Chris turned around and pointed at her body, still draped in lingerie. "Go put some clothes on already!" he demanded. "What's with you? Ever since I got those implants for you, it's like you can't stand to cover 'em up!"

He picked up a plastic jug and drained the remaining few ounces of sports drink into his mouth. Tossing the empty jug across the deck, he looked at Amy. "On your way back in, get the second jug of sports drink from the fridge, will ya?"

She wanted to ask why they weren't heading back in but didn't dare press her luck. "Okay," Amy said, slowly walking toward the galley, still rattled from Chris's earlier outburst. Halfway along the hallway she stopped and slapped her forehead. *Oh no! Now he's really gonna freak.* She turned around and walked back onto the deck empty-handed.

Chris looked over. "Where's the drink?"

"I forgot to mix it."

"Well, why don't you just mix it *now*?"

Amy nervously replied, "I . . . I forgot the water."

"That's great." Chris was on the verge of another rage rant. "Three miles from the coast and nothing to drink!" He took a step back, slipped on the empty jug, and nearly fell. In frustration, he kicked it across the deck.

Gary tapped him on the shoulder in an obvious attempt to distract Chris. "Bro, check it. There's another fin. Looks like a hammerhead. A lobster dinner says you can't hit it on the first shot."

"You should know better than that." Chris snatched up the spear gun and turned his attention to the waters off starboard.

Running to the helm, Gary fired the engine and accelerated the boat until it was parallel with the fin. Amy stepped back, arms crossed and heaving a deep sigh, to give them plenty of room to pull their next victim on board.

"That's it! Keep her steady!" shouted Chris as he trained the spear gun on the fin. A spray of whitewater trailed behind the gray triangle as it glided through the night. His finger tensed on the trigger, his left eye squinted. "Come on . . . come on. Yes!"

Chris squeezed the trigger.

Ssssap. A perfect shot. The spear found its mark just below the dorsal fin. Chris fist pumped the air with a victorious shout. "Bro, you should have known better than to make that bet!"

But the shark didn't flinch.

When the small fin began to rise, he noticed another fin in front of it. Another fin appeared behind it.

Two more.

Six more fins rose from the water, all lined in a row. Rising higher, the fins merged together, and Chris realized in horror that they weren't fins at all—but the tip of an enormous jagged frill.

Chris's jaw dropped. He looked up and saw his spear dangling like a toothpick on a piece of the frill. He dropped his spear gun to the deck in disbelief. Then the water surrounding the boat turned black as the frill rose above the mist.

"What the—? Get us outta here!" Chris's voice cracked in fear.

Gary pressed the throttle and the bow lifted, speeding forward. But the frill remained off port, matching their pace. As Gary drove like a madman, Chris looked past the bow, then the stern, trying to estimate the creature's length. But there was no end to the black shadow in either direction. Then the frill cut the waters in a forward shift, plunging beneath the surface. The spear gun danced across the deck and flew over the boat's side as the enormous shadow disappeared behind a spray of whitewater.

After a few seconds, Chris motioned Gary to slow the boat. Gary eased back on the throttle, bringing the roaring engine to idle. As the boat slowed, Gary stood up. "Tell me I didn't see that!"

"That had to be a whale," said Chris, eyes wide. "Some kind of humpback."

Gary shook his head, doubtful. His eyes darted around the waters.

Clouds drifted before the moon, and the sea grew darker.

Chris motioned everyone to be quiet. All eyes stared into the pitch. At first they heard only the waves slapping against the hull.

A bellowing roar echoed from the blackness.

"Where did that come from?" shouted Chris.

"I don't know!" yelled Gary, his head on a swivel. "Everywhere!"

Another roar. Closer. Palpable. No one uttered a sound.

Amy began to weep from the doorway to the galley. Chris brought a finger to his lips, signaling her to keep quiet.

She looked down at the deck, her voice a mere whisper. Terrified. "Chris! What's that? Can you feel it?"

The ocean began to rumble. The sound was distant, barely perceivable, but grew steadily louder. Chris's eyes darted over the surface of the water.

In all of their years together, Amy had never seen him express such genuine fear. The deep sound grew louder like an underwater volcano. Then the deck began to tremble as they felt the vibration nearing the surface. Amy stepped back farther into the hallway. "What are you waiting for?" she screamed to Gary.

Gary slammed down the throttle.

The boat lunged upward as the gigantic nose shot above the starboard in an explosion of whitewater. Chris fell back, the deck collapsing beneath his feet as he disappeared into the darkness behind the upper row of teeth.

The impact propelled Gary twenty feet in the air.

Amy was thrown back across a counter in the hallway. She tumbled to the floor. Through the doorway, all she could see was a blur of gray-striped flesh of the massive upper jaw across the starboard. She felt the deck and the entire hallway rise from the surface. The creature held the boat firmly in its awesome jaws. A heartbeat, and then the head rolled, plunging into the water, tearing the vessel in half.

There was a moment of weightlessness. Everything whirled. Through the hallway, Amy saw a blur of the night sky until she felt the boat crash against the sea. Instantly, the hall and galley flooded. Cool water swept above her head, taking her breath.

She felt her section of the boat swirling toward the depths. She swam through debris from the galley. Her blond hair flowed like a part of the ocean, clouding her vision on occasion, as she searched for a way out. She slipped her body through the large window in the hallway.

Once outside the sinking wreckage, Amy looked up at the moonlit surface. Dozens of severed shark fins spiraled toward the depths, leaving trails of blood like red ribbons. She pushed the hair from her eyes and swam through the surreal underwater setting. Debris fell around her like confetti. A few strokes more and the blue water transformed into pink— she'd risen into the chum line. Amy burst through the surface, screaming Chris's name at the top of her lungs, which slowly gave way to realization of her circumstances: the frill, the mouth, the boat in shreds. She stifled her cries, now silent except for an occasional whimper. She moved slowly, only enough to tread water. Her eyes scanned the surface. No trace of Chris or Gary, only floating debris and the faint smell of fuel in the air.

Suddenly, several fins appeared at the opposite end of the chum line and began to close in on something orange in the water. She squeezed her eyes shut, refusing to watch the inevitable.

~~~

Gary swam out from behind a large piece of debris, his orange life jacket glowing in the moonlight. The second he hit the water, he remembered that he'd planned to tell Chris today was his last day out. Now, it was—in more ways than one. He looked at the swarm of fins and the realization hit him. This was the last night of his life.

At that moment, something tugged at him from below. His mouth dropped beneath the surface, and he fought, rising above the surface again, gasping on the bitter taste of blood. Warmth swept over his torso, and he looked down at a red billowing cloud rising beneath him. *No.*

Refusing to comprehend what had happened, Gary frantically swam back, but the warm cloud followed. Then, through the perimeter of the bloodstained waters, he saw the figure of a bull shark swimming away with something in its mouth that looked like a shoe. Before his eyes, another shark rammed the bull shark, tearing the foot from the severed limb.

All around him, the water was moving—alive. Gary was then jerked to his left. Frothy pink water splashed into his face. He tried to draw his left hand back to his chest, but it was brutally snatched away. His free right hand pounded blindly into the water, grazing and connecting with sandpaper skin. Another fin rose, waving in front of him. His head swirled. He heard screams and pleas filling the air—louder and louder— but he did not recognize them as his own. Another shark hit from the front, and he felt the strap of the life vest pull into his back as it was torn away.

Bloody gray skin flashed before his face. A searing pain raked across his abdomen, and he was pushed back across the water, then he was floating free. More warmth flowed upward. He didn't have to look down to know what had happened—he was torn open. His guts were spilling into the sea.

The moonlit sky disappeared, replaced by red water as his screams turned to bubbles. Then Gary closed his eyes and waited for the next hit.

The wait wasn't long.

~~~

Amy swam back in horror, watching the orange life jacket dance amid the thrashing fins. She tried not to hear Gary's screams, though it was impossible. All at once, the surface split and the great mouth stretched open, lifting Gary and the two bull sharks tearing into his body. Unaware of their impending demise, the sharks continued to fight over the torso until they disappeared within the pliosaur's closing jaws. Then with a final crash of water, the giant head slammed back beneath the waves.

As the shockwaves settled, Amy nervously looked across the water, not seeing a single fin. She hoped that maybe the huge creature had scared all the other sharks away.

No such luck. A single fin broke the surface.

Amy held her breath, watching the two-foot fin slowly veer back around into the chum trail and align itself for the kill—hers. She frantically looked for something to hide behind, but there was nothing. She floated helplessly in the freshly chummed waters. When the shark drew nearer, she could see its hammer-shaped head oscillating beneath the waves. The shark picked up speed, slicing through the chum line straight for her.

Amy let loose a scream. That's when the giant frill broke the surface, towering behind the approaching fin. Then an enormous swell appeared in front of the monster's interlocked teeth, which soon parted to reveal a mouth wider than a set of double doors. The great nose cast a shadow over Amy as she watched the cavernous mouth completely swallow the large hammerhead. The pliosaur's nose plowed into the surface and it dove. Amy quickly spread her legs as the long frill glided between them, missing her by inches.

Behind her, the pliosaur exploded from the surface, a hammer-shaped head protruding from the side of its jaw. With a kick of a massive paddle fin, a shower of water covered Amy.

The enormous shadow was gone, fading into the sea.

Amy continued to tread water, hearing only the sound of her racing heart echoing in her ears. She frantically searched the surface waters around her.

Is it done?

Out of the gloom, the vast head slowly rose beneath her. Less than eight feet away, an enormous red eye broke the surface. Her field of view filled with gray, pebbled flesh as the huge orb examined her from point-blank range. Clouds of blood gushed from its jaw.

This is it. I'm done.

The head rose higher, water cascading down from the rising teeth. Twenty feet above her, the huge jaws stretched open and unleashed a roar—so immense and terrifying, she could not move, only stare in wonder—as the great creature called out to the night. Then with a tremendous splash, the head rolled back into the sea and was gone.

~~~

John peered forward through the chopper's windshield, the walkie-talkie at his ear, fire in his eyes. "Are you sure the signal was moving east? As long as we've been tracking it, the pliosaur's been headed west." He listened for a moment, "Okay. Out!"

Clicking off the walkie-talkie, John said to Kate, "Nathan said it's no mistake—the creature is definitely headed east. Said it must have caught a scent to make it change course like that." He stared down at the communication device in his hand. "He also said he would have picked up a signal sooner, but he noticed the generator powering the surveillance equipment had cut out. It took a while, but he finally fixed it." John shook his head. "Unbelievable. Countless lives resting on a five-dollar spark plug."

Kate peered into the distance. "Maybe our luck is starting to change. Look at the moon—it's completely full. And the fog's starting to break up."

John gazed up at the full moon and felt an unmistakable sense of unease.

~~~

Alone, three miles from the coast, Amy continued to tread water. Her lower jaw trembled uncontrollably as she nervously looked around the surface. The boat's debris was scattered widely now with the exception of several large pieces of fiberglass that lingered close by. She felt certain that by now the chum trail had disbursed, and the boat's underwater frequency device used to attract sharks had been destroyed. Her chances *seemed* better.

She prayed for a break—that if there were nothing to attract the sharks to her, she would survive this. Amy knew sharks weren't the mindless killers Chris made them out to be. But it did little to erase

Gary's gruesome death from her mind. For the thousandth time, his life jacket, still bouncing in the bloody waters, flashed before her. She closed her eyes, and it was still there.

Then there was the hammerhead. She recalled how the shark came straight for her, rationalizing that it was only because she was in the chum trail. But the other thing . . . the monstrosity that came up beneath the boat was beyond her comprehension. And the bizarre way it had just stared at her. Maybe she was just a morsel too small to bother with. Maybe that's why it left her alone.

The water felt cooler. Amy wondered how long it would be before anyone knew they were missing. *What a joke*, she thought. Chris was so secretive about what he was doing that no one probably even knew they'd gone out. *It could be days.*

Her mind went back to the huge creature. She tried to convince herself it was gone, but unbelievably, she could feel its presence. She thought about the frill she'd seen just a few moments ago. Once or twice she had felt a slight undertow, as if something enormous had passed beneath her. She refused to look down. There it was again . . . or was it her imagination?

Whimpering, she fought the urge to look down, then gave up. She lowered her eyes, seeing the shadow of her legs rippling against a passing wall of gray-striped skin. The mass of flesh then tapered down into a sweeping tail and soared off into the darkness. In the distance she saw a ripple of water, the frill. It continued on a forward path, then slowly arced around. The creature was making huge circles around her.

It had never gone away.

She could now see the massive beast more clearly beneath the full moon—its body flashing in and out of the moonlight as it patrolled the waters around her.

Why not just take me, monster?

Her mind raced, but her arms barely moved; just enough to tread water.

Or . . . are you protecting me?

She reasoned with herself that perhaps it was keeping the hungry sharks at bay. She felt a glint of hope, however unreasonable. She rationalized that the creature somehow knew she wasn't here to harm it, that she wasn't like Chris and Gary. Maybe the creature, with its complex brain, could sense she was innocent.

Her theory of hope was short-lived.

The wide circle began to close.

The creature flashed by her. She lost sight of it.

Amy screamed. She drew her legs up as the beast, approaching from behind, sailed beneath her. A paddle fin missed her by inches. She turned frantically in the water, catching sight of a trail of bubbles. The white froth divided and the towering frill rose, veering around toward her, cutting through the night water, closer, rising.

Nowhere to go, Amy admitted her luck had run out. She was next. She could only watch the horror close in. The huge mouth stretched open before her, then closed, and the enormous head plunged beneath her. She screamed when jagged skin scraped her left thigh.

Amy rose above the surface, spitting from the undertow.

She felt it then—the pain of a hundred bee stings sweeping up her thigh from where the monster had brushed her.

She wondered at the game this creature seemed to be playing. As if it wished to torture her more than kill her quickly.

After cruising away from her, the pliosaur once again came around for another pass. The beast rose higher until its striped back broke the waterline. The huge eyes appeared beneath a pressure wave.

But this time it didn't dive.

Instead, the pliosaur merely rolled its head.

Beneath the water, the giant neck brushed Amy's chest and thigh, sending her bouncing and rolling off the passing flank. Blood rose from her abraded skin.

Hysterical with fear, she rose in the creature's wake.

"Just do it! Get it over with," she spat angrily. Treading water, she glanced down at the stinging warmth. Amid the red haze, she saw that her teddy was little more than a few shards of waving black material. The water was cold, but the entire left side of her body was on fire.

Then her vision lightened and a rush of dizziness overtook her. Her mouth slipped beneath the surface and she tasted the bloody sea. She actually prayed for drowning.

Her mind raced, pondering her options. The frill headed away from her again, readying itself for another pass at her, she had no doubt. *Can I do it?* she thought. Facing a certain horrible death, a self-inflicted end had some appeal. *There's no time left. I have to do it now! This is the best way, if I can just make myself do it.* Amy closed her eyes. She softly whispered, "God forgive me," then drew her final breath.

She threw her head back, and the red-stained water closed over her. Beneath the surface, she forced herself to dive. *Pretend it's a dream*, she thought, keeping her eyes clamped shut and descending into the cool blackness. The pressure around her intensified with every stroke. *Soon it will be over.* Once she reached a certain depth and inhaled, she knew there would be no going back; she wouldn't be able to surface in time to save herself.

Reaching a depth of about forty feet, she forced herself to do the unthinkable.

Instantly, salt water burned through her nasal cavity. Her arms and legs flailed uncontrollably with a surge of panic, her scream muted by incoming water. *God, no. What have I done?* But she kept her eyes shut . . . she was far too deep to come back up. She inhaled more water. Her lungs were on fire.

She was jolted forward from a sudden impact to her back.

Seabed?

But then she heard the sound of crashing water. Opening her eyes, completely disoriented, she saw the full moon and black smoky clouds. Amy felt a pebbled coolness beneath her back. Coughing and spitting seawater, she rolled to her stomach. Her eyes and mouth widened in disbelief, though she couldn't utter a sound. She was gliding across the night sea on this horrible creature's head.

Amy rose up on one elbow, catching her breath. In the moonlight, she could see her bloody body glistening as it lay across the gray skin. Just in front of her hands was an enormous eye. Behind her, she recognized the dreaded frill, towering above her.

It's keeping me above water, she thought in wonder. *It won't let me drown.* Immediately, her mind went back to earlier that night, when the hammerhead came straight at her, and the way the creature had killed it.

She went back to her original hope that maybe . . . just maybe . . . the creature was protecting her.

Why? Why would it care? Why not let me die with the others?

Then it hit her.

She recalled a documentary she'd seen on killer whales. She remembered how the orcas would attack seal colonies. After having their fill of several seals, they would play with one "lucky" member of the colony and then bring it safely back to shore. Researchers had no explanation for the bizarre behavior, but the whales did it nonetheless.

Is it possible?

On all fours and remaining as still as possible, Amy looked ahead with yet another glint of hope.

But the beast didn't appear to heading for shore, or anywhere in particular. It was still swimming in a huge circle.

With the night wind whipping through her hair, she felt life creeping back into her body. Gazing down at the behemoth beneath her, she caught a glimpse of herself as well. Her torn left breast, void of its implant, hung grotesquely low. Her left hip and thigh was a mass of tattered flesh. Her beautiful figure and flawless skin—her entire reason for being—was gone, yet it barely registered. None of it seemed to matter as she watched the water and froth divide before the massive head, dreading the horror to come, hoping . . . always hoping.

The pebbled skin dropped from beneath her suddenly. *What? The creature is diving, dropping me back into the sea.*

Swimming upward, Amy surfaced in the cool water.

It's not done. Surely not . . .

The colossal head rose beside her, rising higher and higher until it eclipsed the full moon. The enormous maw opened wide and unleashed a bellowing roar. Again, the giant head cocked back and emitted another roar, as if calling out to the sea.

Then the towering head rolled back and slammed into the water in a mass of waves.

~~~

Inside the Sky Hawk, Kate stared forward, scouring the sea while John talked to Nathan on the walkie-talkie. "Good job, Nathan," John said. "Let us know if the signal moves again. Out." He lowered his hands and turned to Kate. "Nathan said the new signal is about—"

Kate cut him off, "We don't need it! Look!"

John followed Kate's gaze and felt his heart pound in his throat.

~~~

It's coming back it's coming back it's coming back . . .

Bathed in her own blood, Amy watched helplessly as the merciless beast closed in. Again, it glided by, scraping her cruelly with its jagged skin. It tugged her face below the surface, her hysterical screams transforming into gurgles.

Below the surface, more blood rose from her abraded body as she rolled off the passing flank. Her face rose, spitting and spinning in the monster's wake.

Methodically, the creature veered back around.

~~~

Inside the cockpit, John and Kate stared at the spectacle below, foreboding growing in their hearts and minds as they watched the pliosaur brush by the woman as if teasing her, as if it were pushing her around for the sole purpose of heightening her terror.

Kate closed in, lowering altitude. "What's it doing to her? I've heard of killer whales playing with seals before killing them, but never—"

John interrupted as he rose from the passenger's seat. "It's not playing with her . . . it's toying with us."

Kate looked at him in disbelief. "Come again?"

"It waited," John said, sliding off his headset. "Somehow, that thing knows we can track it . . . just like at the pier. It knew we'd come."

Kate stared at him like he was crazy.

"All right, then," John stepped between the back seats, "you explain it!"

Entering the cargo bay, he reached the doorway. His hair blew back from the wind of the main rotor. Forty feet below, he saw the woman turn and look up at him—pleading, terrified . . . hopeful?

Immediately, John recognized the blue eyes glowing in the chopper's light. The Sea Ray's debris scattered around her confirmed that she was the young blonde he'd seen earlier. Clearly, the two men with her were nowhere in sight.

Dead.

John watched as the pliosaur brushed by the woman again, then headed away, only to circle again. The monster turned on its side, a red eye glaring up at the doorway.

The enormous jaws swung up from the water, letting loose a roar that could be heard above the rotor blades.

John met the creature's gaze. "I get it. At the pier, you didn't like how that played out. So you waited. Now you want me to try it again, give you another shot." He backed up to a bundled nylon ladder.

As if in reply, another roar.

"That's it! You expect me to jump in after her . . . like at the pier?" said John, sliding the ladder to the doorway. He saw his shot. The beast was still thirty yards away from the girl.

"Sorry to disappoint you!"

With that, he hurled the nylon ladder through the doorway. It fell, unwinding toward the surface.

The pliosaur kept its distance.

John's heart sank when the girl reached up into the glaring light. It was a pitiful sight. Her torn open left breast hung grotesquely. Below her reaching arm, light glistened off her exposed ribs. The sides of her torso, hips and thighs were torn to ribbons. The merciless monster had literally skinned her alive.

He looked at the creature with a fury.

And then the beast dove.

"Hold on!" John screamed.

The moment her hand connected with the ladder, a luminous shape appeared beneath her.

It rose.

A mound of water pushed her upward, then exploded into a perfect black tunnel around her. The jaws slammed shut, and the ladder sprang up from a plume of water. For a gruesome moment, John glanced a severed hand still clutching the bottom of the ladder . . . until the ladder whipped, sending the appendage off into the night.

John stood frozen, looking down at the froth of bubbles beneath the swaying ladder. Losing sight of the creature, he returned to the cockpit. His blood boiled. His heart ached.

Kate turned in her seat. "What happened?"

"You know what happened," barked John, looking through every window in the cockpit. "You saw it, didn't you?"

"But animals don't think that way."

"It could have taken her at any time," John said, "but it waited. It knew we were on the way and would try to save her . . . like at the pier." He looked Kate in the eye. "I couldn't tell if it was trying to lure me back into the water, or if it just wanted to make sure I saw it happen. Either way, that thing's pure evil!"

He crawled across the passenger's seat, looking through the window. "Where? Where is—?" He paused when he spotted the tip of the frill. He pointed and Kate nodded, swinging the chopper around. The giant tail appeared in the glaring light. John ran to the cargo bay. Through the doorway, he saw a huge paddle fin pump beneath the swells.

"GET ME OVER IT!" he screamed toward the cockpit with fury. Pulling a depth charge from the crate, he carried it to the doorway. He stared down at the colossal back of the creature. "Come on . . . can't miss. Not this time."

He pressed the button . . . 1 . . . 2 . . . 3 . . . and let it go.

The pliosaur rolled at the same split-second the charge exploded beneath the surface. A plume of water reached up to the doorway.

A direct hit. John couldn't believe his eyes.

Without looking to see if the creature was still alive, John snatched the last depth charge from the crate. In a single motion, he activated it, hurling it through the doorway.

Kaboom! Another shot right on the money.

"Brrravooo!" Kate shouted from the cockpit, pumping her fists in the air.

For a long moment, John didn't dare take a breath as he watched nothing but boiling bubbles rise beneath the searchlight.

Nothing . . . nothing . . . it's gone. He sighed deeply, relieved, exhausted.

Then the frill broke the surface, the red orb of its eye almost winking at him. And just that quickly, it was gone, again. Alive.

Eventually, John made his way back to the cockpit and slowly took a seat, stunned. His last nerve fried. He stared blankly at the frothy swells and boat debris. "No way . . . there's no way I missed. That first shot was square on its throat." He raised his gaze to the full moon, and an eerie sensation crept over him. "Maybe they were right . . . something else is playing a hand in all this."

"Look," Kate said, "I'm not sure what you're getting at, but that thing's just a reptile . . . fifty tons worth, but still just a reptile." She caught sight of the fuel gauge. "Wow! We're at bingo fuel!" She gave a nervous glance through the side window. "I can think of better places to run out of petrol."

Twisting the throttle, she flipped a switch on the instrument cluster. "I'll call the admiral and relay the pliosaur's last coordinates." Glancing at John, she added, "It couldn't have gone far; they can still find it."

"Not tonight." John's vacant eyes stared down at the dark water. "It's gone . . . it's already proven its point."

Chapter 9
THE NECALA

Moments after receiving the pliosaur's position from Kate, the naval demolition team reached the site. Immediately, Admiral Henderson saw the boat debris sprinkled in a long chum line. He barked into his headset, ordering the helicopters to disperse and scan the area. When he raised his binoculars, there it was–about seventy-five yards from the debris, a huge splash. Closing in, he could make out the enormous shadow just beneath the surface. Playing the chopper's spotlight over the creature, he saw the knotted back gliding above the waterline. It was heading into the fog bank.

The admiral motioned to the pilot. "Sit me on its back!" Instantly, the lead helicopter closed on the great silhouette. The cargo door slid open. Below, they could see the giant shadow gliding beneath the misty waves, part of its jagged back cutting the waterline. The fog grew thicker, obscuring the beast. Quickly, the first depth charge was handed to a man harnessed inside the cargo bay just inside the doorway.

With a splash, the gray cylinder pierced the surface then exploded beside the shadow. The blast dispersed the fog. Amidst walls of water, the enormous underbelly rolled to the surface. The second depth charge detonated beside the flank, spewing water up against the bottom of the helicopter.

The flight crew cheered as the vast underbelly rolled. Then without the slightest trace of movement, the great bulk descended to the depths of the sea.

~~~

Just as Kate's helicopter touched down behind Simon's Town airport, John received a call over the radio. "John, this is Tom Hayman with the Sharks Board. Do you copy?"

John eagerly responded, "I copy. What's the latest, Tom? Over."

"We're a couple miles off Pearly Beach on our way back in. John, we got it! We saw the debris Kate described and picked up a visual on the pliosaur immediately. The demolition team dropped a couple depth charges near the creature—not direct hits, but the monster rolled over on its back and sank like a stone. Then they dropped four more depth charges in the same vicinity just to be sure. It all just happened . . . maybe just ten minutes ago. And you weren't exaggerating about the size! That bloody thing was enormous!"

Shutting off the helicopter's engine, Kate looked over at John, whose face could barely hold his wide smile. Kate whooped and tossed a high five. Suddenly, John's smile vanished as a guarded thought popped into his head. "Tom, was there blood? Did they recover any part of the carcass?"

He looked at Kate, who frowned.

There was static, then Tom's voice was clear. "It was hard to tell if the blood was from the creature or the chum already in the water. As far as the carcass, the pliosaur sank after they hit it, with no movement at all. We're going back out tomorrow morning to recover what's left of it. Oh, and to be on the safe side, we're not releasing any of this to the media until we do find the carcass. Don't want anyone to get to it before we do."

"Okay, thanks," John said quietly. "If there are any further developments, you can reach me on Kate's cell. Out."

Taking off his headset, John battled with this feeling of unease. He tried to recover his original sense of relief: *they hit it! Even if they didn't kill the creature, they had to have seriously wounded it. Right?* The doubt wouldn't go away, but he knew there was nothing more he could do. *Just wait and see . . . again.*

He reached over and cracked the door open, allowing Kate to exit first. She didn't say a word. Then Nathan's voice crackled over the walkie-talkie beneath the copilot's seat. John picked it up. "Hey, Steven, I've got some pretty good—"

Steven cut him off. "I just picked up a signal on the monitor a minute ago. Wait . . . argh, it just went out again. But I've got the pliosaur's new coordinates!"

"When? Exactly when did the signal go out?" Nathan hesitated at the urgent sound in John's voice, and then said, "Uhhh, just now, less than a minute ago. Why?"

"I just got a call from Tom from the Sharks Board chopper. He said the demolition team destroyed the creature more than ten minutes ago. If that's the case, the transmitter should have gone out *then*, not a minute ago."

"That's true," Steven said, "but there is a possibility that the pliosaur is dead and the transmitter's still sending a signal." He paused, then repeated in a softer voice. "It is possible."

"I don't know," John said. "If the depth charges didn't do enough damage to take out the transmitter, I don't think we can assume they did enough damage to the creature. I mean, they said the hits weren't spot-on."

"Wait!" Steven said with urgency. "It's back on."

"Did it move? Did it move at all?"

Kate grabbed John's arm in a death grip as she listened to the conversation, her eyes wide with disbelief.

Steven replied, "Wait, it's hard to tell. I've marked the last spot on the monitor. Let's see . . . yeah, not much, but it looks like maybe two hundred yards from the previous transmission. *Annnd*, there it just went out again." His deep sigh could be heard clearly over the speaker. Kate kicked the dirt with her boot, cursed a flash of angry words, and walked away from the chopper. She stood there, her back to John, head tilted back as if praying to the heavens.

"All right, I'm going to call the admiral!" John said, his eyes on Kate. "Do not turn away from that monitor, okay? Let me know if that signal comes back. We'll refuel and probably stay here at the airport for the night. But I'll keep the walkie-talkie close by. If I don't hear from you tonight, I'll call you in the morning. Out."

John set the walkie-talkie down and walked over to Kate who now stared blankly through the chain-link fence and at the back of the airport office. He stared with her, both silent for a long while.

Kate spoke first. "Don't worry. I'll run into town and pick up another couple barrels of meat. While I'm out, I think I'll pay a visit to an old mate." She smiled, a newfound determination in her tone. "Maybe he can help us with something." She slapped John on the back and winked. "If Big Ugly is still out there, I assure you this is his last party!"

John's mouth hung open as he watched her walk away. A smile crept onto his face as he shook his head. *The woman doesn't give up easily.* He walked after her into the building. *I like it.*

~~~

John smoldered as he hung up the telephone in Kate's office at the Simon's Town airport. He looked at Kate who was downing a sports drink in the kitchenette. "I can't believe it! The Navy won't admit even the possibility of the pliosaur still being alive." He looked at the clock which read eleven fifteen. It had been hours since the demolition team had supposedly destroyed the creature, which John knew in his bones was not the case.

"How can they not, based on the facts?" Kate said, disgusted. She tossed the empty bottle into the garbage can.

"Admiral Henderson insists the so-called movement after death was probably caused by underwater currents. He even disputes the homing device, saying that its accuracy is highly debatable." John pulled a chair in front of the computer desk and muttered, "The thing is . . . his argument sounded convincing, but his tone did not. He doubts it too."

Kate walked out of the kitchenette. "Guess all we can do is wait until tomorrow and see what turns up when they drop down to look for the carcass. We both need to get some sleep, so let's wind it down for tonight and start fresh in the morning. I'm going out back to prep the chopper. Back in a few."

After Kate closed the door, John took a seat in front of the computer. He switched it on, thinking back to the beginning of this bizarre assignment. When he'd first heard the prophecy on the island, he dismissed it as nothing more than tribal folklore. But a lot had happened since then; things that were gradually turning him into a believer. There was a mention of shed blood and the strange part about the full moon. But what haunted John most of all was one Zulu word spoken by Kota, the meaning of which he did not know: *necala*.

Once online, he did a search for a Zulu translation dictionary. He keyed in the word, spelling it phonetically. The translation floated on the glowing screen: *guilty*.

~~~

The small fishing boat slowly cruised alongside a dimly lit dock off Pearly Beach. Kota continued to look for a place to tie off the boat while Kolegwa stared awestruck at all of the strange people and their foreign attire. A young man pulled his bikini-clad girlfriend to his side and leered back at them as if he did not approve of Kolegwa's gaze. Kota blew him a kiss and laughed.

Finally, Kota spotted a slip near the shore. Pulling closer, their attention shifted to a roaring sound over their heads in the night sky. The two tribesmen watched as five naval helicopters flew in formation past the Seaside Hotel and headed inland.

Kota stepped across to the dock and tied off the boat. Kolegwa looked up and said, "They find Kuta-keb-la!'

"Do not worry!" replied Kota, turning his attention to the full moon glowing above the night sea. "Tonight is only the beginning!"

~~~

Thoroughly exhausted, John sat in a wooden chair in the airport office, staring at a small television. The walkie-talkie was silent, balanced on his thigh. He peeled off his damp, tattered shirt and tossed it on the floor. His naked back was littered with the cuts and bruises from his rescue at the pier.

He clicked over to another station. Like the others, it showed a reporter at a location he would never forget. The young black woman stood on a dark shoreline, while behind her searchlights scoured the ravaged Pier 16. It all seemed surreal. Broken pilings protruded hideously from the sea while hundreds of planks washed in and out with the tide.

The reporter summed it up with a dramatic tone. "Yes, you heard it right. Numerous eyewitnesses claim to have seen a reptilian creature—

massive, estimated at eighty to one hundred feet long—demolish the pier behind me. A gruesome attack that would have claimed a second life had it not been for a heroic rescue from an unidentified bystander."

Heroic rescue, John scoffed, and he dropped his head, his elbows now balanced on his knees. His efforts were not near enough. He vividly remembered the daughter screaming for her father who'd been a victim on that pier. *If I'd only gotten there sooner, she would still have a father. If only . . .*

He looked back up at the television. He didn't want to watch, didn't want to hear more, but he couldn't look away.

The reporter glanced at some notes in her hand then looked straight into John's eyes.

"Many are linking this to yesterday's Montanza tragedy. Even before tonight's attack, fishermen who claim to have seen the creature under the net, all insist it had paddle fins." She then went on to explain briefly how marine reptiles that'd swum by this means of propulsion hadn't existed for millions of years. "Now, we're going to take you live to Professor Lenny Brennan at the South African Museum in Cape Town to help shed some light on what this mysterious creature may be."

John slid his chair closer to the television. The camera cut to an elderly man, maybe in his sixties, with a long, gray beard. The camera pulled back to reveal an enormous set of reconstructed pliosaur jaws set up just behind him.

"Oh yeah. It's way outta the bag now," John muttered.

A female reporter held a microphone in front of Professor Brennan. His voice was gruff, and his words were clipped, matter-of-fact. "Pliosaur—meaning 'greater lizard', was a prehistoric marine reptile, one that we thought to have been extinct for over sixty-five million years. However! . . . much more than 'just a reptile.' Note the jaws." He stepped back to give the camera a better view of the jaws.

The professor then picked up a huge, black, fossilized tooth from a table.

"A giant possessing the most formidable teeth in the animal kingdom," he said, turning the tooth in his hand. "The reptile could reach a length of sixty feet or more. Undoubtedly, the greatest predator in history. And I believe this creature is swimming off our southern coast. This very minute!"

"Professor, what makes you so certain?" asked the reporter.

Returning the tooth to the table, Professor Brennan stepped closer to the jaws. "In the last few days, there have been at least nine eyewitnesses to the beast. The two lads and young woman on the speedboat yesterday, the surviving surfer from the Jeffrey's Bay attack, and then only hours ago, five more witnesses from the Pier 16 incident—all who claim the creature they saw was at least eighty to one hundred feet long. Considering that the largest marine croc ever actually measured was only twenty feet long, and did not possess paddle fins, this particular creature must be a pliosaur." Ignoring the reporter, he eyed the camera with his wrinkly glare and concluded, "There is simply no other logical explanation!"

The reporter pushed for more answers. "So, assuming this creature *is* a pliosaur, would this be big news in the world of marine biology?"

"Marine biology?" Professor Brennan spat and gave a resounding "Hhha!" to punctuate his opinion. "This is brilliant news the world over. Nothing short of finding a living T-rex roaming through the jungles of Africa, young lady. Already, I've heard from dozens of paleontologists from around the globe who are catching flights to South Africa tonight. After today, the history books will have to be rewritten!" He jammed a finger into the air.

John watched the wrap-up and muttered, "Well, Admiral Henderson, looks like you've finally got your Black December." He flipped to another station and paused. The moment he saw the young blonde's hypnotic blue eyes, his body tensed. How vibrant she looked in the photograph compared to the woman he saw only hours ago reaching up to the helicopter. He could still see it clearly: flesh hanging from her torn body, the terror in her eyes as the pliosaur circled her. He thanked God that her family would never know how horribly she suffered before the creature finally killed her.

The woman's image moved to the corner of the screen to bring another female reporter into view. "Also among the reported missing from the wreckage discovered this evening is Amy Lawrence. At twenty-two years of age, she is the wife of the vessel's owner, Chris Lawrence. Both being retired lifeguards, the couple owned and operated Lawrence Bait & Tackle on Pearly Beach."

John's heart sank, and his eyes immediately glazed over with tears. He'd finally reached his breaking point. The reality of the nightmare stared back at him in Amy's blue eyes. *Three kids out fishing for tuna, slaughtered in the prime of life.* He lowered his gaze, staring blankly at the floor. The burning rage inside him, the only thing that had kept him going, disappeared. There was nothing left but sorrow.

The reporter continued, "In a possible twist of fate, we've just been notified that last October, Chris Lawrence was fined for finning sharks."

"Finning sharks," John whispered as his gaze rose back up to the TV screen.

Guilty.

The word from the prophecy echoed in his mind and realization crept into his eyes. He looked through the window at the full moon, and a chill ran up his spine. Had he completely lost his mind, or was it all starting to make sense?

~~~

Finished with chopper prep, Kate headed back to the office. Swinging open the door, she saw John sitting in front of the television. She stared at his naked back, knowing the scratches were incidental compared to the deep scars he carried inside. Then she saw what was on the screen—the young lady they could not save. Her heart broke, knowing John was reliving every moment of the nightmare, one of many he could not save.

Stepping closer, she saw a long gash on his shoulder. Kate gently slid her fingertips beside the wound to take a closer look. It could require stitches. She didn't mean it as a romantic gesture, but when John reached up and took her hand, she didn't mind. Kate leaned forward. Their fingers interlocked for a moment, then released, and her hand slid down following the contours of John's chest. Leaning closer, her hair fell down around his bare shoulders, and her lips gently touched his neck.

John's fingers were lost in her hair.

Her lips followed the outline of John's neck until they met his in a long kiss. He leaned his head back, fully giving in—respite from the torment, Kate supposed. More . . .

In the heat of the moment, he pulled away. His eyes were riddled with guilt, confusion.

Kate sighed and stood up, pulled her hair back in place. She pointed to the television. "Why do you keep doing this to yourself? Haven't you seen enough?" she said firmly, and reached over to turn it off. "Let's give this a break for a while, shall we?"

John grabbed her hand with a look of panic. "No, don't! Something new could turn up, prove it's still alive."

"Listen," Kate said. "You weren't there with the demolition team, and the Navy insists they got it. Besides, Nathan hasn't picked up a signal in over an hour. Can't you even entertain the possibility that the creature is dead?"

John didn't utter a sound.

As if taking a child's toy, she removed the walkie-talkie from his lap and placed it on an end table. "We can at least put this here. It's still in earshot, so you won't miss it if Nathan calls with another signal." She eased back on the edge of the table, arms crossed in front of her, and looked at him curiously. "Earlier, after trying to depth-charge the creature, you mentioned something . . . that whole 'playing a hand' bit

. . . what were you getting at?"

John stared at the black screen on the TV. "Tonight, I dropped that depth charge square on its throat . . . and nothing. Now, the Navy swears they killed it . . . but the transmitter inside the beast suggests otherwise." He gave a sardonic laugh. "What would all of the world's great scientific minds make of that?"

"What are you trying to say?"

"Maybe science doesn't hold all of the answers."

Kate's eyes narrowed. "Come again?"

"Once released, that thing could have easily returned to the open sea, never to be heard from again. But it didn't. It turned up here—just like the tribesmen prophesied. I didn't quite understand parts of their prophecy until tonight when I looked it up—the meaning for the Zulu word 'necala.' Kate, it means 'guilty.' The prophecy says, *Before the first full moon, the blood of the guilty will be shed to mark the beginning. Then innocent blood will fill the sea.*"

Admittedly, the words painted an ominous picture. Kate felt herself shiver.

John added, "Tonight was the first full moon since it was released."

"Okay." She nodded with growing concern.

"Listen." John had a crazed look in his eyes that Kate had not seen before. She nodded again and John continued, "Look at the first major attacks. The Montanza . . . remember the activists protesting the cruelty of the nets that trap dolphins and other sea life . . . and the way the tuna are butchered? Then the fishermen at Dyer Channel—both of them men who have illegally slaughtered sharks for decades. What do these two incidents have in common?"

Kate threw her hands up. "You got me." Still, she felt the answer just beyond her grasp, drawing nearer with each word John spoke now.

"Can't you see it? In the villagers' eyes, they were defiling the sea. It's just like they prophesied. These victims are the *necala*—the *guilty*, whose blood would be shed first. Before the first full moon!"

"I think you're stretching things a bit, John," Kate said, and she saw his eyes flare with frustration.

"No, I'm not, Kate. Somehow it all marks the beginning of the prophecy!"

Clinging desperately to her comforting voice of reason, she quickly countered, "Hold on!" She rose from the end table. "For all this tribal mumbo jumbo to hold up, one of the next attack victims would had to have been guilty, by the full moon, tonight . . . right? That would have been the elderly bloke on the pier, or the three mates out fishing for tuna. How were any of them guilty?"

John pointed to the television. "Afraid I was just getting to that," he said blankly. "Just saw the three kids from the boat on the news. Two months ago, they were busted by the Navy."

"Busted for what?"

"Earlier tonight, looks like they tricked us; all that blood on their deck . . . they were really finning sharks."

Kate's heart skipped a beat, but she tried to maintain a realistic demeanor to balance John's emphatic claims. "What are you saying? Are you implying that this is all part of some divine retribution; that God would actually side with those savages?"

John looked away. His eyes shone in the night. "On the island there's a huge clearing sprinkled with fifty or so painted conch shells. Each shell marks the grave of a child . . . a child that died after eating fish tainted from a chemical spill. Then you factor in decades of over-fishing, dredging the seabed for all she's worth, endless pollution. Take a good step back and look at it all. Who are the real savages?"

His eyes slowly rose to her. "If God were to side with the innocent, what makes you think that's us?"

Kate kneeled to face John. An empathetic look in her eye. "Look, I know you've been through nothing less than a living hell, and I've been right there with you, I have! But those attacks had something else in common, and do you know what that is?"

John waited.

She finished, "They all had fresh blood in the water. That's what drew the creature to them, not some tribal prophecy . . . right?"

John fought her argument as she'd expected he would. "But you saw it, Kate—the look in its eye. Then the way it waited to butcher that girl in front of me. I'll give you this, though. You're right about one thing: whatever it is, it's not from God. It's straight from hell."

Kate blew some hair out of her eyes with a long sigh. *Stubborn.* She glanced at her watch, effectively ignoring his last comment. "Look, I almost forgot . . . I have to run out and get something." She ruffled his hair as she passed. "Try to get some rest, John. You'll send yourself to an early grave next if you don't."

"That's rich!" John said with a genuine laugh.

"What?"

"We're chasing the most lethal predator in history . . . and you're worried about lack of sleep taking me out."

Kate shook her head and headed for the door. *He's absolutely impossible.*

~~~

The dark figure of Kota stood at the edge of the Seaside Hotel parking lot, staring out to sea. He waved to Kolegwa who was carrying the two briefcases along the dock. "Come, we don't have all night."

Brakes squeaked behind them, and Kota smiled. "Ah, our ride is here." They turned to a black Jeep that had just pulled into the parking lot. As they approached, a door cracked open, and a man's sandaled foot slipped out. Kota unsheathed his machete and raised it behind his back. He spoke in Afrikaans, "Sir, could we trouble you for a lift?"

Chapter 10
TOP STORY

John continued to flip through the channels in amazement. He knew that once the story broke it would be big, but he had no idea. In the last half hour, he'd seen at least six different paleontologists discussing the possibility of pliosaur's existence. There were numerous interviews with the two boys on the speedboat and the eyewitnesses from Pier 16. And everyone was an expert; there were endless theories on relict, mutated, and genetically altered crocs from every oddball in South Africa.

Then there were the reports on the news from Cape Town International Airport showing frantic ticketing agents trying to deal with the amount of booked flights. Tomorrow scientist and curiosity seekers from around the world would be flooding the terminals. Even worse were the hotels. Already they were saying that it was impossible to get a room in Cape Town. Practically the entire city was booked.

Flipping to another station, John saw a female reporter standing on a crowded shoreline. Behind her was the now infamous red speedboat with the huge bite mark in its stern. The reporter was saying, "As you may have heard, the small vessel behind me was allegedly attacked late yesterday by a creature of gigantic proportion. Already, the enormous bite mark in the boat's stern and testimonies of those on board are making headlines across the globe."

A photograph of a young man appeared in the corner of the screen. "Yesterday, naval authorities were quick to classify this sighting as a hoax. But many dismissed the 'hoax theory' when Ron Fernan came forward. You may recall Ron as being the survivor of an alleged shark attack that claimed the life of Dorian Anderson two days ago while they were surfing near Jeffrey's Bay. According to Ron, the creature that attacked them was no shark, but of the same proportions described by the boys in the speedboat as well as by witnesses from tonight's Pier 16 attack.

"As of now, naval authorities won't deny or confirm the existence of such a creature, stating the situation is under investigation. Now, we're going to take you live to Pier 16 for an update."

As the media frenzy continued to unfold before his eyes, John couldn't shake an uneasy sensation. He wondered what would happen tomorrow morning if the Navy went out and didn't find the carcass. He could hear the admiral now: "The currents must have moved it," or "The scavenger sharks must have already consumed the remains." He looked at the walkie-talkie sitting on the end table. *Come on, Nathan. If we could just pick up one more signal . . .*

It was going to be a long night.

~~~

It was well after one a.m., and Admiral Henderson was still on the phone in his Simon's Town naval office. A small television in a bookcase showed the ravaged Pier 16. With his phone at his ear, he kept one eye on the news and said, "I don't care about the bloody headlines. For the last time, it doesn't matter. The beast is dead, and we'll prove it in the morning when we go down to retrieve the carcass."

He listened for a moment, his blood pressure rising. "Absolutely not!" he barked, "There will be no press conference. Just tell them we still have the matter under investigation. I'm not about to address those vultures until I have a photo of the carcass and can put this mess to an end!"

Hanging up the phone, he sat on the corner of his desk. It wasn't ten seconds until he heard the annoying ringing again. Ignoring the phone, he stared through a picture window and out into the dark naval yard. His eyes drifted across the glistening rotor blades of the helicopters and to the waters beyond. He looked back at the news. It showed a reporter interviewing yet another eyewitnesses from the Pier 16 attack.

"Well, it looks like you vultures aren't going to let this wait," he muttered.

~~~

The A109 Agusta LUH naval helicopter soared through the night sky as Tom Hayman sat nervously on a bench in the cargo bay. He was in full dive gear and sandwiched between three naval divers. Ahead in the cockpit he could see Admiral Henderson barking orders to the pilot. A glimpse through the windshield showed that visibility should be good due to the full moon. As the rotor thumped overhead, Tom couldn't shake his earlier conversation with John.

John's voice still rang in his ears. '*I'm telling you it's still alive. I just received a call from the ship where they're tracking the transmitter inside the pliosaur. According to the transmitter, it moved two hundred yards. And that was ten minutes after you called me telling me it was dead!*'

But Tom knew better . . . he'd been there. He saw the first shot detonate just beneath the creature's underbelly and then the second one just above its jagged back. This beast was dead. But he also knew the admiral was right: they'd better prove it tonight before the scavenger sharks strip the carcass down to fragments that could be swept away by the current, never to be found.

This was one answer that could not wait until morning.

Tom glanced at the faces beside him. To his right was Andre Wells, a stone-faced, seasoned naval diver. Tom hadn't heard him yet say a word. Suited up in an orange naval wetsuit, he just stared intently at the closed cargo bay door. The young black men to Tom's left were a different story. Johan and Thabo Madaki, nicknamed the 'Bloodhound Brothers,' were a pair of chatty, wild-eyed boys from Simon's Town. With their hair braided in long cornrows that hung to their shoulders, the boys were nearly identical. The most obvious difference was that Johan's hair was brown, and Thabo's was dyed bright red.

They might not look it, thought Tom, *but these boys know their business.*

Although they were only in the naval reserves, Johan was a local dive master and knew the area like the back of his hand. Both in their mid-twenties, the brothers earned their reputation a year ago when a naval patrol boat went missing in these waters. Naval frogmen scoured the area for weeks with no luck. Then the Bloodhound Brothers pitched in and found the sunken vessel by nightfall the same day.

Quite a contrast to Andre, thought Tom. Maybe it was nerves, or sheer adrenaline, but the brothers were talking a mile a minute.

Thabo zipped up his wetsuit. He glanced down through a window behind them. "Johan, looks like we're going to one of your favorite spots," he yelled above the rotor blades.

"Oh yeah!" said the older brother. "It's a real hot spot for kreef."

Listening in, Tom looked at Johan. "Kreef?"

Johan was sliding on his dive fins. "Kreef. That's what the locals call the Cape rock lobster. The seabed is saturated with them, my friend."

Thabo pulled his long, red cornrows from the neckline of his wetsuit. "But tonight we're looking for something a little bigger and a lot easier to find, hey, bro?"

"A lot bigger, yes," cautioned Johan. "But not necessarily easier to find. There are a lot of deep ravines between the caves. If the carcass fell into one of those, it won't be easy to spot, especially at night." Johan reached down and picked up a large circular light by its side handles. "But don't worry, I've got one of the brightest dive lights on the market. Four hundred watts of halogen. This baby'll light up the seabed like a convenience store in a high crime area." He winked. "Next time I'm out here looking for kreef they won't have a prayer, eh?"

Thabo looked at his brother. "Got that right, bro!"

Tom turned his attention to the cockpit as Admiral Henderson rose from his seat and waved at his divers. "All right," the admiral shouted. "Make sure you're geared up. We're five minutes from the site."

~~~

From a balcony of the Seaside Hotel, Kota and Kolegwa stared out over the water beneath the night sky. Moonlight glistened on the distant waves as Kota's mind raced, pondering the outcome from the explosions he'd heard earlier. If John had already warned the authorities about Kuta-keb-la, Kota knew there was little time.

Kolegwa looked around his strange environment, questioning everything. He peered down at an elderly white man and a little boy sitting by the pool. The child erupted in giggles every time the old man bounced him on one knee.

"What is it that makes all outsiders evil; is it their pale skin?"

Kota remained deep in thought.

"My mother used to say that the elders are wrong; all outsiders cannot be evil." Kolegwa then studied a young black couple on the sidewalk below. "And here some evil ones have skin like us. I do not understand what makes them evil."

"You are not here to understand," grumbled Kota. "You're here to do as I say."

Their attention turned to a single craft flying over the night sea. The two powerful figures watched as the naval helicopter rose and glided silently before the full moon.

Kolegwa looked up and said, "They look for Kuta Keb-la.'

"No!" replied Kota. "They look for death. And tonight they shall find it!"

~~~

Standing behind the pilot's seat, Tom peered forward through the helicopter's windshield. Sixty yards ahead, he spotted the glowing yellow marker left by the Navy to mark where the pliosaur went down. The helicopter descended. Tom watched the marker get closer, growing brighter beneath the fog. Twelve years with the Sharks Board had never prepared him for anything like this.

He headed back to the cargo bay to see how the other divers were making out. He looked at Andre. His cold somber expression that he first took for concentration was clearly masking fear. Beside him, the Madaki brothers were still talking without a care in the world. *Did they have any idea the impact of this moment?* wondered Tom. Thabo high-fived his brother. "Ha, and Mom said the only way I'd ever be famous was on *South Africa's Most Wanted.*"

As Thabo pulled his hand back, Johan noticed a sparkle on his left ear. "Where'd you score that?"

Thabo proudly pulled his long, red cornrows back to display a diamond earring. "Cynthia got it for me. It's a full carat. Not a bad score considering I've only known her for one month, hey?"

"Nice." Johan winked. "Almost looks like a real diamond."

Thabo raked his hair back in place and slid on his mask. "You're just jealous because my ladies take care of me."

Johan nodded toward Thabo's dive light. "If it is real, I'd hock it and get a new light head. Can't believe you're still using that antique."

"Works like new." Thabo picked up his dive light. "Jerry Dunnigan just put a new bulb and battery pack in it."

"Jerry Dunnigan." Johan laughed. "I wouldn't trust that clutch plate to put batteries in a flashlight. You know that boy's not right in the head."

"Maybe, but his prices are right."

Johan shook his head and put on a communication headset.

Seeing that everyone was geared up, Tom slid open the cargo bay door. The rotors thumped louder before the glaring moon. When the Madaki brothers came to their feet, Tom approached them. "Listen up!" he said. "I don't care what the admiral said in the briefing earlier. This is the exact spot where the creature went down. If you don't locate the carcass in twenty minutes, I want you to come back up. Understand?"

Admiral Henderson got up from the cockpit. Giving Tom the eye, he spoke to the other divers. "Split up into two groups to cover as much ground as possible. The currents could have moved the carcass. And when you locate it, I want close-up photos, particularly of its wounds. He looked Tom in the eye and then Johan. "The two of you with communication headsets, make sure you use them. I want you to keep me informed of everything you see. All right, men, you know what to do!"

Tom grabbed a halogen dive light and joined the others at the doorway. Johan clicked on his dive light. The powerful beam shot down through the fog and lit up the blue-green sea. "Now that's a dive light." He glanced at the light Thabo held. "Cheapskate. You really gonna jump in the water with that?"

Thabo just ignored his brother.

Staring below, Tom watched the rotor wash sweep away the fog and reveal the black water. His stomach turned. It was difficult to release his hand from the doorframe. He knew the night dive would be unsettling, but felt completely unprepared for the level of fear welling up.

Okay, John. I sure hope you're not right about this one. That thing better be dead!

Reluctantly, he looked at the other divers and gave them the thumbs-up. Then one-by-one, they dropped through the night and splashed into the black sea.

~~~

At two a.m., Kate backed through the door of her Simon's Town airport office carrying a small cardboard box. She saw John lying on the couch, television still yammering.

"I'm back with a surprise!" she announced. "Just visited one of my husband's old military mates. Wouldn't care to ask where he gets the stuff, but he scored us a crate of depth charges. I've already loaded them onto the chopper."

She set the box on the kitchen table. "I also got us a set of night vision binoculars. Now we can see what's under all that fog." She smirked. "He wasn't sure if phantoms of the sea show up on them or not, though."

Not hearing a response, Kate clicked off the light. She prowled over to the couch like a panther in the night, eased down over John, and heard him snoring. *So much for another shot at romance*, she thought. She gave an empathetic whisper, "Guess it's been a rough day, huh?"

Sitting down on an arm of the couch, she looked at John's body glowing in the light of the television. It was a pitiful sight; the numerous cuts and bruises on his bare back and shoulders, and the way he cradled the walkie-talkie against his chest, he looked like a frightened child clinging to a doll.

Thank God, he's getting some sleep.

Careful not to wake him, she slid the walkie-talkie from beneath his arm and laid it on an end table. She clicked off the television and curled up alongside him, slowly easing her head down onto his chest. When he snored again, she couldn't help but smile. She closed her eyes, fully content.

~~~

Beneath the surface, Tom quickly turned on his dive light. The short distance the beam traveled in the pitch did little to calm his nerves. Now that he was in the water, the possibility of the pliosaur's survival didn't seem as farfetched as it had at the office. With a camera dangling from his neck, Andre hovered close by.

A glance back showed two specks of light moving farther away as the Madaki brothers headed in the opposite direction. Tom gave Andre a thumbs-up and turned his light toward the seafloor.

~~~

The two dark figures hovered at a depth of around thirty feet. Johan was adjusting the beam on his dive light, while Thabo gazed up at the full moon, watching it shimmer eerily beyond the waves. Sixty yards east, he saw a faint circle of light where the naval chopper waited above the sea.

A bright light swept across his face. Looking down, he saw Johan motioning him to get a move on. Descending beside his brother, Thabo shone his dive light into the abyss. He was quick to notice that the beam from his light traveled about half the distance of his brother's. The beam flickered. It weakened then disappeared. Thabo gave the light a few good whacks, but to no avail.

He turned to his older brother. Johan was mockingly giving him the "L" shape with his fingers on his forehead: *loser.* Then Johan shook his head and motioned Thabo to follow him.

Piece of crap! thought Thabo as he hooked the dead dive light to his belt. *I'll never hear the end of this.* The duo descended into the inky blackness, the beam from Johan's powerful dive light leading the way.

Thabo looked up when his brother shined the light on a school of passing angelfish. Suddenly, a barracuda shot out of nowhere and scattered the fish. Thabo paused for a moment, waiting for his heart rate to return to normal. All the while, he could tell his brother was laughing behind his regulator.

Johan again shook his head at Thabo. Then motioning Thabo to follow him, Johan dove toward the seafloor. It was time to get down to business.

~~~

Descending deeper into the abyss, Tom glided behind the kicking fins of Andre. The beams of their dive lights crisscrossed over the seabed. On their way down, Tom did not take lightly the fact that both of them naturally searched around them in all directions instead of directly on the seabed where a carcass would most likely be found . . . as if they expected the creature, alive and well, to tap them on the shoulders.

Tom glanced at his dive watch. Fifteen minutes had passed, and every instinct told him it was time to start heading for the surface. As he turned to get the other diver's attention, he saw something white contrasting against the murky bottom. He cautiously swam closer, but discovered it was only part of an old boat hull. He flashed his light in all directions from the boat.

Again, Tom went to check his watch. And when the light's beam shot straight down, he gasped into his regulator. He couldn't believe his eyes. At the bottom of a deep ravine, the light illuminated a massive, jagged back. Tom slowly moved the light. It was the creature, undeniably. *Absolutely enormous.* He motioned to Andre, and the duo descended.

As they got closer, Tom could see that the colossal beast was wedged between the walls of the ravine. Only the top of its back was clearly visible. As far as he could tell, the carcass was fully intact— thankfully—and there were no scavenger sharks milling about. In fact, he found it strange that not a single shark was in sight. Descending, he could make out scarring above the left flank from one of the depth charges. Looking at Andre, Tom then pointed to an area where deep chunks of flesh were missing. While Andre stopped to photograph the wounds, Tom glided farther along the knotted back. Cautiously, he dropped down in front of the enormous head. His light reached the mouth, and a chill shot up his spine. Tom swung his gaze in all directions, the light following. Motioning Andre, he frantically pressed a button on his communication headset to call the admiral.

~~~

Reaching a depth of about sixty feet, the rocky seabed finally appeared in the beam of Johan's dive light. Thabo slowly looked around. There was nothing but blackness in every direction. Peering up, he saw that the faint light from the helicopter had long since faded away.

Whooosh!

Something flashed by Thabo, tossing and disorienting him in its wake. Turning back around, he found only a huge swath of bubbles and Johan's dive light dropping to the seafloor. The beam twirled crazily through the darkness as it fell.

Thabo hovered in the inky blackness, absolutely terrified. He'd never felt so alone.

Far below, the dive light stopped spinning, its beam painting a white stripe across the seabed.

Thabo couldn't move or breathe. *Where's Johan? If he were beside me, I wouldn't know it in this blackness.* His mind raced. *What if it was a shark?*

He had to get to the dive light.

A pump of his fins, and Thabo dove toward the light, all the while looking in every direction for Johan. Although he could see nothing, he sensed he wasn't alone.

Thabo touched down on the rocky seabed. He snatched up the dive light, playing it toward the surface, searching madly for his brother. The glaring light sliced through the blackness, and still there was no sign of Johan.

A crimson cloud drifted in front of the beam. Thabo turned the light, trying to find its source. He lost track of it. Then he picked it up again, the red cloud growing thicker as he followed it to the seafloor.

Thabo's heart stopped. Just a few feet in front of him, an enormous set of interlocked teeth presented themselves in his light. Above the teeth, pebbled skin faded back to a pair of red eyes which glowed threateningly from the pitch.

The monster was waiting for him.

~~~

Inside the naval helicopter, the pilot again questioned the admiral. "Sir, what's going on down there? Are they okay?"

The admiral stared at the sea in panic and rage. "It was a humpback whale," he muttered in a dull voice. "We used six depth charges to destroy a harmless, fifty-foot plankton feeder. The pliosaur . . . is still alive."

"But what about the Madaki brothers?" asked the pilot. "Did you reach Johan?"

The admiral nodded. He turned around and faced the pilot with the glassy eyes of a zombie. "We made contact. All I heard was screaming . . . he was screaming."

~~~

Thabo stared at the colossal head glowing in his dive light. A stream of blood seeped out from between the interlocked, spiked teeth. A belch of bubbles rose from one of the nostrils, but the creature remained perfectly still.

Thabo did not move. *Maybe it's like in the movies—if I don't move it can't see me.*

The jaws swept open. The light illuminated a huge serpentine tongue writhing in a swath of blood. *His brother's blood.*

A gurgling roar sprayed bloody bubbles around Thabo as he spun, tossing the light. Pumping his fins, he lunged forward, his screams echoing in his regulator. Another stroke, but he only felt the forked tongue slither beneath his left leg. The blackness of the open mouth surrounded him. Thabo swam madly below a row of spiked teeth, his arms reaching for the outside ocean. His hands groped the seafloor, clawing and pulling him through the silt. He crawled and crawled until a searing pain sank into his lower back–then his abdomen. A crushing snap made his neck go limp as his dive mask kissed the sand. He rose violently from the seafloor, and the last thing he saw were the bubbles exploding from his own mouth.

~~~

Tom desperately swam for the surface. Trailing five yards behind him, Andre kept pace with camera in hand. After failing to contact Johan over his headset, Tom made an attempt to warn the brothers in person. But when he peered over a rock formation and saw the shadowy head thrashing beside the abandoned dive light, he realized their fate. In that instant, Tom tossed his dive light so he could swim at full speed. Now only one thought crossed his mind: *did it see him?*

In spite of Tom's fear, he couldn't help looking back down. Seventy feet below, he saw glimpses of the gray skin still reflecting in the light.

Tom turned his attention to the approaching surface. He could see the chopper's glaring light above the rotor wash.

He glanced down again. He saw three flashes—the camera? *Is he insane–snapping shots of the pliosaur?* Andre pointed at the camera, then at Tom. He shook his head frantically, trying to indicate that he hit the button by accident.

Turning his attention above him again, Tom swam madly for the chopper's rotor wash. He spotted the end of the nylon ladder dangling beneath the choppy water. Bursting through the surface, he felt the pounding wind from the rotors. He climbed up the ladder without looking back. The admiral was leaning from the cargo bay with his hand extended. Latching onto it, Tom rolled into the doorway and pulled the regulator from his mouth, gasping. "Don't take her up. Andre's still down there!"

They both looked back at the water and saw Andre rising beneath the rotor wash. He now swam with both hands free, the camera apparently dropped—and soon they understood why. A horrible blackness appeared beneath Andre. Illuminated in the chopper's light, the jaws stretched wider, Andre silhouetted in the pitch. The giant teeth defiantly slammed shut at the surface, spraying the chopper with whitewater. Blinded by the splash, Tom and the admiral were forced to look away until the colossal head rolled back into the sea.

After the shock waves settled, there was nothing but rotor wash and a red haze glowing in the chopper's light. Not far off, they saw the giant head rise beneath the fog. Tom ripped off his dive mask and turned to the admiral. "Where are the depth charges?" he demanded. "We can still stop it!"

The admiral turned away and headed silently to the cockpit.

Tom frantically looked around the cargo bay. There was nothing but diving gear, video cameras, fluorescent balloons, lights, and other types of markers. He grabbed the back of the pilot's seat.

"There aren't any," said the pilot flatly. "This was only supposed to be a recovery mission."

Tom looked at the admiral who refused to face him. Releasing the pilot's seat, Tom fell back, disheartened, heartbroken for his fellow divers, for what this all meant. He looked down through the doorway, watching silently as the chopper kept pace with the pliosaur until finally it disappeared completely, leaving behind only the mist-covered sea.

~~~

At three twenty a.m., the airport office was silent as John sat on the couch studying the television news. Kate was sprawled out beside him, asleep. On the screen, an anchorwoman was reporting in front of the ravaged pier. ". . . according to our sources, the creature responsible is somehow linked to a mysterious expedition funded by a Port Elizabeth college professor."

A voice whispered from the shadows of the office. "I see you're about to make headlines again."

Startled, John turned, staring into every dark corner of the office. The voice laughed, then said in a Spanish accent, "I know you remember me, amigo. We've been together for a long, long time." A young Mexican man stepped out of the shadows. He was in his early thirties, decked out in black leather motorcycle attire, a battered helmet tucked under one arm. A long tear in the left thigh of his leathers was slick with blood. Beneath his sunglasses, his face was milky white like a corpse— and with good reason. It was Carlos Rodriguez, the man John had run off the road in college.

"*Si*, we've been together for a long time." Carlos nodded at John. "It's been so lonely here, but now I've come to say gracias for my new compadres." Carlos stepped forward with his left arm around a young boy. "I'd like to introduce my new amigo, Andric Wells." The boy's hair and clothes were soaking wet. His eyes were glassy, and his skin so pale it glowed. John recognized him as the young boy that had drowned in the net of the Montanza. Then one by one, five more faces materialized in the darkness—the fishermen who also met their fates at the fishing festival.

Two more men appeared beside Carlos. "Then, of course, you've already met these compadres, Drew and Al." Dripping with bloody seawater, both of the old anglers stared at John, their sightless eyes glowing in the night. Carlos waved graciously, and another man appeared. His face was obscured. "And now we have a late arrival, Louis Jones, the husband of the woman you rescued at the pier." Carlos grinned. "Too bad you didn't get there sooner, hey, amigo?"

John found himself standing in the middle of a cool, dark abyss. The floor was wet. He could hear the seawater dripping from the victims who now surrounded him. Slowly, the bloody water and tangled seaweed beneath his feet rushed upward and curled around his boots. Like a cold hand, he could feel the icy darkness rising inside him.

"Oh, there's more!" Carlos bellowed like a game show host. "Let's not forget the lovely *Aaaaaamy* Lawrence, our newest arrival!" He winked. "She's a real looker, John!" The young blonde appeared before him, and John could see that her once-piercing blue eyes now held no terror, no hope, nothing. Her torn left breast hung hideously beside her exposed ribs. Yet she still reached out, as if longing for him to pull her from the sea.

Carlos put a cold arm around John's shoulder. "Still, I need one more favor, amigo." The circle of victims opened, allowing Carlos to walk John back to the couch. "There's someone else I would like to join our little fiesta . . . I've had my eye on her for a long while." He stopped, looking down where Kate was asleep on the couch. "I want you to bring her to me, John, like all of the others." He slapped John on the back, and his hideous laugh echoed throughout the room. "I know you won't let me down!"

Then laughter gave way to a ringing.

John woke up screaming, "KATE, NOOO!"

Rising from the couch in a panic, he inadvertently knocked Kate onto the floor. He looked around, groping in the night for her.

Kate rose from the floor, squinting in the dark. "Hey, I'm here, right beside you . . . or at least, I was." She saw John still flailing in the darkness. She whispered, "Hey, hey, it's okay. It's okay. It's just my cell phone." Answering it, she turned on the light next to the couch and responded to the caller, "Sure, he's right here."

Still shaking off the nightmare, John looked up groggily as Kate brought him the phone. "Is it the admiral?"

"No, I think it's the mate from the Sharks Board."

John could hear the sound of a helicopter in the background. It muffled the familiar voice.

"John, this is Tom from the Sharks Board. After all the press the pliosaur was getting, the admiral decided to take a dive team out and locate the carcass tonight."

John stood up and pushed his hands through his hair as Tom continued. "Apparently you were right. It looks like they used six depth charges to blow up a harmless plankton feeder—a humpback whale. I mean, it was a big one, and its back was extremely knotted for a humpback . . ." John was pacing, letting the words sink in. Tom continued to offer excuses; he grew defensive, "And the way it was covered by the fog . . . you have to remember none of us had ever seen the creature before tonight—"

John interrupted, "But once you found the carcass, realized your mistake, you . . . the dive team came straight back up. Right?" There was a long pause on the other end. "Out of the four-man dive team, I was the only one that made it back."

John sat back down on the couch. He realized he'd wakened from one nightmare into another. "Was the demolition squad with you? Did they at least drop—?"

"No," Tom's voice was dry. "We were in a single, unarmed chopper and were only able to maintain a visual for about a minute." John could hear the man breathing deeply, and then he said in a more perky tone, "But don't worry. I've already talked to Admiral Henderson. I thought you'd like to know the Navy will be continuing its search tomorrow morning, for a living pliosaur. So let me know if your guy gets another signal from the transmitter. Okay? John?"

John hung up slowly, not responding to Tom. He looked at Kate with a somber expression. "Guess what?"

Chapter 11
THE HUNT FROM LAND

From a balcony of the Seaside Hotel, Kota continued to stare out over the night sea. *So far so good*, he thought. In the last half hour he'd only seen one helicopter and heard no more explosions. *I must get moving. There is much to do and little time.* He turned around and looked through the sliding glass door where he found Kolegwa sitting at the foot of the bed, mesmerized by the magic of television.

As Kota entered the room, Kolegwa stood up, still in his lime green pants, and excitedly pointed to the images on the screen.

"Relax . . . I'll explain it to you later!" Kota said, then picked up the remote and turned down the volume.

Kolegwa raised his shoulders, palms up, as if to say, "Why'd you do that?" Kota just waved him away.

Sitting on the side of the bed, Kota took John's wallet out of his shirt pocket. Carefully, he slid each item from the wallet and spread them out on the nightstand next to the telephone.

He pulled out a tattered business card. Turning the card over, he saw the word "cell" and a telephone number written in faded red marker. He laid it on the nightstand and dialed the number. Eight rings later, the voice of an elderly woman answered, "Hello." Kota did not respond immediately and the woman prompted, "Kate, is that you?"

"Is this Professor Atkins?"

"Yes, it is. Who . . . who's calling me at this ungodly hour?"

"I'm trying to reach John," replied Kota as he quickly opened the wallet to John's driver's license. "John Paxton."

"No, John isn't here. In fact, I tried to reach him several hours ago myself, but he wasn't in."

"Do you have a phone number or address where he's staying?"

"Yes. I believe he's still staying with Kate at Alexander Aviation, her Simon's Town office. Would you like the number?"

Kota slid his fingers through the business cards on the table. "No, I have it."

"Are you with the Navy? What did you say your name—?" Kota hung up abruptly.

He turned to Kolegwa with a wide grin. "Looks like the hunt is on!"

Kota put on his jacket and slid the business cards into his pocket. Then he leaned over and took out a wad of African rand bills from a briefcase beside the bed. Heading for the door, he muttered to Kolegwa, "I must go out. Do not leave the room until I get back."

Kolegwa nodded without breaking his gaze from the strange vibrant images on the black box in front of him.

Kota paused at the doorway, thinking. Then he grinned mischievously. He walked back to the bed, retrieved the remote, and changed the channel from cartoons to a rerun of *The Terminator*.

"There . . . that's more like it!" He laughed as he walked out the door.

~~~

Kate was pacing the airport office, hands flying in the air as she spoke, while John sat silently on the couch. "Well, at least the Navy's back on our side. And after what just happened, you can bet Admiral Hot Head will be motivated to stop the creature. If the media gets wind that he obliterated a harmless whale, they'll make him look like the fool he is. No doubt, tomorrow morning we'll have all the eyes in the air and the firepower we need."

John still didn't say a word.

Kate glanced at a digital clock beside the couch. "Looks like we can still catch a few winks before sunrise." She reached over to a wall switch and flipped it off. Plopping down on the couch, she snuggled up beside him. Releasing a long breath, she said, "I know how you feel . . . but see, there *was* a logical explanation why the pliosaur was still alive. Now we can put to rest all that tribal prophecy rubbish that's been roaming around in that head of yours. It was a humpback whale; a case of mistaken identity. The Navy simply destroyed the wrong creature."

"Think what you will," John muttered, the night's events replaying in his mind. He recalled the young blonde reaching up to the chopper—the giant jaws taking her before the full moon. He could still see the taunting look in the pliosaur's eye as it glared up at him after taking a direct hit by a depth charge. There was no mistake. The creature he'd hit was no whale. "No way," he whispered. "That still doesn't explain everything."

~~~

Light from the hallway shone through the window, bathing the small hotel room in a yellow hue. Kolegwa sat at the foot of the bed, mesmerized by his strange surroundings: torches with no flames providing light with the flip of a switch; a substance Kota had called glass which blocked the wind and rain; and a bed so soft without the use of leaves or straw. And, of course, the magical black box.

He slowly rose from the edge of the bed. Powerful quadriceps muscles strained the fabric of his outrageous, lime green pants as he cautiously approached the television. He reached out to touch the small figure inside the strange box, but his finger hit against something transparent. Again he tried to reach inside, bumping the screen with his fingertips. But the little man inside the box didn't seem to notice. Curiously, Kolegwa ran his fingers along the sides and back of the box, squinting to find the hidden latch on the mysterious little cage.

Finding no way to free the strange little people, Kolegwa crawled back on the bed and leaned against the headboard. He spotted the remote control beside his knee and remembered how Kota pointed it at the cage. Cautiously, he picked up the remote and pressed a button, wondering if the same magic that had worked for Kota would also work for him.

The channel switched to an old *Tarzan* movie. Kolegwa leaned forward, watching as dozens of tribesmen poured onto the screen. They were chasing a jeep loaded with elephant tusks as it raced through the jungle. Frenzied cries echoed around the walls of the hotel room. Kolegwa leaned closer.

A man in the back of the jeep pulled out a machine gun and fired. The front rows of natives dropped lifelessly to the ground as the machine gun kicked in the man's hand. Kolegwa's eyes bulged. He scurried toward the edge of the bed, desperately trying to think of a way to free the natives before the white man killed them all.

He picked up the television and raised it overhead, the power cord and cable ripping from the wall. Off to his right, he saw the large window overlooking the outside walkway. With all his strength, he hurled the television. In an explosion of glass, the television burst through the window and crashed onto the concrete in front of a young couple on their way to an evening dip in the hotel pool.

~~~

The black Jeep Cherokee skidded to a stop in the Seaside Hotel parking lot. Stepping from the vehicle, Kota reached over the tailgate and tightened the caps of four full cans of gas. "This should be plenty," he muttered with a wicked grin. He then walked past the pool and headed up the stairs to the second floor. As he reached the top step, he noticed the commotion in front of his room. A group of onlookers were standing around a smashed television, its pieces scattered across the hallway.

Kota groaned. *I knew I shouldn't have left him alone!*

Nearing the room, he heard the pleas coming from behind the shattered window. "No! Don't do it mate, please. I'm sorry ... I'm sorry."

A young man ran past Kota and shouted, "I'm calling the police." A woman standing in front of the window screamed hysterically, "There's no time. It'll be too late!"

Kota walked through the doorway and saw Kolegwa holding the

hotel manager against the wall with his forearm. The shivering man's feet hung eight inches above the floor. Just inside the doorway, the manager's little dog barked frantically at Kolegwa, the cold steel of Kolegwa's machete whirling overhead.

The blade drew back. The powerful biceps tightened as the machete whipped through the air.

Slap!

Kota's hand caught Kolegwa's arm. "Let him go," Kota said firmly.

Kolegwa released the middle-aged man, and he plopped back against the wall in shock. The telltale trail of fear dampened the inside of his pant leg.

Kota motioned Kolegwa to back off, and then he reached into his pocket and pulled out a thick wad of bills. The mangy little dog ran to the man's feet, frantically barking to protect its owner.

Peeling off several large bills from the roll, Kota handed them to the trembling man. "Here. This will cover the damages." Kota then looked down at the little dog—the breed impossible to identify. He peeled off another bill. "And get a new dog!"

Kota turned his attention to Kolegwa and motioned him to get the briefcase from under the bed. A distant siren approached. The hotel manager inched toward the doorway, keeping his back to the wall while the tribesmen quickly gathered their belongings. The small crowd looking through the window scattered when the two men emerged from the room. Red flashing lights illuminated the scene.

That didn't take long, Kota thought, and quickly surveyed the area.

Shirt and shoes in one hand, briefcase in the other, Kolegwa followed Kota along the hallway away from the lights and sounds of the law. The two dark figures descended the stairwell and disappeared into the darkness of the parking lot. When they reached the Jeep, Kolegwa finally spoke, his tone defensive. "I just free little men from cage."

Kota pulled the keys from his pocket and shook his head. "I can't take you anywhere."

~~~

Beneath a sliver of moon, the gray jeep wound along a lonely road until it reached the Simon's Town Naval Headquarters. Passing the long building, Kota turned onto a dark, deserted dirt road that led to the back of the naval airport. He handed an unfolded map to Kolegwa who sat silently in the passenger's seat.

The click of the parking brake seemed overly loud in the silence. Kota dipped his finger into a small leather pouch. It contained a substance composed of ground-up pliosaur teeth, found in the shallows of the lagoon, mixed with white paint and minerals indigenous to the island—a concoction believed to give the wearer the same powers as Kuta-keb-la . . . the power to kill and never be destroyed!

After carefully painting the familiar spiked shape on their faces, the two grabbed their machetes, and walked to the back of the jeep.

Adorned in a loincloth, machete clenched between his teeth, and a five-gallon gas can in each hand, Kota headed toward the airport silently on bare feet. Kolegwa brought up the rear, equally equipped. They crept along the edge of the woods and passed an old colonial-style house. A lit window on the second story seemed to float in the night sky.

Just past a small clearing, they saw the back of the airport. They proceeded until a chain-link fence appeared in the mist. On the other side of the fence, fading moonlight danced across the windows and rotors of at least a dozen Agusta LUH helicopters. The moon slowly disappeared. Not uncommon to the Cape area, a thick veil of fog had moved in from the bay and descended on the compound.

The perfect night.

Kota reached the chain-link fence first. They set the gas cans in the tall grass. He slipped a pair of wire cutters from behind the leather band of his loincloth. A few dozen snips, and a small circle of fence fell to the inside.

Kota stepped through first and slowly scanned the dimly lit area. "Good, no guard dogs," he whispered. The two crept forward into the mist.

Suddenly, a flashlight appeared, beaming through the landing gear of the helicopters. Footsteps drew closer. A flash of light glistened off Kolegwa's shoulder. "Who goes there?"

The tribesmen put the gas cans down and quickly disappeared into the shadows of the helicopters. Less than a minute later, the light went out, permanently.

~~~

At three forty-five a.m., the telephone shrilled loudly in Kate's airport office. Two, three, four times. John's snoring continued while Kate fumbled for the cell phone. "Hello?"

"Is this Alexander Aviation?" asked a deep voice.

"Yes . . . yes, it is!" said Kate, unable to place the voice.

"Is John there? John Paxton?"

"Yeah, hold on for a minute!" Kate nudged John until the snoring stopped. "Here, it's for you."

"Who is it?"

"I don't know. Doesn't sound familiar. Here."

"Is it the admiral or Tom?" John asked, sitting up.

"I said I don't know."

John took the phone and greeted the caller with a hello. Then he looked at Kate in bewilderment.

"Who is it?" Kate asked.

"I don't know. When I answered, all I heard was a click followed by a dial tone."

~~~

Leaving the roadside telephone booth, Kota opened the door of the jeep. He slid inside and smiled at Kolegwa. "Looks like we've got one more stop to make tonight. The hunt will soon be over!"

~~~

Twenty minutes later, the black jeep rolled into a dimly lit parking lot. Sliding out, Kota and Kolegwa stayed low and in the shadows as they crept to the small office. Kota raised a business card taken from John's wallet. He compared it to the name on the building: Alexander Aviation. A match.

Carefully, the two silhouetted figures headed around to the back of the building. Moonlight revealed only their half-painted faces and glistening blades as they walked beside a long row of hedges. At the back door of the small building, Kota peered over the hedge into a window of the dark office.

"They must be out," he whispered to Kolegwa. He peered behind the building. Beyond a chain-link fence, he saw a vintage military helicopter sitting on the landing pad, the Alexander Aviation logo painted on its side. He lowered his hand to the wire cutters at his hip, his teeth gleaming in the moonlight as he grinned. "Ah. That's okay. We'll wait."

~~~

An ear-piercing scream shattered the serenity of the airport office. "Noooo!" John lunged, reaching into the night.

Startled, Kate woke and found John lying halfway off the couch as if reaching down from the doorway of the helicopter. She helped him back up onto the couch and cradled his head in her lap. He was soaking wet. His heart was pounding like a drum. "Shhhh," she whispered. She rubbed his sweat-streaked hair as he continued to stir in his sleep. "It's okay. It's just a nightmare. It's all gonna be okay."

Staring into the night, she said it one more time as if to convince herself, "It's all gonna be okay."

But she knew it was a lie. John's nightmares were for real.

Captain Porter paused at the starboard rail, winded from his morning jog around the main deck of the *Indian Princess*. She was a good ship. Small by today's standards—only three hundred seventy-five feet long and carrying just over four hundred passengers—but she was just the right size for him. At sixty-two years old, he was the picture of self-content as he eased his hands along the rail. He paused, taking a moment to watch the rising sun slowly dissolve the morning haze.

It was the last day of their nine-day Atlantic cruise. They had visited several West African islands, including the ever-popular St. Helena: a small remote island best known as the site of Napoleon Bonaparte's exile. Now, it was good to be back in the warm, green Cape waters. Drying his face with the towel draped over his shoulders, he descended two flights of stairs to the lower level.

He entered the galley and smiled at the organized chaos. He shouted over the noise of clanking plates, "How's it coming? Everything still on schedule?"

From behind a large, stainless steel bowl, a robust man in chef's attire gave him the thumbs-up. "With time to spare, Captain . . . time to spare!" He slid a glass of lemonade across the counter.

Captain Porter nodded gratefully. He sipped it while inspecting the items being prepared along the counter. Sixty pounds of roast beef simmered in large pans, its sweet aroma filling the air.

"Mmm, scrumptious." The captain turned his attention to a nearby cooler. Behind the glass, dozens of desserts sparkled, ranging from cheesecakes to sorbets. Completing his inspection of the galley, he walked through a set of swinging doors and entered the pride and joy of the *Indian Princess*: the grand ballroom.

As always, the majesty of the ballroom took his breath away. Rows of ornate crystal chandeliers adorned the vast ceiling. A marble walkway meandered through exquisitely set tables and led to a hand-carved wooden bar. On either side of the bar, two columns boldly reached up to the thirty-foot ceiling. Long horizontal windows spread across the port side added to the room's openness, offering a spectacular view of the blue-green waters.

The captain ambled among employees feverishly setting the room for a formal party. At the top of a ladder, a woman was hanging a glass starburst decoration from one of the chandeliers. At the opposite end of the room, another employee secured the end of a long banner above the doorway. Across the blue vinyl, silver letters read: *Congratulations, Wattington Diamonds.*

The captain approached one of the columns where several people were inflating silver foil balloons with helium. He watched one balloon gracefully float upward until it bounced lightly on the ceiling, joining hundreds of others. He smiled at the brilliance of these balloons in the chandelier light. He paused at the room's focal point: a twenty-by-thirty-foot glass bottom dance floor that peered straight down into the open sea. Like a sparkling sapphire, water beneath the glass bathed the room in a shimmering blue hue.

A bubbly waitress joined the captain. "Hypnotic, isn't it?" she said, staring in awe at the waters before her. "The other day I stood right in the middle of that glass. . . . felt so free, like I was walking on the ocean."

The captain nodded proudly. "Yes, it's extraordinary. Designed an entire ship around that piece of Lexan glass. The pontoon-shaped hull's nothing less than an engineering marvel, and one of only two in the world." He looked up at the suspended stars and exotic decorations. "Yes, indeed, this is going to be one brilliant party!"

~~~

The shrill ring of a cell phone shattered the morning serenity of the airport office.

John opened his eyes to find Kate practically on top of him. He felt the warmth of her body pressed against his chest and didn't want to move. Her eyes slowly opened, glittering in the morning light. She smiled, and they stared into each other's eyes for a long moment until another ring broke the spell.

Slipping off John, Kate reached to the end table, and fumbled for the phone. When she finally answered, her eyes flew open. "It's my mom . . . hurry, turn on the news. Channel eight!"

John quickly turned the television to channel eight and saw an enormous ball of fire appear on the screen just below the word "LIVE."

Kate said into the phone, "Okay, I got it on."

John asked, "What is it?"

She lowered the phone. "That's the Simon's Town Naval Compound," she explained. "It was broken into during the night and set afire. They lost everything except a few choppers."

John sat down in front of the television and raised his hand to his forehead. "No, no. This can't be happening. The timing couldn't be worse—we need as many eyes in the air as possible!"

Kate nodded, then held up a finger. "Oh, no. I'm afraid there's more. The guard on duty was murdered."

Then John saw his face appear on the screen as Kate continued, somberly, "And a wallet with your driver's license in it was found beside the body."

~~~

In the ship's grand ballroom, the men wore tuxedos, and the women, elaborate gowns. Glass stars twinkling beneath crystal chandeliers transformed the ceiling into a night sky. Couples swirling on the transparent floor appeared to be dancing on the blue sea below them. In fact, the room echoed in lights, shadows, and blue hues as its wide window shades blocked out the late afternoon sun.

In a corner of the room, two heavyset black women sat at a table with two well-behaved little girls. "Would you like another soda from the bar?" Joyce raised her voice above the ballroom music.

"No, thanks. I'm still not finished with this one," replied Thelma, looking toward the crowded dance floor.

"Okay. What about you two?" No response. Joyce snapped her fingers to get the attention of her twin daughters.

"No thanks, Mom. We're okay, too," replied one of the five-year-olds, both nodding without taking their gaze from the hundreds of silver balloons pressed against the ceiling.

"Well, I'll be back in a minute. You two be good for Aunt Thelma now."

Joyce rose from her chair and immediately felt as if all eyes were on her. Normally, she wasn't the self-conscious type, feeling that she carried her two hundred pounds of JOYCE quite well, but this was peculiar. After a quick glance down the front of her teal gown to make sure everything was still in check, Joyce made her way along the marble walkway toward the bar. Passing a table, she heard a couple laughing behind her. As she passed the glass-bottom dance floor, a man swooped down in front of her. He waved a dollar bill in front of her face and yelled in a drunken slur, "Hey, baby! I'll take two!"

Suddenly, Joyce felt something rip from the back of her gown. It was Thelma, holding up a piece of paper that read, "Table dances 50 cents."

Joyce turned around and saw two young black boys laughing hysterically near their table.

Thelma ripped the paper in half. "Those two juveniles! They must have slipped this in the back of your chair when you sat down. Too bad we can't just toss 'em overboard."

"What are you gonna do?" Joyce said with a deep sigh as she adjusted the front of her gown. "That little pork chop over there, the one still laughing, is James Wattington—the son of the Guest of Honor."

"Well, isn't that the way," Thelma *tsk*'d as she walked back to her table.

~~~

"Cuz! That was slammin'. Let's do it again. How about that wide load rollin' off the dance floor? She looks pretty good!" said Earl with a malicious grin.

"Naaah, we better keep it down low for a while. Even though it's my old man's party, we can still get tossed outta here," replied the heavyset James. "Besides, I just got off being grounded yesterday." He paused, and then his eyes brightened. "I know! Let's go back to the dance floor and see if any cool fish have shown up yet."

The boys hurried over to one of the raised, wood-framed corners of the floor. Blue light shimmered on their faces. For several minutes, they watched a couple of snook swimming beneath the glass, attracted to the lights illuminating the bottom of the dance floor.

Boredom quickly set in for the boys. Earl looked up from the glass. "These fish are lame. I wanna see something tight . . . like sharks!"

James looked back with a widening smile. "I've got an idea. Follow me!" He struggled to get up, his tight-fitting tuxedo hindering his efforts. He grabbed at the back of his pants. "Ouch! These pants keep giving me a wedgie."

Keeping one eye out for their parents, the two boys crept along the edge of the dance floor, ducking behind the crowd. They passed the DJ booth and stopped at a corner just outside the galley. Then, when no one was looking, they slipped through the set of steel doors leading inside the galley. The room was alive with the clatter of plates and pans.

Kneeling behind two large garbage cans, James pointed at the counter on one side of the room. "Okay, here's the plan. Look over there. See those two pans of roast beef sitting on that counter?"

"No way, dawg! How are we gonna get those outta here without them seeing us?"

"Don't punk out," James whispered sharply. "Just leave that to me. When you hear a commotion, just throw both chunks of beef into that big yellow bucket in front of the table and jet for the back door. I'll meet you up on the main deck. And make sure you get the juice from the pans too. That's where all the blood is!"

"Hold up!" Earl said. "How come I gotta be the one that jacks the meat?"

James pointed down to his beefy body. "Who looks like they can run faster . . . me or you?"

Earl grinned. "I hear ya, cuz."

Carefully, James ducked low behind the long counter and crawled past the chef until he reached the opposite side of the galley. He stopped behind two enormous stacks of plates, each about three feet tall. The moment the chef looked the other way, James placed his hands on the columns of plates and pushed with all his strength.

The tremendous crash echoed above the music from the ballroom. Instantly, the chef dropped his cleaver and raced to the back of the galley to investigate. When the chef disappeared around a corner, Earl seized the opportunity and moved out.

~~~

Ten minutes later on the main deck, Earl anxiously waited by the starboard rail, the full bucket of roast beef at his feet. Finally, James appeared, carrying a milk crate and a ball of kite string.

"What took you so long?" asked Earl.

James dropped the crate onto the deck. "I had to get this crate. Then I went back to my cabin and got my kite string and my Mom's pantyhose." He chuckled wickedly. "Oh yeah . . . how'd you like my diversion?"

"Dawg, that was serious!" Earl laughed. "My ears are still ringing!"

James handed Earl the pantyhose. "Hold these open so I can shove the roast beef into them. It'll help keep it all together and still let the juices seep through."

As James shoved in the second piece of roast beef, Earl shook his head in doubt. "You sure you gonna be able to fit all that into these pantyhose?"

Shoving in another piece of meat, James grinned, "This ain't nothing, dawg. You oughta see my Aunt Ritha. She stuffs a whole lot more than this into hers!" He tied the top closed.

They dropped the beef-stuffed pantyhose into the milk crate. While James tied the string to the sides of the crate, Earl wedged the bucket full of bloody juices between the meat and a corner of the crate.

"You sure kite string is gonna be strong enough to handle all this?" Earl asked.

"It's actually real strong fishing line. After losing three kites, my old man got tired of the string always breaking and made me start using this stuff."

Once satisfied with the bloody concoction, James lowered the crate down the side of the ship until it dropped just beneath the water. A brownish-red haze slowly rose to the surface. James quickly tied the end of the line to the side rail, "Looks good to me, cuz. Let's roll out!" The two boys raced down the stairwell and headed for the grand ballroom to see if their plan would really work.

~~~

"What do you mean they think *I did it*? That's insane!" John paced the airport office while listening to Tom on Kate's cell phone. "It's obviously a setup. I left my wallet back at the island. It had to be Kota, the native I told you about. Somehow, he followed me back from the island and slaughtered the crew on the research ship. Now he's here!" John paused to listen to Tom.

Standing next to John, listening to one side of the conversation, Kate shook her head. "This isn't sounding so good."

"Yeah, I believe you," Tom was saying. "You already told me about the situation with the tribesmen. Why don't you just turn yourself in and explain it all to the police down at the station? You need to tell them what you know about the killings on the research ship anyway."

"There will be time for that later," John insisted. "If I try to sort this out with the local authorities now, they'll want to conduct an investigation. That could take days. They'll also have to go to the research ship and question Nathan and Erick. That'll ruin the whole setup we have for tracking the pliosaur. And what if they want to hold me until they get this whole thing sorted out? I could end up in some South African jail for weeks."

"All right, all right!" Tom agreed. "I just called to let you know . . . and I think Admiral Henderson gave the police the address where you're staying. So, if you don't want to talk to them now, you'd better find a different place to stay for a while."

"Got it, Tom. Thanks for the heads-up. I'd better get going. I'll let you know if we get another signal on the homing device."

After John hung up, Kate pointed to the burning building on the television screen. "They think you're responsible for *that*?"

"Afraid so. Looks like my old buddy Kota wanted to throw a monkey wrench into the works. Tom said the police know where to find me."

"But I was with you last night. I am your alibi. And there's Erick and Nathan. They can prove those blokes are responsible for the murders on the ship! Then, just maybe, the police can link them to the dead guard at the naval base."

"You weren't with me *all night*," replied John, weighing all the positives and negatives. "Remember? You stepped out for a couple hours last night to get the chum and depth charges." He ruffled his hair and sighed. "Besides, we don't have time for all this. We could get a call from Nathan any minute regarding the pliosaur's current position."

"Well, in that case, it's a good thing the chopper's topped off and ready to go," Kate said with a clap of her hands. "Let's get moving!"

~~~

Beneath a flock of nearly one hundred seagulls, the gigantic shadow drew closer to land. Still in calorie debt from the fruitless chase with the speedboat, the fifty-ton creature hungered for large prey.

Using its front paddle fins only in an effort to conserve energy, the beast slowly propelled itself farther west, following an electrical field generated by a pod of southern right whales. Several miles ahead, their alluring underwater groans of communication beckoned. Gliding over the shadow of a deep ravine, the monster sensed something else—close and near the surface. This electrical field was different, stronger. Altering its course, and using all four paddle fins now, the fearless killer drew nearer to the three-hundred-seventy-five-foot shape. The creature's eyes locked in on the rectangular light flickering on the underbelly of its new prey.

As the pliosaur closed in, its sensory devices picked up the magnetic field generated by the ship's massive propellers slicing through the water.

Then the monster sensed . . . something more . . .

Slowly, the alluring scent flowed into its mouth, beyond the spike teeth, and into a pair of chambers inside the roof of the creature's mouth. After picking up the signal from the nostrils, the first cranial nerve instantly triggered the message to the brain.

Blood!

~~~

"Yo, look at that. I think it's a shark." Earl pressed his long, skinny fingers against the wooden frame of the dance floor, looking down through the glass.

"Yeah, it looks like the bait bucket's working. I think that's a baby hammerhead. Maybe the mother's around!" said James, pulling on the collar of his tight-fitting tuxedo. "Still, I think we'd better go up on deck and check on the bucket. Make sure it's far enough below the surface. I left it kind of shallow."

"Aiight!" Earl saluted James, then looked through the dozens of legs on the crowded dance floor. "This elevator music is about to drive me nuts anyway. Race you to the deck!"

Darting through the crowd, Earl glanced over his shoulder to check his lead on James. "Fat boy can't catch me!" Turning back around, his eyes widened as a tray of food filled his vision. Holding the tray was a waiter whose eyes also widened as he shouted, "Watch out!" Earl hit the waiter head-on, then scurried to the doorway, wincing at the loud crash behind him. He couldn't resist a look behind him. The waiter was sprawled across the floor beside several overturned plates of pasta and prime rib. Their eyes met again, and Earl shot through the door to the stairwell.

After tripping an elderly woman in the stairwell, Earl's wiry body allowed him to make it to the starboard rail well before his portly friend.

Eventually, James stepped onto the deck, huffing and puffing. "I think I split the back of my pants coming up the stairs. And I saw you almost take out that old woman. She nearly fell on me," he gasped then pointed to the side rail. "So, how's the bait bucket looking?"

James reached over the side rail and tugged the line until the yellow edge of the crate broke the waves. "Looks like it's okay. I'm gonna leave it where it is."

As James lowered the crate back beneath the surface, Earl's gaze went upward. He pointed. "Yo! What's that? Look at that weird cloud!"

"Where?" James tightened the knot around the rail.

"Where do you think, fool? In the sky!"

"What are you talking about? The sun's out, there aren't any clouds today."

Earl pointed toward the eastern sky. "Well, what do you call that?"

James followed Earl's gaze as the darkness in the sky drew nearer. "That's not a cloud. It's a flock of birds. It's a flock of seagulls. The biggest flock I've ever seen!"

"*For real!*" replied Earl. "Looks like they're heading toward the ship."

"Forget the birds." James started back to the stairwell. "Let's roll out and check out the dance floor before the bait bucket's empty."

Earl caught up with his buddy. "Yo, but keep your eyes open for that waiter I took out on the way up, the one with the ponytail. When he was getting up from the floor, he looked at me like he wanted to throw down. The veins were sticking out on his neck and everything."

Moments later, after creeping down the stairwell, the two boys reentered the grand ballroom. Earl skidded to a stop. James bumped him from behind.

The black ponytail swirled around as the headwaiter locked eyes with Earl. "Hey, you! Stop right there!"

Instantly, the boys disappeared behind the ornate, wooden swinging doors.

~~~

"Morris, just let it go. It was an accident," said a young waitress on her way back into the galley, carrying an empty tray. "They're just bored; trying to have a little fun. Who could blame 'em? Look around. With all this Lawrence Welk music, this isn't exactly the most happening party."

Glancing back at the elderly couples barely moving on the dance floor, the headwaiter adjusted his collar and cocked his head. In his best Rodney Dangerfield voice, he said, "Look at that, will you? The dance of the living dead! Lucky when I dropped that tray earlier I didn't cause a dozen heart attacks. Oooow! Gotta be careful around here, ya know. Make a sudden loud noise in this room, and they could charge you with mass murder."

Laughing, the waitress said, "Well, they're not all *that* old." She backed through the kitchen doors. "I think you just got the early-bird crowd seated at your station."

"The way this day's going, that's just my luck." Morris followed her into the galley. "Just my luck."

~~~

Out of breath, James and Earl reached the top of the stairwell. The moment they set foot on deck, they stopped cold. Dozens of small shadows swirled around them. They looked overhead.

"Wow! Do you believe this?" gasped James, as an enormous flock of seagulls circled the ship. Ravenous cries filled the air. To Earl's left, at least thirty seagulls were perched on the starboard side rail while others landed randomly around the deck. Earl jumped when a seagull atop the stairwell squawked loudly in his ear.

Hesitant to take another step, James watched as the mysterious birds seemed to cover every available space on the ship.

A dropping landed on Earl's shoulder. Had the scene not been so peculiar, he would have laughed. "Look at all of them . . . it's almost like that old Hitchcock movie."

James nodded as three more seagulls landed on the starboard rail. "It's kind of creepy. It's almost like they're waiting for someone to feed them."

Chapter 13
ARRIVAL

The grand ballroom was dark with the party in full swing. Men dressed in tuxedos and women in drop-dead gorgeous gowns flirted, gossiped, and laughed. By now, most were finished with their meals. Some had made their way to the transparent dance floor where couples were swirling to ballroom music. The room's main source of light was the hypnotic blue tint emitted from the waters beneath the glass.

In the middle of the dance floor, an attractive young woman dropped her hands in disgust. "Forget it, Bill. You're on your own. I can't dance to this rubbish."

"Oh, come on, Carla," said Bill, holding her hand to keep her on the floor. "Hey, why don't you just ask the DJ to pick it up a little? I mean, look at him over there. He's half asleep. He's probably more bored than we are." Bill waggled his eyebrows at her and smiled. "You can do it. Just sweet-talk him. It always works on me." He gently pushed her in the direction of the DJ. With a quick wink, the strawberry blonde sashayed her way across the crowded dance floor toward the mirrored DJ booth. Carla caught a glimpse of herself in the mirror, her eyes following the contours of her form-fitting teal gown as light shimmered off her every curve. "No doubt this will work," she muttered with a half smile. She rose to the tips of her toes and peered over the front of the booth to get the DJ's attention.

She looked over her bare shoulder at Bill, winked again, and then turned back to the young black man in his Hawaiian print shirt. The DJ gave a big white smile and nodded as she laid out her request for something more upbeat.

No sooner than she turned around to face Bill with a thumbs-up, the music faded and the room grew dark. The entire room was still and silent for a moment, then . . . A loud *thump.*

Urgent chatter started immediately, followed by . . .

Another *thump.*

Then a streak of light shot against the mirrored ball above the dance floor, and specks of light swirled around the room. From the enormous speakers, a deep voice echoed around the room, "Now it's time to take a trip back to the eighties!"

Slowly, the ten-thousand-watt sound system reached its full potential as a pulsating disco beat thundered through the room. Hops and hollers echoed around Bill, and the dance floor came to life.

Bill smiled at Carla as she met him in the center of the dance floor.

"Babe, if we could bottle what you've got, we'd be rich!"

As if on cue, the elderly crowd quickly shuffled from the dance floor as the hard-driving Whitney Houston song grew louder. The beam from a strobe light shot up from beneath the glass bottom. Then the entire dance floor began to glow in flashes, keeping rhythm with the pulsing beat. Instantly, the dance floor filled with a much younger crowd. Carla started to say something to Bill but knew he'd never hear her as she felt the music vibrating the glass beneath her feet. She leaned her head back, closed her eyes, and let the rhythm take over. The music was now in control of her body. *No doubt, this girl was born to dance.*

Her eyes popped open when she felt her right heel slip from her shoe and nearly fell. Bill caught her, and she gave a thankful nod. *Bloody stiletto heels. They make your legs look great, but they're not much for dancing.* As she tried to work her heel back beneath the strap, there was another moment of darkness. She looked at Bill, then gazed curiously around the room. The gentle blue tint was gone. She slowly looked down. The lights beneath the dance floor illuminated a ghostly gray mass.

At first, she thought it was the sandy sea bottom passing beneath the ship, but she quickly dismissed the notion as impossible because it was moving sideways beneath the glass.

She tugged on Bill's coat and pointed, but she could see he'd already noticed the odd mass below them, heading left to right, contrary to the direction of the ship's course. They looked at each other in confusion. Bill shrugged and pulled her closer to him. Together, they kneeled to peer more directly through the glass.

There was a grinding noise then, and her blood ran cold. She froze, hands splayed across the glass of the dance floor, as the tip of what she guessed was a giant fin scraped across the glass beneath her feet.

Slowly, she stood up, leaving her shoe in the middle of the dance floor. She took a step backward, her eyes glued to the water. Bill remained on the crowded floor, fixated on the object beneath the glass.

"Bill, what is it?"

There was no answer. The moment Bill turned to face her, the dance floor erupted in an explosion of glass.

The crash was absolutely deafening as the tremendous impact hurled Carla back onto the marble. Cold water pounded her. Looking up, all she could make out was a gray wall of flesh that propelled everything upward. Bodies and glass flew through the air. Dozens of people soared along the ceiling, twisting and rolling through the chandeliers, showering the room with crystal. Others crashed like rag dolls onto the tables below.

The DJ dove to the floor as a huge section of glass shattered the booth behind him. The pulsing music stopped—replaced by terrified screams.

Scurrying back, Carla saw another section of the dance floor land on a party of ten, crushing a man at the end of the table. The others fell onto the floor, looking around the room in shock. Near the dance floor, a woman's body, tangled in a chandelier, crashed down on a table of eight. Frantically, the horrified group tripped over their chairs trying to get away from the table.

Carla was on her hands and knees, wet hair strung in her eyes. *This can't be real!* More cool water swept across the marble. She crawled back farther on the trembling walkway, distancing herself from whatever was protruding from the dance floor.

In the darkness, she could see glimpses of a massive head as it thrashed, seemingly in slow motion, with the blinking strobe light. Rows of gigantic teeth and pale, wet skin glistened in the blackness. Carla glanced around her. In unison, the stunned passengers backed away from the dance floor. They struggled to keep their footing after the creature's every movement. Elbows and knees pelted her as people rushed by.

Frantically, she searched for her boyfriend. Looking back toward the galley, she saw Bill's lifeless body dangling from a chandelier. The horrific image made everything spin, and she collapsed onto the walkway, unconscious.

~~~

Emerging from the employee's restroom in the back of the galley, Morris, the headwaiter, grabbed the doorframe as the boat rocked heavily. "Yow! Must have run into some rough weather." He carefully walked along a hallway and entered the back door of the galley. Heading to a nearby cooler, he pulled out a Caesar salad. When he turned toward the grand ballroom, he noticed cries coming from behind the set of doors. "Sounds like things are livening up in there!"

Walking farther through the galley, he caught a glimpse of the chef's back as it disappeared into a stairwell, but shrugged it off. Brushing his ponytail from his shoulder, Morris reached for the stainless steel doors. He paused, listening to the ruckus in the ballroom. These weren't sounds of joy—they were cries of sheer terror. He dropped the salad and slowly pressed his fingertips against the door to peak through. Inside, he found only darkness.

The floor jilted dramatically, sending Morris stumbling forward through the double doors. He took several steps into the ballroom to regain his footing, and that's when the floodlights came on, fully illuminating the room.

Morris grabbed his chest and gasped at the sight before him—not the strewn bodies, not the smashed dishes and tables, not even the blood. His vision focused on one thing and one thing only: the toothy maw of a horrific sea creature thrashing upward through the hole that was previously a dance floor.

The room swayed, and he stumbled to the side, then back into the wall. Slowly, his peripheral vision began to absorb the horror all around him. People splashed across the flooding carpet, stumbling across chairs, clawing over one another in an attempt to reach the doorways. To his left, a woman in a white satin gown lay twisted in a chandelier on top of a table. Not far from her, a man lay lifelessly beside a section of glass. Huge chunks of glass were strewn everywhere.

This is absolute madness!

A sheet of water swept up the walkway, touching his shoes.

Not moving his eyes from the creature, he moved along the wall, back toward the door.

Something black passed over his head. Instinctively, he glanced up to see the bottom of the shoes of a young man dangling from a chandelier. Then he saw the others. Dozens of people were tangled in the chandeliers, some swayed and screamed while others dangled like lifeless marionettes. Shaking his head, Morris continued toward the door. He was in sensory overload, the entire scene more than he could comprehend.

Suddenly, a crack formed in front of the dance floor, the carpet tearing away as the crack widened.

All the way to his own two feet.

He threw his body at the door, but slipped and fell just before reaching it. As he tried to regain his footing, he realized he was sliding. Backward. He flipped over to control the momentum, stopping finally when his shoes hit pebbled flesh.

Shaking uncontrollably, he stared at the monster's throat. Cool water gushed beneath him. His eyes moved upward to witness the underside of its enormous jaws, the massive head writhing in all directions.

Morris threw his arms over his face and waited.

Suddenly, he felt the creature's movement change. Morris seized the opportunity to throw himself to one side, just as the jaw slammed down. The headwaiter continued to roll until he grasped the legs of a table, and he immediately pulled himself behind it. From beneath the table, just ten feet away, he resisted the urge to vomit as he saw the enormous muscles in the creature's throat ripple with its movement.

"Ah, hell no!" he screamed as he rolled out from beneath the table, regained his footing, and dove for an exit door. Doors still swinging, Morris stumbled through the hallway until he finally leaned against a wall, unsure of what to do next or where to go.

His white coat was covered in blood, miraculously not his own. He put his head in his shaking hands and wept.

~~~

On the second level in the main dining room, passengers in formal attire shared looks with people at other tables. There was a loud bump from below. A woman seated at the end of a table of six looked at the floor. Another bump lifted her chair from the floor. The waiter standing beside her balanced a tray with a downward glance. "Dinner is served."

At that moment, the table of six, waiter and all, lifted and then disappeared as a gray blur tore out a section of the floor. A wall of silver balloons rose through the opening, accompanied by horrific screams from below.

People around the room frantically looked for the source of the screams while balloons collected above them in a vast skylight. Then a primal roar shook the floor as an upward blast of air scattered the balloons across the ceiling.

~~~

Frustrated, the pliosaur lifted its head with all its force, tearing through more of the floor of the second level. A shower of tables and chairs fell through the enormous opening, landing on those still struggling to exit the ballroom.

Sensing that its tight-fitted girth could move no deeper into the ship, the leviathan arced its upper body backward, crashing through what remained of the floor, rupturing the portside pontoon. The tremendous suction of his passing ejected those remaining in the ballroom from the bottom of the ship like a bursting piñata.

As the clouds of bubbles cleared beneath the ruptured hull, the uninjured swam toward the surface while unconscious bodies swirled amid tables and chairs. Hundreds of spiraling plates twinkled like fireflies as large steel appliances fell to the depths, littering the seafloor.

~~~

On the ship's bridge, Captain Porter stared through the window overlooking the main deck. Dozens of passengers flowed from the stairwell, their orange life jackets glowing in the sun. Silver balloons soared above as seagulls circled, zipping past the windows.

The captain turned around as the first mate ran through the doorway, out of breath.

"Well? What is it? Did we ram something, hit bottom? What?"

The first mate struggled for words. "No, sir . . . more like . . . it ran into us!"

"*What* ran into us?" bellowed the captain.

"I didn't see it," the first mate gasped. "Some say it was an enormous creature . . . a reptile. Like . . . like a dinosaur!"

"Dinosaur?" The captain screwed up his face and pulled his chin in, doubtful.

The first mate nodded. "Yes sir. Whatever it was, it burst through the glass bottom dance floor." He paused and wiped his brow. "You know, sir, last night on the radio, I heard something on the news about a huge marine reptile in the area that attacked a speedboat yesterday. They claimed the creature was over seventy feet long. But that was just a small speedboat it attacked. We're in a cruise ship nearly four hundred feet long. I would have never dreamed of such a danger. I mean, the Navy hasn't confirmed that the creature even existed, but still, after what's happened . . ." He held his hand to his face, stunned.

"I heard something of that too," added the petty officer, who'd been listening in on the conversation. "I thought it was just something dreamed up by the resort owners to drum up business, like all of that Loch Ness rubbish!"

Looking down at the main deck as more people swarmed from the stairwell, the captain said, "Well, we should be okay. Even if the dance floor is completely missing, we shouldn't be in any danger of sinking with the sealed chambers in the pontoon hull."

The first mate shook his head wildly. "No, sir. The hull is completely missing from the dance floor to the galley. There's nothing there but water now!"

Still looking below at the passengers, the captain stroked his chin. "Hm. Well, we're less than six miles from land. Certainly the ship will stay afloat until we reach port."

The first mate looked down, his tone somber. "Sir . . . the second and third chambers in the portside pontoon were ruptured . . . well, the ship . . . sir, she'll never see land again," he stammered.

"Captain! Take a look at this!" Another crewmember on the bridge was pointing down through the portside window.

The captain strode over to look past the portside rail. One by one, bodies began to appear from beneath the surface. Some swam for the ship, frantically screaming, while others floated face down. Life preservers soared through the air as passengers along the rail tried to help those in the water.

"Well, all right, drop the lifeboats then. We have to abandon ship! We have no choice!" said the captain, his heart heavy with the news. The first mate looked down from the opposite side of the bridge. His eyes grew wide. "Captain, I think you'd better take a look at this . . . I'm not so sure about the lifeboats."

Kate closed the door to her airport office while John eagerly headed toward the helicopter. Just as she put the key into the lock, a call came over the office radio. She cracked the door to listen.

"Mayday! Mayday! This is Captain Porter from the *Indian Princess*. We're a cruise ship about six miles off Betty's Bay. We've been rammed by . . . something enormous! The hull has been severely damaged . . ."

Kate waved John back to the office. "Hey, we've got a distress call. Sounds like the pliosaur's attacked a cruise ship off Betty's Bay."

John ran back to the doorway to listen, but the channel had turned to static.

"Where? Where's Betty's Bay?" John asked, following Kate to the radio on a counter in the kitchenette.

"It's not that far from here. We can be there in less than twenty minutes."

"I'll call the admiral from the chopper, and get them on the move too." Just as they stepped outside the office and started to close the door, another call came over the radio. Quickly, they ran back into the office to listen.

"Mayday! Mayday! We're a fishing boat twenty miles off Hout Bay. We've just been hit by an enormous reptile twice the size of our boat. We're taking on water."

After the distress call terminated, Kate gasped, "What's the deal? The creature can't be in two places."

"Where's Hout Bay? Show me on a map."

Kate wrestled a map down on the counter next to the radio. "It's west of the last attack site off Hermanus. *Wayyy* west!" Kate's finger stopped on an area of water west of Cape Town.

"No way." John looked closer at the map. "That's past Cape Point, more than a hundred miles through Atlantic waters. The admiral said the creature wouldn't go that far in the cooler water. Nathan confirmed it too; in fact, he was adamant about it. That call can't be right. The creature's at the cruise ship. I know it."

"But that fisherman said Hout Bay. You heard him too."

John shook his head, adamant. "Something's not right about that call then. Look at the distance the pliosaur would have had to cover since last night. That has to be at least two hundred miles from Hermanus where the creature attacked the naval divers. Nathan said there is no way the pliosaur would go that far into the Atlantic, not with such a rich supply of whales and other feeding opportunities in the Cape area. Something definitely does not sound right."

"Then what?" Kate asked.

"Maybe in all the panic the fisherman got his quadrants mixed up. All we can do is try to contact him and confirm his location, or wait for another call."

Kate looked at her watch. "Well, we can try to reach him on the radio in the chopper. We've got to get moving. Remember what Tom told you, the authorities could be here any minute!"

Kate picked up her bag, and they headed for the door. The second she turned the doorknob, another call came over the radio. John ran back to the radio and listened. "This is the *Indian Princess*. The distress call we just sent out was a mistake. It seems someone here was trying to play a prank about that enormous sea monster we've all heard about. We will handle the prankster. Please ignore any further distress calls from this ship in this regard. We're in no need of assistance. I repeat: we're in no need of assistance. Out."

John and Kate stared at the radio in confusion. "Wait a minute," John said slowly. He leaned back against the table, arms crossed, thoughtful. "The first call was from the ship's captain, the second caller didn't even identify himself—"

Before John could finish his sentence, another call came through in a panicked voice. "Mayday! Mayday! Please . . . anyone out there! We're on a thirty-two-foot fishing boat off Hout Bay. We've been hit by an enormous reptile. It's still after us—"

Again the channel turned to static. "What's going on here?" Kate said, frowning at the radio. "He clearly said his boat was off Hout Bay. That's at least two hundred miles from the cruise ship and in the opposite direction. Maybe the first call from the cruise ship really was a mistake?"

"No way. That creature wouldn't go into the Atlantic," John said, stepping toward the door. "Besides, there's something about that voice from the fishing boat—sounded very similar to the person who made the second call from the cruise ship, talking about a prankster."

He turned and beckoned Kate to follow. "I know that voice. It's Kota," he said matter-of-factly.

"The tribesman from the island who killed the guard?"

"Yes, I'm sure of it. The calls from the fishing boat are a decoy. He's trying to throw off what's left of the naval squadron and send them in the opposite direction. That cruise ship is in trouble, and we've gotta go help 'em out, Kate. The admiral's probably already fallen for the "fake" Mayday call and is heading for Hout Bay. By the time he and his demolition team get this all straightened out, it'll be too late. The cruise ship is probably taking on water, and if the pliosaur is still in the area . . ." Closing the office door, they walked quickly toward the gray, vintage military helicopter. Neither noticed the three-foot section of fence missing from behind the garbage cans. They picked up the pace and started to jog toward the landing pad.

~~~

Through the Sky Hawk's windshield, Kota saw John and Kate running toward the landing pad. He dropped the radio headset with a menacing smile. "That should confuse them well enough." Even if John didn't fall for his decoy call, he knew the Navy would. Slithering back between the seats in the cockpit, he stepped past the barrels of chum and joined Kolegwa behind a small divider wall that separated the rear section of the cargo area. As Kota sat down, Kolegwa began to wake up, half nauseated from spending the night with the foul stench from the chum barrels. Kota quieted him with a finger to the lips.

Just as the cockpit doors opened, Kota unsheathed his machete.

~~~

The first mate had left the bridge and now scoured the water from the portside rail of the *Indian Princess*, searching for the enormous shadow. Frantic passengers scurried around him, screaming and pointing at the slightest trace of whitewater. Someone pulled his arm from the rail. He turned to see two young black boys, one heavyset and the other skinny, both frantically pleading, faces wet with tears.

One cried, "We're sorry! We're sorry! We didn't know, mister." His friend nodded fervently in agreement.

"Know what?" asked the first mate, pulling his arm back.

The heavyset boy grabbed the first mate's coat. "For real, mister. We . . . we just wanted to see some sharks. We didn't want to see . . . th-that!" The first mate picked up two life jackets from the deck and handed them to the boys. "Put these on, and go find your parents. Now go . . . and stay away from the rail!"

Sending the boys on their way, the first mate returned his attention to the water. He watched passengers swimming frantically toward the ship, the seagulls swirling overhead, the lifeboats splashing down. Debris and dead bodies clipped the survivors as they paddled toward the lifeboats and life preservers, which were then hoisted back up to the ship like manual elevators.

The sheer panic is almost hypnotic, thought the first mate, and he shook his head to focus on what he might do to help.

Immediately his gaze returned to the water when he heard heightened intensity of the screams around him.

The crest of the dragon-like back swept out from behind the ship's bow.

There you are. The first mate gripped the rail tightly, his knuckles whitening, his mind reeling. Passengers at mid-deck pulled the lines faster to lift the overloaded lifeboats higher from the surface. A woman dangling from a life preserver, which was being hoisted up the side of the ship screamed. The enormous shadow glided toward her. The creature rose to the surface, brushing against debris with the side of its nose, clearing its path, while giant red eyes focused on the side rail. The creature's striped back passed directly below the dangling lifeboats. Then, with a slash of frothy water, it disappeared.

The first mate saw one of the lifeboats rise to the rail. As he raced over to help, they all started screaming down at the water. A man in the lifeboat jumped for the ship's rail but missed, falling back into the sea. The first mate's vision flushed gray as he witnessed impossibly massive jaws push from the water between the lifeboat and the ship's rail, then slam shut in an explosion of planks. More bodies. More terror.

Trembling, the first mate staggered to maintain his balance, then looked over the rail. The creature had slid down the side of the ship, leaving a fifteen-foot red streak on the hull, leading to the waterline. Then it dove again with a tremendous splash which shot up the hull and washed the red streak into a diluted pink smear.

~~~

The vintage military helicopter bearing a jagged tooth grimace soared over the shoreline as John shouted into his headset. "You gotta believe me, Admiral! The second call from the cruise ship was a fake . . . not the first one. And the other calls . . . about the small fishing boat in Hout – those WERE fake! The ones from the fishing boat were just a decoy to throw everyone off track. The creature would not go that far into the cooler waters . . . you said that yourself! And look how far it would have to have traveled since the last known attack site just last night." John's eyes were bulged as he ranted. "The pliosaur's at the cruise ship, Admiral!"

After a moment of listening to the admiral disregard his pleas, John shook his head in frustration. "Oh, for pity's sake, sir. I didn't have anything to do with the fire at the station or the dead guard." He threw a hand in the air and made a fist of frustration. "Okay, okay. How 'bout this? Later I'll come in and get this all sorted out. But not now. Right now, we've got to help the people on that cruise ship. Kate and I are heading out there now. Sir, you've got to turn your guys around. Those people need you."

John held the headset close to his ear as he listened again. He sighed, then said, "I know because I recognized the voice. The caller who claimed the cruise ship's distress call was a prank, and the caller from the fishing boat off Hout Bay had the same voice. It was Kota, the tribesman from the island. The same guy that left my wallet by the guard's body at the station."

After another pause, John shook his head. "All right. But when you get to the area and can't find the fishing boat, it'll be because there *never was one.*"

He whipped off the headset. "Stubborn idiot!" he said under his breath.

Just then, a call came over the walkie-talkie beside the seat. He put the headset back on and asked the admiral to hold while he took a call from Nathan. "Yeah, Nathan, talk to me!"

"I've got it on the monitor. The signal came on about a minute ago, still going."

"Is it near Betty's Bay?"

"It sure is," replied Nathan. "About four miles off the coast . . . how'd you know?"

"I-I'll explain it to you later. Just call me back if the signal starts any dramatic move." Putting down the walkie-talkie, John adjusted his headset. "Admiral, Nathan at the research ship just picked up a signal on the pliosaur, and guess what? It came from the exact same coordinates as the cruise ship's distress call. You've got to turn around. The creature is definitely at the cruise ship. This can't be a coincidence."

John listened for a moment then cut the admiral off. "Save it, Admiral! You'll get a chance to explain it all later . . . to the hundreds of loved ones mourning the passengers on that cruise ship." The frequency then turned to static.

~~~

Less than ten feet from the cockpit, Kota and Kolegwa waited, hidden behind the short divider wall beside the barrels of chum. The inside wall of the helicopter vibrated against Kolegwa's back. He sat with his knees close to his chest, careful to keep his feet out of sight. Below his hip, his machete blade glistened in the light shining through a small window behind his head.

He raised up, peeped out that window, and saw the helicopter's shadow gliding across the blue waters far below. Having never been higher than the top of a palm tree back at the island, he found the view more than a little unsettling. He turned and leaned his head back against the vibrating wall and closed his eyes. His stomach was still queasy from the stench of chum. In his mind's eye, he could see his wife and two little girls back on the island. He missed them horribly.

Lightly, he ran the tips of his fingers across the scabbed-over X carved on his chest. It would soon all be over. He only waited for Kota to give him the signal to step from behind the wall and fulfill his vow. He glanced down at his machete, tempted to sneak up to the front of the strange craft, and kill the white devil now. But he knew he must wait. He knew Kota was right, insisting that they avenge the chief's death at just the right moment. Once they saw the shadow of Kuta-keb-la and John stepped in front of the doorway, he'd get the signal.

The placement of the wound was critical. The machete blow couldn't be lethal. No. the evil one must be alive, able to swim when he hit the water, so the attack would take place on the surface in plain view. Then the chief's death will have been avenged in the noblest of ways— by killing his murderer in the same manner in which he was killed. Once accomplished, they would force the woman to take them back to the island, leaving Kuta-keb-lay to fulfill his destiny.

Vengeance. Kolegwa smiled.

~~~

A glance through the side window and Admiral Henderson saw the three helicopters flying in formation, following his command without question. Fighting the growing doubt about the direction of their current mission, he looked behind his seat and into the cargo bay. He studied the four men wearing chest protectors and helmets seated around the crates of depth charges. Through the clear shields on their helmets he saw the anticipation in their eyes. Afraid they would sense his uncertainty, he turned back around. The call with John wouldn't stop playing in his mind.

He looked down at his watch. They were still at least forty minutes away from Hout Bay. Since they'd lifted off there hadn't been another call from the alleged fishing boat in distress. Every attempt he'd made thus far to contact the vessel went unanswered. Maybe they were too late . . . or just maybe that cursed Paxton was right.

Although he hated to admit it, he knew John's argument made sense. Still, could the guy be trusted? Had he started the fire, killed the guard? Who knows what length such a person would go to in order to protect this valuable find—a living dinosaur! Then there was the transmitter allegedly inside the beast. If there was any truth to that, the pliosaur was definitely at the cruise ship, and the admiral was taking his team in the opposite direction. Although he was a proud man, he knew there was more at stake than his ego.

He mulled things over some more. He recalled what Tom Hayman had pointed out to him: if he'd listened to John last night, he would have never gone out to search for the carcass. And three of his men would still be alive.

Suddenly, he was struck with the realization—without a doubt in his mind.

I am wrong. We've got to turn back.

He glanced through the window at the squadron. *But I can't just ignore the fishing boat call.* He pondered his options and decided to send one chopper to Hout Bay and the rest of the crew to the cruise ship's locale. The second he motioned the pilot, a frantic voice came over the radio. "Mayday, mayday. Navy, do you copy? This is Captain Porter from the *Indian Princess*. Where are you?"

"We read you, Captain. This is Admiral Henderson. Over."

"Where are you blokes? We're only six miles off the coast. What's taking so long? The ship's heavily damaged . . . we're taking on water steadily. She won't stay afloat much longer!"

"Is the beast still in the vicinity?"

"Yes. It's still circling the ship. It's so enormous . . . the lifeboats . . . they're useless." The captain's voice then lowered, weary with burden. "Admiral, I have over four hundred passengers on board, actually some of them no longer—" He choked and took a breath. "You've got to get here before everyone . . ."

"We're on our way, Captain. Hold on," the admiral said, trying to exude some sense of comfort. "Out."

Quickly, Admiral Henderson motioned the pilot to turn around, his finger whirling in the air.

~~~

Less than a mile from the sinking cruise ship, a naval patrol vessel that was on maneuvers off Betty's Bay altered its course southwest. Responding to the latest distress call, Chief Petty Officer Greg Benson knew they could reach the sinking ship long before the fleet of helicopters or any rescue vessel dispatched from Simon's Town.

Minutes later, the patrol boat approached the cruise ship's starboard. Officer Benson could tell by the way the ship was listing port that she'd soon be underwater. He pulled alongside the vast hull, looking up as passengers frantically waved to him from behind the rail. Now that he was closer, their behavior seemed odd. *Hysteria*? he wondered. *Almost like they're trying to wave me away from the ship.* Benson knew he couldn't do much with just one boat, but at least he could offer them hope until the helicopters and larger vessels arrived. He recalled hearing something about a dangerous marine reptile in the area. If there were passengers overboard, at least he'd be able to get them safely out of the water.

Cruising alongside the ship's hull, Officer Benson picked up the mike with a glance at the officer beside him. "I'm going to notify the admiral. This looks bad. These folks don't have much time."

~~~

Inside the lead helicopter, Admiral Henderson listened to his headset.

"Admiral, this is Petty Officer Greg Benson. We're approaching the *Indian Princess*. She's listing port pretty hard—we'd better get some help out here quickly!"

"How close are you to the ship?" the admiral demanded.

"We're cruising alongside the hull as we speak."

"Get outta there!" shouted the admiral. "Get outta there now!"

~~~

At the cruise ship's starboard rail, some passengers turned away from the sea, burying their faces in their hands, screaming. Others couldn't look away as the giant maw rose beneath the capsized patrol boat. Slowly, the spinning props dropped below the surface, spitting bloody water into the air like a grotesque fountain.

The sinking patrol boat rolled, sliding down the side of the monster's head. The white hull quickly faded as the spinning props drove the unmanned vessel to the depths of the sea.

A pump of its massive forefins, and the pliosaur moved on from the bloody waters. Eventually, the creature arced back around and continued to circle the sinking cruise ship like a wolf guarding a fresh kill.

~~~

Staring blankly at the console, Admiral Henderson continued to listen to his headset long after the call had turned to static. Enraged, he looked over at the pilot. "I want a call dispatched to every boat we've got! No one—absolutely no one—goes near that cruise ship until we get there!"

Chapter 15
RISING WATERS

Captain Porter watched from the leaning bridge as the nightmare continued to unfold before his eyes. With the deck now too tilted to stand on, passengers and crewmembers alike had crawled up to the starboard side rail where they clung for life. *How long can they hang on?* From bow to stern, the rail was lined with orange life jackets. Like various colored flags, long gowns blew out beyond the rail, waving in the wind. Some passengers stood with their elbows locked behind the top rail. Others, showing fatigue, sat on the deck hugging the bottom rail. In spite of their various postures, they all stared in the same direction.

The captain turned his binoculars and followed the sloping deck to where the portside rail now rested a frightening two feet above the waterline.

Beyond the sinking rail, numerous red stains served as hideous markers showing where some had taken their chances with the lifeboats. Here and there, a few bodies remained afloat without movement. Already ravenous seagulls were starting to break free of the enormous flock, swooping down at random to pick flesh from the floating corpses. One by one, other seagulls soared down to join the feast.

Suddenly, a wave of fear flowed over everyone on the starboard rail. A mere ripple divided, and the frill rose from the sea. The surrounding water turned black with the creature's shadow as it glided alongside the ship, rising higher and higher until several feet of its gray back was visible above the sinking rail. Tilting its head to the side, a hideous red eye appeared just above the waterline, peering up at the rail.

"Why doesn't it just attack and get it over with?" screamed a man from the starboard rail, his torn shirt exposing his left shoulder. "It just keeps circling closer and closer. I can't take this anymore!"

Beside him, a female steward with one arm around a young girl, said, "Sir, please calm down. You heard the captain's announcement. The Navy's on the way!"

"Oh yeah . . . like that patrol boat that just helped us out?" bellowed the man. "What are they gonna do? If they were here right now, there's no way they could get everyone off the ship in time! Look at the port rail. It's practically touching the water. Another couple feet, that thing'll be able to reach—"

"Shut up! Enough!" shouted a burly man, clinging to the rail. "Keep flapping that trap, and you won't have to wait! I'll throw you in there myself, right now!"

~~~

Farther down the rail near the stern, Joyce and Thelma held on tightly to the two girls. Joyce didn't know how much longer she could hold on. Her right arm was numb from being looped around the rail while her left arm ached from holding Trish. Thirty feet below was the ship's swimming pool, its water collected on one side with the leaning deck. Every inch the ship moved deeper into the sea, the pool's heated water spilled over the coping, sending a waterfall down the deck until it disappeared through a pile of pool chairs collected against the portside rail.

"Mommy, why are those two men shouting?" asked little Trish.

Joyce turned her daughter's attention from the arguing men. "Don't you mind them, baby. Just bow your head and close your eyes." She led the two little girls in prayer, keeping one eye on the water.

The massive shadow moved away from the ship, and out to sea. Joyce knew it would be back. They all did.

After a long slow turn about forty yards off port, the monster veered toward the ship and faded below the surface. Seagulls lifted from floating bodies as the massive shadow passed below.

"Mommy, what's it doing?"

Joyce pulled her daughter closer. "Just hold on, baby."

The leviathan launched upward with the force of all four paddle fins. The enormous shadow blurred with speed.

Screams echoed from the rail as everyone's fear was realized.

All at once, the pliosaur's terrible head lunged from the water, jaws tightly clenched. Water spewed over the rail as the enormous head and underbelly slid onto the deck beside the pool. The portside rail collapsed like a pipe cleaner, folding beneath gray flesh.

On either side of the enormous body, waves broke over the railing and washed up onto the deck. Instantly, Joyce and everyone along the starboard rail rose higher as the tremendous bulk pressed the port side of the ship farther beneath the surface. Planks moaned from the creature's weight.

A paddle fin hit the deck, ripping up planks as it thrust for traction. It slipped into the pool, spraying pool water out across the sea. Slowly the creature forced more of its body onto the deck, inching its gaping jaws upward toward the starboard rail.

The horrified passengers held on with all their strength, staring down at the colossal head. More of the tremendous back emerged from the water, sliding onto the deck. The tip of the nose moved to within twenty feet of the rail.

As the portside sank, the passengers climbed over the starboard side rail, a pitiful barrier between them and the monster. Others, unable to make the transition, struggled to hold on to the railing from below, their feet searching for traction on the wet deck. A deafening roar from the creature shook the entire ship as it held down the port side. The colossal head thrashed, the underside of its jaw crashing through a skylight that protruded from the deck. Slowly, hundreds of silver balloons rose through the opening and floated around the monster's head as if in macabre celebration. Again, the creature thrashed, trying to force more of itself onto the ship. A wave shot out from beneath the jaws, showering those above. Directly above the creature, drenched passengers cowered behind the rail, looking occasionally behind them at the thirty-five-foot drop into the open sea. The back arced. The jaws rose high, exposing the white underside of its throat. The head slammed down hard against the deck. The enormous thud resonated through the deck and shook the rail violently.

The ship shuddered and listed farther into the sea.

~~~

Inside the bridge, Captain Porter and the first mate were flung against the portside wall. Another crewmember soared through the window in a shower of glass. The captain scrambled to his knees and watched in horror as the seaman fell forty feet, stopping suddenly when he met the sunken port side rails.

~~~

Leaning into the starboard rail, Joyce held on with all her strength—one hand gripping the rail and the other holding Trish between her chest and the rail. Every muscle screamed for her to let go. Trish whimpered, trembling at the sight of the nightmare below them.

"No, baby. Don't look at it," Joyce said through strained lips.

The creature had begun to slowly slip backward now, the ship's remaining buoyancy hindering its progress. It thrashed harder, as if in a final attempt to loosen its prey. With a roar of inconceivable magnitude, its head slammed against the deck. Grips broken, a flurry of passengers tumbled down the deck, sliding past the creature and into the sea.

Beside Joyce, Thelma lost her grip on her daughter Charmaine, who rolled under the rail and down the deck, disappearing over the edge of the swimming pool. All around them were hellish sounds of wailing and screaming. . . Joyce was certain her voice was in there somewhere.

Now she felt her own grip loosening, and her feet slipped under the rail until her hips were on the wet deck. Trish rolled off her chest, and Joyce caught her by the right hand. Joyce's body slid farther down the vibrating deck, one hand clutching Trish's hand, the other on the bottom rail.

The ship jarred again. Trish's small fingers were slipping from her hand.

"*Hold on!*" Thelma screamed from above.

Just short of dropping her daughter, Joyce released the rail. Rolling over one another, they slid down the deck until it suddenly dropped from beneath them. A weightless moment . . . then Joyce splashed into the tilted swimming pool, Trish landing beside her. Surfacing, Joyce grabbed Trish, and then she saw Charmaine. All three swam forward and quickly grabbed onto the side of the tilted pool.

Her arms stretched over the coping, Joyce looked down the sloping deck just as the seawater shot up, crashing into her face. Sputtering, she looked around her, finding an enormous paddle fin to her right and more spewing water in her face.

"That's it, girls! Hold on!" yelled Joyce above the sound of the creature's skin scraping against the deck.

There was a loud splash from behind. Joyce turned and saw a woman wearing only a bra and panties swimming toward an orange raft in the pool.

The deck quaked. More planks buckled and snapped beneath the creature's underbelly. A wide crack spread to the coping of the pool. An enormous bubble rose behind Joyce, releasing a great belch of air. The woman in the center of the pool grabbed the raft, looking around in confusion as the water level dropped. Joyce looked down and saw the bottom of the pool splitting wider like a gaping mouth. More bubbles rose through the opening. "Girls, hold on!"

Joyce held on tighter to the edge of the pool. The water level dropped below her hips, then her feet.

"Mommy! What's going on?" screamed Trish.

"I don't know, baby. Just hold on to the side!" Looking over her shoulder, she saw the blond hair of the woman with the raft disappear through the bottom of the pool.

No sooner had Joyce looked back up, a wave crashed over the coping, hurling her and the girls backward. Falling twelve feet, Joyce landed back-first in several feet of water collected in the side of the pool, her daughters splashing down beside her.

The ship moaned and rocked again.

Joyce looked up at the towering walls of the pool and knew there was no way they were getting out. But that wasn't her only problem—another huge swell shot over the top of the pool. She grabbed her two daughters just as the wall of water crashed down across her chest, washing them back through the enormous crack in the bottom of the pool. Splashing into the cabin below, Joyce frantically surfaced, yelling for her daughters. But her cries were unanswered.

~~~

With its upper body strewn across the deck up to its fore paddle fins, the pliosaur continued to thrash, pushing the vessel farther beneath the surface. Beneath the port side rail near the creature's underbelly, an explosion of bubbles shot out from the hull.

The stern dropped deeper, sending more water racing up the deck and throughout the lower cabins.

The Indian Ocean was claiming the ship.

The pliosaur began to tire, lying still for a moment with the upper third of its body sprawled on deck. Unblinking red eyes stared up at the people clinging to the rail, its giant, tooth-studded jaws slightly agape. Fifty feet beneath the surface, the rear paddle fins swept just enough to keep the monster's head and neck on the ship, while just above the water an enormous front paddle fin curled into the empty swimming pool in a final attempt to hang on.

Finally, the ship's buoyancy won out, causing the creature to slide sideways from the ship with a tremendous splash. The ship's port side quickly rose above the waterline, revealing the bent side rail pressed down against the deck. Slowly, a thin sheet of water flowed from the side of the ship, exposing a massive section of deck deeply scarred by the creature's ragged skin.

The beast rose beside the mangled port rail and turned its attention to the screaming in the water.

~~~

Flying off the coast of Hermanus, Kate's eyes were drawn to the side window. She focused on a long, red trail leading to the stern of a fishing boat. "That's about the tenth boat we've seen chumming the waters since we've been heading east." She shook her head. "And all of them less than half the size of the pliosaur. They'd better hope they don't find what they're looking for."

She squinted and pointed in another direction. "And look at those buggers! On the news last night they show a pier less than five miles from here that was attacked by the pliosaur ... and there you have it. Look at them. See that chum line? Maybe a hundred feet long there at the end of Pier 21, people lined up three rows deep along the rail. Unbelievable. And look at all those black dots in the water. I've never seen so many sharks this close to land. All this chummin' is really bringing them in."

John gazed at the various areas Kate pointed out. He was silent, shaking his head, mouth drawn into an angry line.

She picked up the binoculars from John's seat and trained them on the end of the pier. Black dots, too numerous to count, took on the form of torpedo-shaped bodies gliding beneath a red haze. "Looks like everyone's having a go at it," she said. "I heard that one of the local newspapers put up a ten-thousand-dollar bounty for the first photograph of the pliosaur." She grinned at a somber John, trying to lighten the mood. She nudged him. "Knew I should have brought my camera!"

He rolled his eyes.

As Kate veered away from the coastline and headed farther out to sea, she couldn't believe the number of boats in the water. It almost looked like a regatta, except the vessels varied in size and lacked formation. She glanced at John as he continued to stare silently at the horizon. "I know what's bouncing around in that head of yours."

"If we both know, then you don't need to tell me."

"You're thinking about last night . . . how the depth charge didn't faze it. John, that beast has gotten inside your head. Now, you think it can't be stopped because fate or some unseen justice is about to be served on that cruise ship."

John turned to her. "You saw what happened last night. Everything is lining up with the beginning of prophecy. His eyes shone with intensity. "Now the second part: 'And then innocent blood will fill the sea.' Can't you see it yet? The cruise ship is the innocent blood. Kate, it all fits perfectly."

Kate threw a hand up in the air. "Why do I ever open my mouth?"

"Why can't you admit it?" he challenged. "You saw the way it waited to kill that girl in front of me, then how it took a depth charge square on its throat. There's more to all this than 'logic,' Kate . . . can't you feel it?"

"Listen!" Kate spat. "Ever think that last night the depth charge didn't explode as close to the beast as it appeared? The water and fog only made it look like a direct hit when it wasn't." She looked him in the eye and pointed to the cargo bay. "We've got four depth charges left. One dead-on shot, John. That's all you need."

Kate looked back at the windshield before he could see the uncertainty in her eyes. Although she would never admit it, when she first heard the ship's distress call, it sent a chill up her spine. Immediately, she had thought of the prophecy. She didn't know anymore. Were the parallels of the prophecy getting harder to dismiss, or was it all playing tricks on her mind too? In an attempt to change the subject, she said, "Would you mind checking the chum barrels? That smell is wretched." She wrinkled her nose.

John unbuckled his seat belt. "I'll go back and crack the door."

"While you're back there, you may as well pop the top off the crate of depth charges. We're less than two miles from the ship."

~~~

Entering the cargo bay, John carefully stepped over the rope ladder coiled in front of the chum barrels. "She's right. We could use an air freshener back here." He reached to unlatch the door, but surprisingly found it already unlatched and slightly agape. His hair blew back from the wind as he slid the door all the way open. The sound of the main rotor thundered around him.

Facing the breeze, John took a deep breath, allowing the salty sea air to clear his head. His thoughts turned to the cruise ship as he dared to imagine what they would find. He pictured hundreds of life jackets scattered across the water, women and children screaming in horror as the long frill turned their way. He prayed the image in his mind was wrong. *Come on, Paxton. Keep it together.* Slowly he took a step back from the doorway and steadied himself against the short divider wall. His thoughts remained on the cruise ship as he stared down at the passing water.

The back of his boots were less than two feet from Kolegwa's toes.

~~~

Swimming up along the submerged port side of the ship, Joyce broke the surface near the port rail. She immediately looked around for Trish and Charmaine, whom she'd thankfully found once they'd fallen through the pool to the cabins below. She'd directed them through the water-filled rooms, keeping their eyes averted as much as possible from the dead bodies floating around them. She shuddered, freezing from the nightmare as much as the ocean water. Finally, the two girls popped up in front of her, gasping for air. "Oh, thank you, God." She pulled them close as they, too, shivered. Suddenly, she saw both their eyes widen at something behind her. She didn't have to turn to know. But she did anyway.

Twenty yards away, she saw the back of the creature's head drop as a series of chilling cries were suddenly muted.

Swimming away from the sight, Joyce encouraged the girls to follow, pulling them close to her side. "Come," she said. Then in a whisper meant only for herself and the Almighty, "Lord, help us." She reached over and grabbed a nearby body by the wrist. Cringing from the feel of the ice-cold skin, she slowly pulled the floating corpse in front of them, careful not to disturb the seagulls feeding on its back.

The pliosaur turned then, and Joyce saw the mound of gray-and-white striped flesh coming their way. "Girls, look down at the water," she said urgently. The girls immediately complied, all of them now with heads down, chilled to the bone, holding onto a corpse even colder.

Slowly, the gigantic head passed before them, sending out a wake that rocked the dead body. Wind brushed across Joyce's face as the seagulls fluttered their wings to maintain balance. She lifted her feet as a paddle fin passed beneath her. An upward surge of displaced water rolled up the back of her legs.

"Mommy!"

"Shhh!"

The seagulls settled as the creature slowly moved away from their location. Joyce looked up to glimpse its glowing red eye and the red stream that trailed from the side of its mouth. She said another silent prayer and held the trembling girls.

~~~

Forty yards out from the ship a male steward continued to tread water. His shoes already off, he slipped his left arm out of his jacket and relinquished it to the sea. He saw how quickly the woman screaming behind him had been taken by the beast. The creature seemed to be less interested in the floating bodies, so he lay forward with his arms spread out. He turned his head just enough to keep his mouth above the water. Another glance at the sinking ship, and he decided to take his chances with the open sea.

Slowly, he moved his cupped hands beneath the surface. Moments later, he felt the current taking over, and he no longer had to paddle with his hands. He glanced back slowly, careful not to make any sudden movement. He saw the black woman and two little girls hiding behind the corpse as the giant shadow slowly passed them. He could hardly breathe from fear. Despite being a retired Durban police officer, this was the most horrifying moment of his life.

Again, he looked back at the woman and two girls. Although ashamed of the thought, he truly hoped the creature would soon discover them and be distracted long enough for him to slip away. "Come on, they're just behind the corpse," he muttered. "What are you . . . blind? How can you miss her? She's as big as a bloody house!"

The ship and the creature drew farther into the distance as the current continued to move him in the opposite direction. Two more minutes passed as the man floated motionless, when suddenly he felt something land on his back. Without flinching, he noticed two more scratchy feet land beside his left shoulder.

A beak full of flesh was ripped from his neck.

"Hey! What the—?" The man twisted around, swatting at the birds. He missed and slapped the surface with his cupped hand. As the startled seagulls took flight, he looked up, realizing his mistake. The giant shadow slowly turned his way. Three sweeps of the powerful paddle fins, and the creature was on him before he could utter a sound.

Kate looked back from the cockpit as John pried the top off the crate of depth charges. "Remember how to use those? You've only got four shots. Better make em' count!"

John looked down at the shiny tops of the depth charges as wind from the cargo doorway beat against his back. "Same as the others; just push the red button, then drop . . . right?"

"That's right," Kate shouted over the sound of the helicopter's chopping blades. "Make sure you push the button all the way in until it clicks, or it won't discharge. And remember, if the target's shallow, give it a three-second count . . ."

John threw his hands up. "I know . . . or it'll detonate too deep. Got that part."

Just as he unlatched the top of the first chum barrel, Kate yelled, "You'd better get ready. That's it just ahead."

He walked toward the cockpit and stopped behind the passenger's seat. Through the windshield, he saw the faint outline of a distant ship. The image of women and children screaming from the water again played in his mind. He knew the reality of that image was soon coming.

He heard a noise behind him and whirled around. It was a light clank, like the sound of something hitting the floor. Looking through the cargo doorway, he saw a splash fifty feet below the chopper.

"What's the matter?" Kate asked. "You see something?"

John walked back into the cargo bay and looked around the chum-stained floor. "I saw something splash below the chopper." He stepped over the rope ladder lying beside the open doorway. When he looked at the crate in front of the chum barrels, he noticed that one of the depth charges was missing.

"So what did you see?" Kate asked. "What kind of splash was it?"

"I'm not sure . . . but it looks like one of the depth charges rolled out."

"Rolled out?" Kate shouted. "They're in a bloody wooden crate. They can't just roll out!"

"I don't know, but somehow it did." John walked back toward the cockpit wondering how the depth charge managed to get outside the crate. When he reached the back of the passenger's seat, his attention shifted again to the distant ship. Even at this distance, he could tell by the tilted silhouette that the distress call had not been a hoax.

~~~

No sooner than John's attention shifted away from the cargo bay, Kota stepped out from behind the divider wall. He lifted two more depth charges from the crate. Quietly, he laid the cylinder-shaped objects on their sides and rolled them toward the open door. Then Kota quickly slipped back behind the divider wall and sat down beside Kolegwa. His right hand lowered to his machete.

~~~

Kate's attention was drawn to her side window. "Hey, there goes another splash . . . and another one. Are those coming from our chopper? What's going on back there?"

"Nothing, I'm right here," John spat as he walked back to the cargo bay and looked into the crate. "I don't know how, but two more depth charges are gone."

"Well, you'd better keep an eye on that last one. We're almost at the ship . . . and it doesn't look good," Kate said, squinting beneath her hand at her brow. "Look at that. What are those shiny things rising from the ship . . . some kind of signaling device?"

John slid the crate with the last depth charge to the back of the cockpit and peered over the seat. For the entire flight, he had tried to imagine what they would find, but he was totally unprepared for the spectacle below. The sight of the ship's portside rail even with the waterline took his breath. Leading up from the water was a large section of scarred deck that could have only come from one thing. In disbelief, his eyes followed the angled deck up to the opposite side of the ship where hundreds of passengers clung to the starboard rail.

Kate gasped. "I knew it was going to be bad, but I didn't expect this."

In front of the windshield, the strange twinkling in the sky revealed itself, taking on the form of silver balloons floating through the largest flock of seagulls John had ever seen. As the helicopter descended, his stomach tightened. He made out several bodies floating on the surface amid a series of red stains and scattered debris from the lifeboats. Overwhelmed by the amount of people still on the ship, he knew there was only one way to help any of them: he had to make that last depth charge count!

He scanned the surface for the frill. "Where is it? Maybe . . . maybe it—"

The question was soon answered as the seagulls swarmed in on an area above the port rail. The giant head emerged from beneath the ship. Shafts of sunlight penetrating the surface glittered along the neck and gray, tiger-striped back. Then, sprawling paddle fins in excess of thirty-five feet from tip to tip, slid slowly from beneath the hull.

John looked at Kate in confusion. "What can we do? We can't drop the last depth charge with it right there by the ship. And there are too many people still in the water," John moaned.

They looked at the nightmare in the ocean and weighed their options.

~~~

Joyce and her two young daughters continued to float with the corpse near the ship. Desperately, she scanned the surface from behind the corpse covered with seagulls. The ghastly sight of beaks full of flesh being ripped from the pale back no longer fazed her. Her only interest was with what lay beneath the surface. She looked up to a wave of excitement on the ship. People along the starboard rail were screaming and pointing to the water in front of her. She pulled the girls close to her side as she saw the tall frill.

This time, it didn't glide by or veer back around and continue to patrol the ship. *It's seen us. It's coming.* Through trembling lips, she vocalized her prayer, increasing in volume as the frill picked up speed. "Dear Lord, protect these babies. I place them in your loving hands. Help us!"

The head broke water, seeming to swell in size as it rose. Cannonball-sized eyes locked in on them from beneath a glistening mask of water. Joyce swam backward, away from the corpse, taking her children with her. "Hold on to me," she gasped. The seagulls took flight, squawking at the sight of the approaching monster.

Exhausted, she paused, treading water, and pulled the girls closer. She pushed their heads down. "Don't look, babies." Her trembling voice surprisingly strong as she shouted to the heavens, "Dear Lord, if this be your will, please don't let them feel any pain. Help us, Jesus!"

The blazing eyes rose high above the surface behind an enormous set of nostrils. The snout lifted, showing hideous pink gums above the water. Rows of giant spiked teeth skimmed the waves. The nose shot up and the water's surface collapsed, spilling into the cavernous throat.

A GURGLING ROAR!

Joyce hurled herself backward, pulling her children. But the vacuum from the swelling mouth drew her forward. Small hands clawed at her arms, trying to hang on. The surface whipped around her. Joyce screamed as blood flew everywhere, splashing in her mouth and eyes. There was another splash off to the side, then another roar—both coming, not from the beast, but from the chopper above them. She looked up to see a waterfall of blood flowing from the side of the helicopter, falling between her and the enormous jaws.

Joyce watched as the shower of blood moved behind the pliosaur's head. The girls screamed, opening their eyes. Just in front of Joyce, the tremendous head rolled sideways and plunged into the sea. The sudden swell pushed her and the children back as a kicking paddle fin spewed water thirty feet into the air.

Joyce's right hand thrust into the air. "Hallelujah! Thank you, Jesus! Thank you, Lord!"

Trish and Charmaine looked at her with their big, beautiful eyes, and her heart swelled. Trish asked, "Mommy, what happened? Are we gonna be okay?"

"Yes, baby. Don't you two worry none, we're gonna be just fine. We've got someone a whole lot bigger than he is on our side."

"Who do you mean, Mommy? The man in the helicopter?"

"No, baby . . . the One who sent him!"

~~~

Just inside the cargo doorway, John tilted the chum barrel even more. "That's it, keep coming, you piece of crap. I've got something to feed you." He watched the waterfall of blood slap the sea.

Kate shouted excitedly from the cockpit, "Keep pouring, John. It's working!"

~~~

Through the small window in the cargo bay, Kolegwa continued to peer down at the water. His emotions were torn as he stared at a black woman and two children who had just escaped a horrible death. A woman and two girls, who from that distance, strongly resembled his family back at the island.

He felt a tap on the shoulder. For the moment, he ignored Kota's signal telling him to attack and allowed John to draw Kuta Keb-la farther from the woman and her children. Kolegwa turned his attention to the doorway. From his vantage point behind the divider wall, he could see the back of the white devil as he struggled to tilt the heavy barrel toward the open doorway. *An easy kill.*

Yet, he hesitated in confusion. It made no sense to Kolegwa that John was risking his own life to save people, people who didn't share his same color of skin. For the first time in his life, he questioned Kota's motives, wondering if this white man really possessed the great evil that Kota claimed.

Kolegwa turned back to the window. Looking down at the water, he thought maybe it was wrong to let Kuta-keb-la kill freely. He glanced along the starboard rail. Over half of the passengers looked like the people from his own village, except for the clothing. For the first time in his twenty-eight years of life, he questioned the teachings of Kota and the elders. Maybe his mother, who lost her life for disputing the teachings, had been right after all. Maybe the rest of the world outside the island wasn't evil. His eyes narrowed as his new thoughts consumed him. *This is not how it should be.* He knew he was on the wrong path. He felt another tap on the shoulder.

"What are you waiting for? Do it now!"

Kolegwa looked at John's back as the white man continued to pour blood from the doorway. Again, Kolegwa paused, hesitant to lift his blade.

Then Kota leaned forward until his mouth was at Kolegwa's ear, "Remember how he killed the chief? Remember your oath?"

Kolegwa nodded slowly, inhaled deeply, exhaled. He stood and raised his blade.

~~~

"Lock and load, baby!" Kate said as she monitored their progress with the chum from the side window. "That's far enough, John. Drop it now!" She looked back at him and noticed the bloodstained floor. "And watch your step back there. This is no time to be taking a dip!"

John rolled the barrel clear of the doorway. He ran to the crate and pulled out the last depth charge. Carefully, he stepped over the rope ladder and carried the awkward object to the doorway.

Forty feet below, he saw the massive head rising beneath the choppy water. The shadow transformed into rocky, gray skin. As they dropped down closer to the water, he saw the huge eyes lock on him from beneath the scarlet cloud. He raised the depth charge to his waist, holding steady. "Come on, just open that big, ugly mouth!"

"Yeah, come on," Kate shouted. "You can do it. Just drop it right down the gullet like a big breath mint!"

~~~

Behind the divider wall, Kota repeated himself in a harsher tone. "Now is the time. Do it now!"

Kolegwa turned toward Kota and raised his blade between them. "No! This wrong. You wrong!" he spat in his native tongue.

"No!" Kota's nostrils flared in rage. "You kill him–you kill him now!" He planted his palms on Kolegwa's chest and shoved him backward.

~~~

John looked over the edge of the depth charge as he steadied himself inside the doorway. His hands trembled not out of fear at what he was looking at, but at the thought of missing. Then, he saw his shot. The great mouth opened directly below the helicopter. The nose broke the surface, water rushing back from hellacious spiked teeth. "Come on, hold it steady," he muttered, forearms straining. The moment his finger touched the button, he felt the floor dip behind him. He whirled around and saw the back of a huge black man falling toward him. John's eyes widened in shock.

Mid-fall, the tribesman turned around and raised his machete to John.

The loincloth, the white tooth painted on his face. In that instant, it all made sense. John stepped back, only inches from the doorway, and raised the depth charge to block the machete. Sparks shot through the cargo bay as the steel blade skimmed the metal. In a single motion, John sidestepped Kolegwa, swooped down behind him with the depth charge, and hurled him through the doorway.

Kolegwa flew from the helicopter screaming, his eyes opened wide as he looked down at the massive head. The machete twirled through the air. The pliosaur lunged from the water and its open mouth met Kolegwa midair, thirty feet above the surface.

John watched, frozen in the doorway as the enormous maw caught the tribesman at the waistline, shearing his lower body while his upper body somersaulted higher into the air. A trail of intestines uncoiled over the sea. Face twisted in horror, Kolegwa continued to scream until his torso crashed into the water beside the beast.

~~~

Through the pilot's side window, Kate saw the breaching monster roll back into the sea. Having only glimpsed a swath of blood trailing the falling jaws, she assumed it was only chum. Feverishly working the stick, she tried to maneuver the craft back over the giant shadow.

~~~

Shaking, John collapsed on the floor, depth charge still in hand. Seeing motion at the divider wall, he then looked in that direction. Exhausted, all he could think to say was, "Oh crap."

Swoosh!

John ducked a swipe of the blade. Kota whirled back around, machete cocked. Then curiously, he halted the attack, staring at John's hands. John looked down. His eyes bulged when he realized he was still holding the depth charge—*the activated depth charge*. Without aiming, he hurled it through the doorway.

Kaboom!

The helicopter dipped violently as an enormous spray of water hit the bottom of the craft, spewing in front of the doorway. John and Kota slid across the bloody floor.

Kota scrambled on his hands and knees until he found his machete. He came to his feet. The white spike on his face distorted with hatred. Powerful pectoral muscles rippled as he tightened his grip on the machete. With every step, his eyes smoldered deeper into rage. He paused. A smile widened on his half-painted face. "So, I hear you lost your wallet?"

"Yeah, that was a nice touch." John slowly stood, trying to get better footing.

Kota took another step forward, effortlessly tossing the machete into his opposite hand. "Relax," he said. "Soon you will meet your friend, Brad! Brad . . . how he entertained us that night on the island. What a sport! In spite of the way we carved him up, he still almost made it out of the lagoon." Kota laughed wickedly, a twisted glee in his eyes. "When Kuta-keb-la came to him, your big strong friend cried out like a woman." Kota took another step closer. "Come on, John Paxton, now it's your turn . . . let's see how loud you can scream!"

At that moment, John's fear disappeared, replaced by an accelerating rage. The noisy cargo area seemed silent to his pulsing heart. He stepped sideways over the rope ladder, his right foot shifting for traction on the chum-slick floor.

Kota lunged forward. John shifted to the side, his foot catching on the ladder as the blade whipped beside his head. He whirled back around, driving his elbow into the back of Kota's ribs, but the strong tribesman didn't flinch. John turned. Gripping the top of the barrel beside the doorway, he hurled it at his foe. The remaining chum gushed onto the floor. Kota stopped the barrel with his foot and kicked it through the open door.

~~~

Oblivious, Kate was squinting down through the pilot's side window, searching for the beast. She shouted back to John. "Think you missed it. Now what?" Then she saw the barrel splash below. She turned back to the cargo bay. "Hey, what's going on back . . . whoa! Where did he come from?"

~~~

A powerful shoulder crashed into John's chest, driving him backward. John felt his boots sliding on the bloody floor. Wind from the thumping rotor blew the shirt tight against his back as he neared the open doorway.

The floor disappeared from beneath his feet.

John soared backward out of the helicopter, arms flailing. In midair, he looked below him. The familiar jaws stretched open, exploding from the water to meet him. Plummeting toward the creature, John felt something grab his left leg and jerk him back—the tangled rope ladder stopped him like a bungee cord. The closing jaws missed him, and the pliosaur rolled sideways and splashed beneath the surface, showering him with water.

I'm still alive I'm still alive I'm still alive . . .

He hung there upside down, head and chest pounding, swaying thirty feet above the water. His wet shirt rolled up under his arms, and he fought to keep it from covering his head. He peered down the remainder of the rope ladder to the water, its free end teasing the creature just above its nose.

Again, the vast open mouth launched from the surface. John's vision filled with blackness until the creature's teeth closed on the ladder just a few feet below his head. Instantly, John's upper body was under water as the monster pulled the helicopter toward the sea, like a balloon controlled by a wild child. The helicopter's whining engine was no match for the creature's tremendous bulk.

On the ship's starboard rail, hundreds of passengers watched in disbelief.

~~~

Beneath the surface, John freed his tangled leg and righted himself on the ladder, the clenched teeth only two steps down from his feet. The beast exhaled through its nostrils, enveloping him in bubbles. Three quick steps up the ladder and John broke the water line, gasping. The downdraft from the chopper pounded his face, and he was glad to feel it.

He climbed.

The pliosaur pulled harder.

The helicopter lowered.

The surface rose back up to John's waistline, then his neck. Quickly, John climbed up another step lifting his shoulders from the sea. The taste of the bloody water was bitter in his mouth.

I'm alive I'm alive I'm alive . . .

Looking up the twenty-five feet of nylon ladder leading to the cargo door, John's hope burst.

Kota raised the machete blade just above the ladder, grinning. He waved at John then sliced the left side of the rope.

The ladder fell sideways as the left rope was severed, dropping John's shoulder beneath the waves. His feet slid off, swinging through the water above the creature's snout. He struggled to climb another step with his hands.

Then he didn't try to climb another step when he looked up and saw the blade rise again.

~~~

Kate looked back from the cockpit and saw Kota raise his machete above the ladder. "Oh, no you don't, you—" With that, she jerked the stick, dipping the chopper.

~~~

Still looking upward, John saw the chopper dip and Kota tumble from the doorway. The big man howled like a cat, his hands clawing at the open air. John felt the water explode behind him as the monstrous jaws opened. Instantly, the ladder sprang away from the creature, and John, barely able to hang on, passed Kota in midair. Glancing back, he saw the tribesman's head crash directly into the creature's upper row of teeth as his decapitated body disappeared behind the closing jaws.

Thirty feet above the water, the helicopter reeled back as if being released from a giant game of tug-of-war. Momentum carried John higher than the doorway of the cargo bay. He heard the ladder clank against the swirling rotor. It caught the ladder and threw John sideways until he latched onto the bottom of the cargo doorway. He pulled himself inside with part of the ladder tangled around his leg.

Kate looked back and shouted, "Get your foot out of the ladder! Get your foot outta' there! The ladder's caught in the blade!"

Suddenly, John felt a tug on his leg. He looked toward the doorway and saw the ladder uncoiling upward toward the main rotor. Another tug, and he was pulled across the cargo bay. His arms caught the doorframe. Just as his legs slid outside into the open air, he rolled around and freed his foot as the ladder zipped from beneath him. With every ounce of remaining strength, John pulled himself back into the helicopter. After rolling to the center of the cargo area, he slowly climbed to his knees.

Kate said, "So. Any more friends of yours back there you forgot to introduce me to?"

"No." John said between gasps, "I think that's about it." He leaned back on his knees. "You wouldn't happen to have an extra pair of pants on board, would you?"

Kate looked at him, puzzled. "Why? It's just a little seawater. It won't kill you to be a little wet, considering what you've just been through!"

John shook his head. "I'm afraid it's a little more than seawater."

Kate turned back toward the windshield, laughing aloud.

When she finally composed herself, she asked, "So, what's the plan now, without any depth charges?" She worked the stick, steadying the helicopter.

Coming to his feet, John peered down at the ocean. As he expected, the red eyes were glaring up at him from beneath the waves. "We definitely have its attention." John glanced at the barrel strapped to the wall. "We still have one barrel of chum left. With any luck we can keep it away from the ship until the Naval Demolitions Team arrives."

"Okay, I guess that'll work." Kate said, and she looked back with a smile. "But this time, no swimming." Then her smile faded. She wrinkled her nose. "What's that . . . smell?"

"What?"

"That smell . . . can't you smell it?"

"Come on! Give me a break! If you were down there in the water with that thing, you would have done the same th—"

"No! I don't mean your trousers . . . it's coming from . . ." she sniffed, "up there!" Kate pointed to the top of the helicopter.

John nodded, "Yeah. It's like a burning smell!"

The main rotor let out a high-pitched shriek . . . just before it started to slow.

"Crap!" Kate growled, as she smashed her hand on the instrument cluster. "The ladder's still caught around the main rotor. It's burning out the engine!"

John looked up toward the ceiling. "You mean . . ."

Kate's back was ramrod straight as she looked out the windshield and nodded. "We're going down."

Chapter 17
IMPROVISATION

"Here?" John eyed the doorway. "No! No, not here!"

Kate fought the stick. "I don't think we have much choice." She twisted the throttle all the way open. The engine accelerated but didn't reach maximum RPM. The tortured engine lifted the helicopter for a moment then started to lose altitude.

Kate worked the collective pitch control. "I'll try to get us as far from the pliosaur as I can. We'll stay up for a minute or so–but we're definitely going down! Hurry! Get up here and buckle in!"

John looked out at the ship. His eyes drifted across the lifejackets along the rail, and his heart sank. He knew he'd failed them all.

"What are you waiting for?" Kate shouted, working the stick. "Buckle in!"

The helicopter soared away from the ship, sputtering–gaining and losing altitude. Kate angled the main rotor to move straight ahead as far as possible before hitting the sea. Grabbing the walkie-talkie, John jumped into the passenger's seat and buckled in. A glance through the side window showed the sinking cruise ship getting further away. When he turned back to the windshield, he saw the surface coming up fast.

"That's about as much distance as I can get us!" Kate yelled. "Gotta save some of the altitude to cushion the impact! Hold on!"

Not again, thought John. *Two chopper crashes in the same week.*

At the last second, Kate yanked the stick back, angling the main rotor backward in an attempt to use the spiraling blades as a parachute.

The windshield filled with sky. The back of the landing gear slammed down, skimming the water first, then the front caught–hurling the helicopter forward.

Water smashed the windshield, flooding the rolling cockpit. Something slammed against the back of John's seat, throwing him forward, and everything turned red. The cold water rose over his head. Through the billowing blood cloud, he saw that Kate was no longer in the cockpit. The craft rolled further on its side, sinking fast. As he unbuckled his seat belt, John saw the top to the chum barrel float by and realized with relief it wasn't his or Kate's blood.

He swam through the cabin door and was blinded by streaks of glaring sunlight reflecting from the broken rotor blades. Once free from the craft's undertow, he glanced down. A billowing red cloud rose from the cargo door as the helicopter continued to roll to the depths like a wounded creature bleeding from its side. Then, looking up, John saw

Kate swimming toward the surface light.

John broke the waterline, gasping.

"You okay?" a familiar voice shouted from behind. Turning around, he saw Kate bobbing in the waves and swam close to her. He quickly wiped the wet hair from her cheek. He felt a rush of relief at the sight of her.

"Sure you're okay?" Kate squinted. Pointing, she said, "All that blood."

"Just the chum barrel." John took a minute to slow his breathing. He glanced back at the distant ship. "Good job. Looks like you were able to get us about three quarters of a mile from the ship!" He saw the walkie-talkie floating nearby and quickly stroked over and grabbed it.

Treading water, Kate looked around. "You know, with all the sharks in the area, not to mention Old Big Ugly, we might want to find a better place to float than in the middle of this chum stain."

John looked down at the water. "I was just thinking the same thing."

As they slowly paddled away from the stain, they heard a rumbling on the water. The sound of a powerful engine behind them grew louder, until it suddenly ceased. John turned around. The blue hull of a thirty-two-foot Sea Ray drifted to a stop right in front of his face. At idol speed, John could still feel the powerful engines thumping the sea.

A stout, curly-haired man peered down from the side of the boat. "Saw you coming down. You mates okay?" He ducked behind the gunwale, but John could still hear him talking. "Best get you two outta there. This ain't a good day to be in these waters."

The man reappeared with a ladder. He hooked it over the gunwale and helped them board. With a smile, he thrust out his right hand. "Henry Peterson, welcome aboard. What happened? Engine trouble?"

"Yeah, something like that," said Kate, scaling the ladder first.

As John stepped onto the deck, Henry looked at him, squinting. There was eagerness in his voice. "I know why you were up there. You were looking for that big critter like everyone else. Well, did you see it?"

Neither responded.

Kate looked back at the cruise ship, which didn't seem so far away now that they were out of the water. She rested her hand on Henry's shoulder. "Come on, Henry. Let's get this thing of yours cranked up, and head back to shore. What do ya say, old boy?"

"Yah, sure," Henry replied, stepping back to the helm. "I just need to take care of a little something, and then I'll get you two mates back to shore."

Kate eased down beside John on the gunwale, just behind the driver's seat. They were both dripping wet. As the boat slowly accelerated, Kate looked past the stern and whispered to John, "Correct me if I'm wrong, but isn't the shore back there?"

Wringing the water from the front of his shirt, he said, "Just give him a second to veer back around."

The boat maintained its course, heading farther out to sea.

Kate tapped John on the shoulder and nodded toward the back of the boat. "What do you make of those?" They stood up and approached the stern.

At the stern were two large barrels, and flowing from the barrels out the back of the boat and into the sea for thirty yards behind them was a red trail.

Kate looked over the transom. "Ah, Henry . . . care to explain why your boat is bleeding?"

Henry glanced back from the driver's seat as he eased into the throttle. "To get the big critter's attention. Ya gotta lay down a good scent, ya know!"

"Get its attention?" Kate gasped. "That's bloody great. Well, turn it off, Henry. Turn it off now!" Kate's voice was almost pleading.

Undeterred, Henry did just the opposite and continued to accelerate. As he did so, a large dorsal fin rose behind the boat. Kate and John's eyes shot open, and they stepped back from the stern.

Henry looked back, laughing. "Relax! That's just a twelve-foot great white—my bait fish. Got a hook in her. Didn't you mates see that thick line attached to the transom? Come on, fellas. You act like you've never seen a shark before." As the shark rolled to the side sending up a spray of water in the middle of the chum line, Kate looked at John, her eyebrows arched. "*That's* the little something he had to do before taking us in?"

John approached Henry at the wheel. "You mean you're trying to catch the pliosaur with *that*? And pull it all the way in to shore with *this* boat?"

"Well, that was part of the plan," said Henry. "But—"

Kate broke in, "Well, you can just stop and let us off here then, because we're better off in the water!"

Henry looked at her, holding up his camera. "No, mate, I'm not that dof. I just want to catch it on film. The plan is to get the beastie close enough to get a good shot of it, then cut the bait shark loose to keep it busy while I get away."

"Ahhh, brilliant plan, Henry," Kate said, her voice bristling with sarcasm. "A kamikaze would question the safety of that mission!" She glanced back at the rolling bait shark. "What happens if the 'beastie' decides to go for the boat rather than the bait?"

"Why would it do that?" asked Henry, clearly puzzled by the question.

"Aaauuughhh!" yelled Kate, at the limits of her frustration. "That's it! Turn those chum barrels off now, or *you're* going in the water!"

With a nod of approval, John said, "Yes, I believe it's time to commandeer this vessel!"

Henry puffed out his chest and bellowed, "This is my boat. No one tells me what to do on my own boat!"

Kate walked up to him, poked a finger into his chest. "Well, it's *my life* you're trying to end. So turn it off now, or it's time for swim class!"

John held up a finger and pointed at the waters behind the Sea Ray.

"What bloody now?" said Kate in a defeated tone, and she turned to look, as did Henry.

A group of fishing boats were coming straight toward them, motioning them to slow down. Henry eased off the throttle, and seven boats surrounded them.

Henry was quick to notice the chum barrels on most of the boats. He yelled over the noise of all the engines, "Hey, you skeefs . . . this is my spot. I've been laying down a chum line for hours. You go somewhere else!"

A Hatteras pulled along their port side. The driver called out, "No, you got it all wrong, mate. We're not chumming anymore. We heard a distress call from a cruise ship in this area. We're all on our way to help 'em out. Come on, turn off that chum line and follow us. Over three hundred passengers still on the ship. We need all the boats we can get."

John had heard enough, waved his hands in the air. "Stop! Wait a minute, everyone. We were just over the cruise ship in a chopper. The creature responsible is at least three times the size of any of the boats I see here. You'll never make it to the ship, much less save a passenger. It's a nice thought, but it'll never work."

"You mean that leguaan is as big as those lighteys in the speed boat said it was, eh? 'Bout eighty feet?" the driver of the Hatteras said in an incredulous tone.

"Leguaan." John squinted at Kate, "What's a leguaan?"

Kate muttered, "It's local slang for lizard."

John stepped closer to the rail, and shouted, "Yes, every inch of it. Probably bigger!"

"Well, what are we gonna do then?" yelled a man from the bow of another boat. "The Navy hasn't shown up, and we're the only boats in the area. We can't just park out here and let them all die!"

Anglers from the other boats murmured amongst themselves.

A barrel-chested, red-bearded man yelled from an old fishing boat,

"Ahhh! Forget these blokes, they're just afraid . . . a couple of pansies. Come on, let's get going. We're wasting time."

One by one, engines began to fire.

John turned to Kate in frustration. "He's right," he muttered. "We can't just sit here." All the while, his tortured eyes were fixed on the distant cruise ship. The clock was ticking, and he knew it. Then John noticed the blood splatter on the deck. His eyes rose to the huge drums on the stern and stopped on the powerful engines between them. "Henry . . . how fast'll this thing go?"

It was Henry's favorite question. "Got twin Merc 400s on her. She'll hit close to ninety."

"What about the boats around us . . . any of them faster than this one?"

"In their dreams," Henry scoffed good-naturedly.

Kate clearly didn't like the sound of this, but it was all John needed to hear.

After a long moment of looking in the direction of the cruise ship, John nodded to himself.

Kate looked at him with growing concern. "What?" she said, hands on her hips. "No . . . no, John. I'm not sure what you're thinking . . . but no."

John was at the side of the boat again, calling out to the boats about to depart. "Wait, guys. I've got an idea."

All heads turned in his direction. Kate's frown line deepened.

"Okay, we're listening," yelled the man in the Hatteras. He motioned for the other boaters to cut their engines.

John spoke up. "First, I need all of the chum you have on board to refill our barrels."

There was silence as all the men listened intently.

"Then, all of you will follow us to the ship, but lagging behind about a hundred yards or so," he said with growing confidence. He put a hand on Henry's shoulder. "Henry, we're going in front of the beast with the chum lines flowing. With any luck, it'll follow us far enough from the cruise ship, so the rest of you guys can go in for the passengers."

Henry looked at the hand on his shoulder. "Yeah, that oughta work. Like I said, this baby'll do close to ninety."

"Not towing fifteen hundred pounds of shark behind it, it won't!" Kate said with a pout.

"I reckon that might slow her down a little." Henry gave his neck a scratch, then with a hesitant nod, he put his foot on the gunwale. He stepped across to the Hatteras tied off beside them and looked back at John. "If it's all the same to you mates, I think I'll go with these gentlemen and help rescue the passengers. That way your boat'll be a little lighter."

"That's very noble of you, Henry," muttered John with a smile.

~~~

Once safely on the deck of the Hatteras, Henry glanced back, wringing his swarthy hands. Looking along the metallic-blue hull of the Sea Ray, he sighed heavily. "That's too bad. I really loved that boat. Wonder if my policy will cover this?" he muttered to himself.

~~~

The driver in the Hatteras yelled to the stocky fisherman, "Hey, Red. So much for the pansy theory, eh? All right, blokes. Let's load up their chum barrels and chivvy along!"

Kate jerked John aside and got in his face. "The words 'one-way trip' mean anything to you? What are you doing? This is a suicide mission!" She tried unsuccessfully to keep her voice low, spittle flying from her clenched teeth. "Look, I know this whole thing's eating you alive, but getting us killed isn't gonna do anybody any good either."

John pulled away and pointed at the transom, determined. "You gotta hear the rest of it, Kate. First I need two more bait hooks."

Kate squinted with suspicion.

"No, seriously," John insisted. He pointed to the boat alongside them. "I just need two more. Get the ones from those guys?" He forgot the magic word. "Please?"

Giving John a long look, Kate rolled her eyes and stepped across to the other boat.

The moment she was stabilized on the other boat, John jumped into the driver's seat of the Sea Ray and slammed the throttle. The nose shot up, hurling John back in the seat.

Kate's eyes bugged when she heard the roaring engines. She took off along the fishing boat, raced along the gunwale like a cat, and bound across the water, landing in the back of the speedboat.

John heard the thud and turned, eyes wide. "Hey! This was supposed to be solo."

Kate rose from the deck, her face boiling red with anger. "You expect to survive this? Have you completely lost your—" She paused when she saw his tortured eyes—the burning guilt and rage. The realization hit her, and she put her hand to her mouth. "You didn't plan on coming back . . ."

John turned back to the windshield. He couldn't look her in the eye. His tormented mind raced. *Now what? She's ruined everything.* "I'm taking you back," he finally said.

"No, I'm not getting off this boat!" She ran to the cockpit and grabbed his shoulder. "There's no way you can pull this off alone. One person can't work the chum lines, cut the bait shark loose, and maneuver the boat at the same time. Besides, what happens if that thing gets to you before you lure it far enough from the ship? You know those fishing boats will go in anyway and add to the slaughter." Her eyes narrowed. "You need my help . . . because if you fumble this, yours won't be the only life lost!"

After a long moment, he eased back to half throttle. "All right," he said. "But do you know how to work the chum lines?"

"Sure, I do it every day!" She smirked.

Leaving the boat at half throttle, he walked her back to the stern. He knelt and pointed to the bottom of one of the barrels. "Under here, there's a handle just like on a water cooler. Feel it?"

When Kate reached down to the handle, John rushed at her, grabbing her legs, and tried to throw her overboard. But Kate's cat-like reflexes allowed her to sidestep the attempt. She tumbled back onto the deck. John stumbled against the gunwale.

Kate rose from the deck, stunned. "You . . . you tried to toss me overboard!"

John groaned as he slowly stood.

"Not quite quick enough." She laughed at him. "Or clever enough. Your eyes tipped me off. On our way back to the chum, I saw you glance at that life jacket under the gunwale."

John stormed back to the wheel, gripping it tightly. "You're going back!"

Kate latched onto the steering wheel, not letting him turn around. Between clenched teeth, she growled, "I refuse to let you . . ." The fight went out of her suddenly, and John followed her gaze—to the sinking cruise ship. Clearly, there was no time to argue. He hit the throttle as they slammed into their seats.

Chapter 18
LIVE BAIT

Wrists swollen from gripping the warm metal of the starboard rail, a young steward named Betty looked down the sloping deck and into the water. Four feet beneath the surface, a long streak of sunlight shimmered from the portside rail. One thing pounded her mind: were they still out of reach?

Beside her, lifeless postures suddenly became rigid. Fatigued muscles found new strength as legs and arms locked tighter around the rails. The frill again split the sea. One by one, passengers looked across the angled deck as the rippling shadow passed below them. Just beyond the sunken rail, the giant silhouette rose, transforming into the now-familiar gray back as the creature glided parallel to the ship. Wet, pebbled skin twinkled in the sun. Slowly, the head tilted sideways, lifting a red eye just above the water line. Horrified passengers watched as the burning orb passed before them, peering upward, searching.

~~~

From the ship's tilted bridge, Captain Porter peered through his binoculars. *Surely we've reached the end of this horror*, he thought, and then he had a morbid side to that: *though some nightmares never end.*

He focused on a black woman and two little girls who'd defied death, thanks to the helicopter which had appeared out of nowhere. Now back at the ship, they clung to each other in the swimming pool that was even with the waterline. For the moment, they appeared to be safe behind the coping.

He puzzled over the helicopter. It appeared to be commercial, not a naval chopper. Why had it gone down? The captain focused on the sunken port side rail, a horrifying gauge he used to determine their remaining time. Although the ship was listing dramatically, he could tell her rate of descent had slowed. *Air pockets trapped in some of the submerged cabins might be partially responsible*, he thought. But the main source for their buoyancy was without question the undamaged starboard pontoon.

Looking down toward the stern, he saw the giant shadow come around for another pass. It circled closer, much closer than before.

The captain scooted beneath the leaning port window, trying to keep the creature in sight. He watched until it disappeared around the bow. He turned around and looked up at the angled floor leading to the starboard window. He crawled along cabinets that ran the width of the bridge, gripping inside each one, and pulling himself closer to the window.

Finally at the window, he looked down and regained sight of the giant shadow. Slowly the creature rose, rubbing its snout along the starboard hull. Then the water swept over its wide head, and it disappeared beneath the waves.

The ship trembled, almost knocking the captain from the window.

Regaining his balance, he looked out again. No trace of the beast. He pressed his face against the glass to get a better angle, and his greatest fear was confirmed. A parachute-sized cloud of bubbles rose from the starboard pontoon.

~~~

The engines whined as the vessel jerked and lunged forward under its heavy load. With every wave that passed beneath the Sea Ray's keel, John's self-doubt grew stronger. His earlier encounter with the pliosaur replayed in his mind. Looking down at that thing from the chopper was some sight, but from the waterline, just above the enormous jaws as they clenched the ladder beneath his feet, that was a different story. *The sheer size of the head was incomprehensible! And now I'm going back . . . in a boat . . . laying a chum line . . . and pulling a bait shark. What's wrong with this picture?*

He glanced at Kate. She put up a good front, but he could tell by the way she refused to make eye contact that she was pissed off and terrified. Now, with her on board, it all seemed wrong, like he was transporting the condemned to their execution. *What am I doing?* He questioned everything.

A sudden jolt of the wheel made him regain his focus. A wave had caught the bait shark. Looking up, he saw the tilted cruise ship less than a quarter mile away. He could tell there was only about half as much of the vessel remaining above the surface as when they'd first flown over it in the helicopter. He began to see movement of orange life jackets along the starboard rail. At that moment, in spite of the risk, he knew he had made the right decision. He glanced over at Kate and gave a half smile.

Kate looked back with an uncertain nod.

"I'd still feel better if you put on that life jacket."

"Life jacket!" Kate gasped. "If this all goes south, what's that supposed to do? Clog its intestinal tract?"

John twisted around in his seat. The cluster of boats were trailing about thirty yards behind. "Argh, they're too close. They need to drop back more." John tried to wave them back, but the boats continued to close in.

When he turned back around, the tip of the giant frill glided out from behind the cruise ship's stern. It passed along the sunken port side rail, slowly rising until several feet of its hide was above the water.

Behind John, the roaring engines ceased.

"Looks like that did the trick. They've backed off a bit now," Kate said, looking back. The fishing boats continued to slow until they were about eighty yards behind them.

John looked over at Kate, his mouth too dry to speak. He swallowed hard. "You know how to open the chum lines?"

"Yes. I got the gist of it before you tried to hurl me over the gunwale. All I have to do is turn the handle in front of each barrel."

John eased back on the throttle. "Okay, you ready to go in?"

"No. Are you?"

"What do *you* think?" said John, looking at the enormous frill.

"Well, at least I know you're still sane."

"I wouldn't go that far." John cautiously eased into the throttle.

Slowly, they pulled away from the seven fishing boats, toward the cruise ship. After reaching about half speed, John nodded toward Kate. "Okay. Go ahead and start the chum lines. Turn on both barrels. We want to make sure we get its attention."

"Okay." Kate got up from the passenger's seat. "And then you better drive this bloody boat like you stole it!"

The vessel skimmed across the water at half throttle as she made her way back to the chum barrels. She turned the handle on each and made her way back to the cockpit.

With the chum flowing, they slowly proceeded. John could feel the shark carcass in tow shifting the boat slightly with each passing wave. How the boat would handle at top speed, he was afraid to imagine. Moving closer, obscure lumps in the water gradually took human form, while circling seagulls landed on them at random. Among the corpses were several life preservers and fragments of what appeared to be a lifeboat. Debris from the ship was everywhere. All this John saw through his peripheral vision—without moving his eyes from the frill gliding slowly through the water ahead of him. They drew within sixty yards of the cruise ship and watched the towering frill disappear behind the ship's bow.

John slowed the engines. He waited impatiently; rapidly tapping his fingers on the steering wheel until the frill came back around. His heart pounded loudly in his ears. He recalled the nightmare he'd recently had of the victims—their pale, lifeless eyes. He could see the ghost of Carlos pointing to Kate. "Bring her to me, John, like all the others. I know you won't let me down!" The ghastly voice seemed to echo above the idling engines.

"Shut up!" John blurted.

"Are you speaking to me?" Kate questioned.

"No," muttered John, "just clearing my head.

Kate glared back. "Oh no . . . don't you go nuts on me now!"

"A little late for that."

John's hand trembled when he reached for the throttle. It shook so bad it felt like the throttle was jiggling on its own. The huge frill passed, and John pulled in behind its wake. The air filled with fluttering wings as startled seagulls lifted from various points in the water.

The Sea Ray closed in.

Along the ship's starboard rail, passengers looked down in disbelief, frantically waving and pointing at the water as if John didn't see the pliosaur. Their cries of warning rose above the boat's engines.

Guiding the boat closer behind the giant shadow, John could see the powerful striped tail gliding beneath the surface. Every instinct screamed at him to turn around and head in the opposite direction. A glance at the starboard rail showed passengers still pointing to the dark water just in front of him.

Kate shook her head. "That thing looks a lot bigger from down here than it did in the chopper."

Carefully, John veered the boat twenty yards to his left and pulled ahead of the pliosaur. Then he slowly cut back toward the ship, drawing the alluring scent just ahead of the sensitive nose.

But the creature didn't take the bait.

John looked back and saw the frill moving away from the boat's crimson wake. Perplexed, he thought of slowing down, but knew that would be too dangerous. If the creature lunged suddenly, considering the load they were towing, they couldn't accelerate quickly enough. There was only one other way—try again, but closer and faster. "We gotta go back and make a closer pass." He noticed that his voice trembled, and he hoped Kate didn't catch it.

"Closer?" Kate looked at him with round eyes. "That looked bloody close to me!"

"No, not close enough because he didn't pick up the scent." John banked to port and veered the boat away from the giant frill.

He approached for the second pass, estimating the creature's speed. He accelerated enough to pull ahead of the vast back, turned toward the nose and slammed the throttle. The boat sped toward a spot a mere ten yards in front of the monstrous snout.

Closer . . . and it appeared as if they were going to ram the beast!

Kate looked over in disbelief. "This is the plan?"

At the last second, John cut the wheel away from the enormous head when he realized he was way off course. The boat had drifted twenty yards wide due to the fifteen-hundred-pound carcass in tow.

The hull slid sideways across the water just in front of the creature's nose as the bait shark skimmed across its head. The pliosaur thrusts its nose upward and roared so loud John's body hair stood on end.

He looked behind him, Kate clinging to his arm. The shark carcass soared through the air beside the boat's starboard. It reached the end of its tether and jerked the stern from the water. The props screamed in the open air. Then the bait shark plunged into the surface beside the boat, stopping them dead in the water like an anchor. The deck trembled. The wheel spun wildly out of John's hands. He felt the bait shark rolling between the boat's hull and the top of the pliosaur's head. The immense shadow of the beast shot beneath the hull. Regaining control of the wheel, John slapped the throttle, making sure it was wide open. The boat lunged forward. The props sputtered, dropping in and out of the water. The hull scraped across armor-plated skin until it passed over the enormous head.

After they gained a short lead on the surprised creature, Kate looked back, wide-eyed. "Was that close enough for you? I think you got its attention now." She circled an arm around his shoulders and said sarcastically, "You have driven a boat before, haven't you?"

"Not towing four hundred pounds of chum and a great white shark tied to the back of it, I haven't!"

~~~

A cheer rose across the starboard rail as passengers watched the cluster of fishing boats pull alongside the cruise ship. Before the boats even reached the ship's sunken port side, people began jumping from the rail and sliding down the deck like a carnival slide. Women's long gowns twisted, rolling up around them as they slid toward the water. Others lagged behind, having trouble prying their cramped fingers loose from the rail.

The fishermen pulled in closer, looking up, overwhelmed by the avalanche of bodies flowing down the ship's deck. Overhead, the majority of seagulls had already dispersed, heading northwest to follow the giant shadow.

Near the bow of the cruise ship, a woman sitting atop the rail screamed hysterically, refusing to let go. "No! No! I'm not letting go. What if it comes back?"

"That's why we have to go now!" demanded her husband. He pulled on her hands until she fell forward and slid down the deck behind him.

Joyce and her two daughters were among the first pulled from the water by the captain of the Hatteras. Once on board, tears of joy swelled in her eyes as she pulled the two little girls tight to her sides. "Thank you, Lord. Thank you." She repeated her thanksgiving over and over.

There was continuous splashing. More people slid down the deck, crashing into the water behind her. The boat started to tilt from people climbing over the starboard, not waiting to use the ladder.

"Now, use all the boats. You blokes don't all have to load onto this one," the captain of the Hatteras hollered, trying to keep his starboard above water.

Holding her girls, Joyce watched while dozens of people continued to slide down the angled deck, landing on top of one another as they crashed into the water in front of the boats. Almost instantly, the surface was crowded with nearly three hundred lifejackets huddled against one another—arms splashing, reaching out from the sea.

The overloaded fishing boats struggled to hold as many passengers as possible, their hulls pressed deep below the surface.

As the Hatteras quickly filled, Joyce walked to the corner of the stern to help make room. She heard a thumping in the sky. Looking up, she saw three naval helicopters approaching in tight formation.

"Look at that; better late than never!" said a man in front of her. The helicopters broke formation and began to search the area surrounding the ship. Joyce turned her attention toward the distant waters. From her vantage, it was difficult to tell if the frill was as close to the speedboat as it appeared. Gusts of spray lifted behind what she guessed was some kind of bait. As the boat and the creature raced toward the horizon, Joyce tightly closed her eyes. "Give that boat speed, dear Lord. Give that boat speed!"

Chapter 19
PIER 21

Knuckles white on the throttle, John looked down at the speedometer. *Thirty-five miles an hour.* Something was wrong. The boat was nowhere near top speed.

He looked back as a spray of whitewater soared through the air behind one of the pliosaur's front paddle fins. Just beneath the surface, he could see the creature furiously driving its head up and down to accelerate its bulk forward. Then water rolled up, shooting out to the sides of the accelerating frill as it knifed through the boat's wake.

Kate looked back, clearly terrified. "What are you waiting for? Hit the gas!"

"I am! Something's wrong. When we ran across its head it must have damaged one of the props!"

"Was that part of the plan?" Kate shouted.

Another glance back and John saw the monster growing closer, plowing through the sea like a locomotive. The colossal head rose and dropped with each thrust of its powerful paddle fins.

John considered his options. He wondered if he could outmaneuver the pliosaur, but quickly realized they wouldn't have a chance with the drag from the bait shark.

"Okay," John shouted. "This is far enough! Go back and get the hatchet. We're gonna see what she can really do!"

"You don't have to tell me twice!" Kate said gratefully and sprang from her seat.

John cautioned, "Wait as long as you can before you cut it. We want to draw the pliosaur as far from the ship as possible!" Kate reached into a compartment in the stern and pulled out a hatchet. "Okay, ready to go back here!"

Leaning over the transom, Kate raised the hatchet above the thick nylon rope connected to the bait shark. She glanced back at the beast. "Okay, Big Boy, let's see if you can hang with us now!" She slammed down the hatchet with a sense of relief. But, the rope didn't cut; the dull blade only pressed it into the transom.

"Do it!" John shouted.

Kate raised the hatchet again and came down with everything she had. The nylon rope cut part of the way through, exposing a shiny steel cable in its center. "What? This fool used rope lined with cable! How am I supposed to cut through that?" Kate desperately tried to chop the cleat loose from the boat.

As Kate hacked away at the transom, John looked portside to see nothing but armor-plated skin gliding beneath the surface. The water in front of the boat darkened as the blunt nose raced ahead of the bow.

"Forget it, Kate! I don't think it's interested in the bait anymore!"

Kate looked up from her hacking and saw the towering frill almost touching the back of the boat. The hatchet dropped to the deck. Kate stepped back and screamed.

At that moment, the frill disappeared, and in its place the pliosaur's head burst from the surface. Suspended above the stern, gigantic jaws sprang open wide, showering Kate with water. She stared up in disbelief as the creature caught the bait shark in midair. Swallowing the twelve-foot carcass whole, the creature rolled into a dive beside the boat, sending up a tremendous swell. The boat listed, tossing Kate into the gunwale. The cable stretched taut until the cleat and a small section of the transom ripped from the stern and followed the great mouth into the water.

Out of control, the boat rolled so far starboard, it nearly capsized. John fought the wheel, trying to ride out the fifteen-foot swell. The craft leveled off and lunged forward, its speed increasing after losing the bait shark. The trembling boat ride became noticeably smoother as the hull rose higher above the surface.

Getting up from the deck, Kate scrambled back to the cockpit. "Did . . . did you see that?"

"What happened?"

Kate caught her breath. "Let's just say that earlier, when I laughed at you for soiling your trousers . . . my apologies." Laughing and crying at the same time, she looked past the bow. "So, you think it's gone?"

"I don't—" John stopped midsentence. The frill was thirty yards off starboard, easily keeping pace with the boat's increased speed.

"How fast are we going?" Kate shouted, her drenched hair blowing back from the wind.

"Forty-two miles an hour. And we're at top speed," yelled John glancing down at the speedometer. "The chum barrels must be weighing us down."

Slowly, but steadily, the gigantic frill inched its way up the boat's wake. John yelled, "I think it's safe to turn off the chum lines now."

"I'll do better than that." Kate raced back to the stern.

From between the two barrels of chum, Kate looked back as a mound of water rose in front of the speeding frill. Resembling a surfacing submarine more than a creature of the sea, the leviathan continued to rise. Unhooking a nylon strap, Kate placed a hand atop the first barrel. "Time to lighten the load! Okay, big boy, catch this!" The barrel hit the surface, throwing up a red curtain behind the boat. It rolled across the monster's head, shot up the frill, and spiraled off twenty feet into the air.

With a grunt, Kate pushed back on the second barrel. "This ought to lighten the load a bit more. This one's still half full!" The barrel slammed the water, spitting blood as it bounced end over end past the speeding giant. Still the creature did not alter its course, but only lowered itself beneath the surface.

For a moment, the frill dropped back another thirty yards and then began to close in. "It's as if we're slowing down, it's coming up so fast," Kate yelled, and behind her, John indeed was pulling back the throttle. With one eye on the approaching monster, Kate backed up to the cockpit, catching her breath. "You know this isn't about the chum line anymore. That thing's after *us*!"

"I know," John said, easing a bit more off the throttle.

"Hey, we *are* slowing down," Kate looked at John then at the throttle. She did a double take. "Hey! What are—? Push that back down!"

Without looking away from the windshield, John said, "When you dumped the chum barrels, we gained too much of a lead."

Kate's eyes were bulging as she swept around to face him. *"Excuse me . . . but isn't that the general idea?"* Another glance back and John saw an empty wake. The creature was gone. He squeezed the throttle in frustration, then eased it back. "I knew we shouldn't have dropped the chum barrels. Now we've lost it. I knew it!" He was enraged.

"That thing was right on top of us!" Kate gasped. "We didn't have a choice. If we hadn't dropped the barrels, we would have never picked up enough speed to get away."

John scanned the surface in frustration. *It's almost like the thing can read my mind.*

"Well, look at the bright side." Kate looked toward the distant shore. "At least we got the pliosaur a good ways from the cruise ship."

John knew Kate was right. He realized that their plan had actually seemed to work, not to mention the small miracle that they were still alive. But this was far from over. Slowly, he brought the boat down to idle speed.

Kate's face flushed pale. "What are you doing? We've accomplished our mission; it's away from the ship. We can go in now . . . John?" She saw the burning rage in his eyes, and the realization sank in. "Your plan was never *just* to lure it from the ship . . . all this time you were baiting it." Her eyes darted over the water. "Now, only God knows why, but you're waiting for it!"

John raised a finger to his lips, listening.

Kate shook her head, "No way." She lunged across the cockpit, reaching for the throttle, but he caught her wrist.

"NO!" he demanded. "Not yet!"

Kate jerked her wrist from his hand. She backed away, eyes glaring. "What's that thing done to you?" She glanced at the sea. "Don't you remember what Steven said about it being an ambush predator? This is insane!"

John's heart rate began to slow. His adrenaline faded, and his mind started to clear. He heard the idling engines, saw Kate's terror-filled eyes. *What am I doing?*

Something tapped him on the shoulder. He looked down at a golf ball-sized clump of seagull droppings on his shirt. Slowly they both looked up as nearly a hundred squawking seagulls collected over the boat.

"That's not a good sign," Kate whispered.

The boat trembled.

"Hit it! GO! GO!" Kate shouted looking down toward the water.

John went.

~~~

Below the surface, the creature twisted through a curtain of bubbles. All four massive paddle fins pumped wildly to bring the tremendous bulk back on pace. The giant head moved from side to side, seeking the familiar vibration. Almost instantly, the highly developed sensory cells inside the creature's snout pinpointed the churning props. Speeding toward the sound, the surface light revealed the torpedo-shaped hull soaring above. The beast rose, speeding toward the surface.

~~~

Thirty yards off port, John saw the enormous head rising beneath the waves. He cut the wheel in the same direction and pressed the throttle forward, amazed at how much better the boat handled without the heavy barrels of chum. Glancing back, he eased off the throttle until the frill drifted into their wake. *That's it. Come on.* Three powerful strokes, and the monster was back on track.

Kate flopped back in her seat. John could see she was exhausted, thoroughly soaked, and panicked—not typical form for Kate. Suddenly, she grabbed John by the shirt and shook him. "Are you ever gonna tell me what you're trying to do, or am I supposed to die confused?"

John kept looking ahead. "Do you remember near the final scene in *Jaws*?"

Kate released his shirt and stared at him like he'd finally snapped.

He locked eyes with her. "Just go with me on this, Kate. Remember on the boat, when they tried to lure it into the shallows to drown it?"

"Not really. But the part where it sinks the boat and eats its occupants is *quite vivid!*"

John returned his gaze to the waters in front of him. "Do you know if the beach straight ahead has shark barrier nets?"

"I don't care about what's ahead! I'm more concerned with what's behind us!" She pointed at the frill which drew horribly close now that John had eased up on the throttle. It was John's turn to holler now. "Come on, Kate! Do you know if the beach is netted or not?"

Kate frowned and looked ahead. Her mouth twisted as she thought, then said, "See that pier in the distance, at eleven o'clock? That's Pier 21. That's the pier we saw on our way out earlier. The one with all the sharks at the end of it; where those fools were chumming for the pliosaur."

"Yeah, I remember. But what about the shark barrier nets . . . does the beach that's straight ahead have them?"

"That's what I was getting at. On the news this morning, I remember hearing someone from the Sharks Board complaining about the chumming so close to land. He said some of the great whites that were drawn in kept getting tangled in the shark barrier nets beside the pier. I'm not sure about the beach straight ahead, but I know the beach area beside the pier is netted!"

That's what he wanted to hear. With a nod, he altered his course slightly to the left.

Kate looked ahead and asked, "So you think the nets will stop it?"

"I don't know," replied John, glancing back at the frill, "But if they don't, the beach will!"

He eased up slightly on the throttle to keep the frill close, hoping the creature would focus solely on the boat's churning props rather than the rising seafloor.

"Come on. Can't you go faster?" Kate yelled above the whining engines. "I can see its eyes. They're less than thirty feet behind the stern."

"No. Gotta keep it close. Can't let it lose interest this close to shore." John used the pier to gauge his distance from the shoreline. As the distant pier became clearer, he could make out the yellow buoys lined across the surface, marking the shark barrier nets. They were about one hundred yards away.

"That's them, dead ahead!" Kate pointed. "The net isn't continuous. It's actually a series of nets spaced apart. So try to go over where the buoys are spaced close together. Don't want the beast to go between the nets."

After a nod, John yelled, "Is it still back there?"
Kate's eyes told John all he needed to know.

~~~

From the crowded Pier 21, dozens of fishermen and spectators adorned with cameras looked up from the chummed waters. As the whining engines of the Sea Ray became louder, all attention shifted to the approaching boat.

"Look! There it is!" shouted a man, raising a camera.

"The boat! Look how close it is to that boat!"

A woman screamed, and several cameras flashed. Everyone along the east side of the pier flooded to the end of the pier. People five rows back pushed forward, eager to get a glimpse. Reporters and tourists jostled for position while struggling to lift their phones, cameras, and camcorders above the heads in front of them. The pier groaned from the weight.

~~~

The string of yellow buoys grew closer in front of them; the pliosaur, behind them. John felt the boat lunge forward from the creature's rising snout.

Thirty yards . . . twenty . . . ten . . .

Whap!

John felt the string of buoys slide beneath the hull. He glanced back and saw the net bow out as the pliosaur rammed it at full speed. The line of buoys dropped beneath the surface, whirling behind the giant.

~~~

In front of the netted head, the churning props moved farther away. The creature's left front paddle fin was tangled in the net, forcing it to dive. The sandy bottom came up fast. The startled beast instinctively adjusted its right front paddle fin and lifted its nose.

Huge clouds of sediment shot up as the paddle fins propelled the creature through a long sweeping turn to evade the shallow waters. The massive belly scraped bottom, and its head lifted.

A row of thick pilings appeared before its blazing red eyes.

~~~

Behind the wooden railing, stunned photographers and onlookers fought to maintain their footing from the sudden jolt. Water spewed over the rail. The pier trembled, thick pilings and planks moaning.

Searching for the source of the jolt, an elderly fisherman looked down from the end of the pier. The slow-circling shark fins suddenly knifed through the surface, scattering in every direction. Then, as his eyes followed the pointed cameras past the east side rail, he saw the enormous netted frill swaying beside the pier.

~~~

Nearing the shoreline, John looked back, expecting to find the pliosaur tangled in the shallows. But the waters were clear. He slowed the boat, searching.

"Over there!" Kate shouted.

John turned to where Kate was pointing. Seventy-five yards away, he saw the enormous netted head jammed beneath the pier. Like distant fireflies, cameras twinkled from the end of the pier, while eighteen feet below, the water came to life.

Every thrash sent spray shooting above the crowd.

John rested a hand on the throttle, waiting, wondering whether to go in to shore or approach the pier. Another piling burst. Two more. He couldn't believe people weren't running like hell for shore to get off the pier. The tangled creature thrust its head sideways. Another piling gave way, collapsing the pier's east corner. He saw the crowd stumbling, finally moving back while the corner of the pier dangled down toward the water.

John hit the throttle and banked away from the shoreline. He knew all too well what this thing could do to a pier. "We've gotta go back. If anyone falls in, they won't have a chance with all the sharks in the area."

"Okay. I think we'll be okay." Kate nervously watched the tangled creature. "Don't think he's going anywhere. Looks like he's jammed in there pretty good. Right?"

John didn't respond, just headed toward the pier. As they neared, Kate stood and scanned the water around the pier. "That's weird! Looks like all the sharks scurried off . . . probably because of the pliosaur. Can't say I blame them."

John eased off the throttle. He guided the boat around a sweeping rear paddle fin and moved closer to the pier. The idling engines became muted by the churning water. The deck started to rock. He looked up at the swaying frill, amazed by the sheer power being exerted by the thrashing giant just forty feet away. Spray kicked up by a front paddle fin fell over him in a fine mist.

Idling closer, a giant left eye turned toward the boat. The red orb locked on John, and the beast froze. Then the netted head twisted furiously, trying to rip through the maze of pilings.

It's furious it can't reach me, John thought. Then a thunderous bellow from the creature shook the pier as if in response. *Oh yeah, it's pissed.* Kate took a step back and her voice shook. "I-I saw that thing looking at you. I mean, it was like he was looking *at you,* John." She nodded rapidly. "Earlier when you said the creature had it in for you . . .

you might have been on to something."

John ran to the stern, waving to get everyone's attention. "Get off the pier." Kate joined in as they desperately tried to convince everyone to clear the area. Clearly, no one understood how much damage was going on beneath them.

But the cameras continued to roll.

~~~

Frank Baumann, a photographer from the *Durban Sun,* acknowledged the boat's presence. Cupping a hand beside his fluffy beard, he yelled down to the driver. "Hey, mate, pull it in a little closer to the tail, will ya? I need to get the boat into frame to give it scale!"

Behind the photographer, the frenzied crowd stepped back as the pier's dangling corner collapsed and crashed down onto the surface. The photographer stepped toward the missing corner, looking down through the hole. Eighteen feet below lay the stony, tiger-striped back. For the moment, the entangled giant lay still beneath the surface, soulless red eyes peering up through the net.

The water settled.

A hush fell over the crowd as everyone stopped, listening. Was the beast finished or merely gathering its strength? Two more photographers stepped closer to the opening. Waves rolled across the armor-plated back while murmurs spread through the crowd.

At a squat two-hundred-sixty pounds, Frank was no lightweight, and the unruly crowd let him know it. "Hey, wide load!" yelled someone. "Pull it over so the rest of us can see!"

Ignoring the crowd, Frank stepped closer to the edge. "Just one more shot."

More photographers followed suit. A myriad of flashes went off, which ignited the creature. The nose thrashed suddenly, kicking water up through the opening, splashing his lens. Another bellow shook the pier. A loud snap. Another snap, then a crack. The pier quaked, and the splintering sound of pilings bursting could be heard.

Behind Frank, planks buckled and split. A gap appeared, separating the end of the pier from the rest. The end of the pier collapsed, dangling down toward the top of the creature's head. Screams spread through the backing crowd. Frank wheeled and dove over the widening crack. Tossing his camera, he fell onto the slanted surface. His fingers clawed across the wood and the front of his shirt pulled up under his chin until he caught onto a gap between the planks.

He watched the crowd above pull two other men up onto the stable section of pier, keeping them from sharing his fate. Another loud snap . . . and he was weightless.

Freefalling with the crumbling section of the pier, the photographer splashed down in front of the creature's snout. Large planks and fragments of wood rained down alongside him.

Beneath the surface, Frank saw only a layer of net separating him from the cavernous mouth and shimmering, spiked teeth. Desperately, he kicked off from the monster's nose, but his foot slipped through the net and became entangled.

The pliosaur thrashed, pulling Frank back and forth beneath the surface. The man frantically twisted his foot trying to kick free. Suddenly, the creature plunged its head straight down, pulling the photographer twenty feet below the surface, ligaments and tendons ripping in his ankle.

His lungs filled with water. Frank was on the verge of blacking out when he felt his ankle snap. The jolt of pain seemed to waken him, and he slipped his ankle from the net. He swam up through the churning waters. He broke the surface, gasping. The blessed sound of a roaring engine filled his thankful ears.

~~~

John carefully guided the boat backward, closer to the end of the pier. His right hand ready to slam the vessel into forward gear if the creature showed any sign of loosening. He watched Kate lean farther over the transom. "That's it," she yelled back at him. "Almost got him!"

The pliosaur suddenly rolled beneath the pier. A massive paddle fin scooped up from the surface, throwing a wave over the speedboat.

The surge of water pushed Kate back, away from Frank's reaching arm. The desperate hand slipped beneath the waves. Thirty feet away, the leviathan twisted violently to free more of its body from the net. It's massive flank hurled into a piling. The wooden column snapped, sending its jagged end into the pliosaur's side. The beast released a bellowing roar.

Kate plunged her hand back into the water as the photographer latched onto her arm. But instead of bringing him up, the big man was pulling her in. Kate screamed.

John saw Kate's feet lift from the deck. He leapt at the stern, grabbing Kate by the waist and pulling her back. The boat rocked violently from the creature's desperate attempts to free itself. The photographer's shoulders rose above the surface–and he hooked his free arm over the transom. The stern bucked, and John lost his grip. Kate flew in the air again, heading for the water. John lunged for her, again catching her, but not before they both splashed into the water behind the photographer.

~~~

One hand gripping the transom, the photographer managed to grab Kate by the shirt. He did not see John.

~~~

After tumbling through the waters, John finally surfaced, gasping for air, and wiping water from his eyes. He looked around, saw Kate safely inside the boat now with the photographer. Treading water, he glanced back at the pier. Most of the monster was still tangled in the net, but a free front paddle fin was pumping madly to reach him. The creature inched its way closer, blood billowing up from its side.

And that didn't cover all John's woes. Kate was screaming from the back of the boat, pointing, screaming, pointing. So was the photographer. He looked up at the pier. So was everyone. He looked behind him.

Two gray fins were speeding toward him. Just as soon as he noticed them, several more fins sliced through the surface, closing in from every angle.

I'm surrounded!

He saw the terror in Kate's expression—*that beautiful face.* Not wanting her to witness the inevitable, he dropped beneath the surface. Ahead, he saw two torpedo-shaped heads shooting through the red-clouded waters. Behind him, the prehistoric jaws moved in closer.

~~~

"GOD NOOO!" Kate screamed from the boat, burying her face in her hands.

~~~

Below the waves, John watched the first great white zero in on him, jaws spreading in that terrifying tooth-filled grin. Unbelievably, the shark missed, its passing pectoral fin slashing across John's ribs. A streak of blood rose from his side. He quickly lifted his feet as another massive great white sailed beneath him. *Not a bite. Didn't even notice me!* John watched in disbelief as the sharks continued to pass him—only to barrel straight into the pliosaur's open wound, mouths open wide.

John swam to the surface. Like speeding torpedoes, huge great whites flashed by him. The creature's giant head lurched above the water, his roars continuing to give weight to the air.

He shook his head, slapped his ears. He couldn't believe what he was seeing, these man-eaters flying past him, the creature injured . . . it was all surreal. And Kate . . .

~~~

When he came back to reality, he was laying on the deck of the Sea Ray, Kate crying and tugging at his shirt—*and that God-awful roar.* He quickly sat up and kissed Kate without any explanation or ado on the forehead, then scrambled on his knees to the side of the boat and looked toward the pier.

His eyes were locked on the water beneath the pier. Kate and the photographer were now on either side of him, following his gaze. Two more fins sliced through the water and closed in on the pliosaur as it struggled to free itself from beneath the pier. It was being picked and prodded as it struggled for freedom. And then it seemed to have had enough.

Taking on a defensive posture, the giant head swept in front of an approaching great white. A red smear shot to the surface. With a sideways chomp of the pliosaur's jaws, all that remained of the scavenger was seven feet of gray flesh and a twitching tail.

No sooner than the severed shark fell to the depths, another white shark sank its jaws into the leviathan's flank, then another swooped in to disable an enormous front paddle fin. Water from the thrashing beasts rose twenty feet into the air. People screamed. The giant roared. Even the sea seemed to cry out. The battle of the predators was in full swing, and everyone was watching.

Navigating the turbulent water, another frenzied shark ventured too close to the enormous mouth. In the blink of an eye, the pliosaur caught the creature in its jaws and threw it clear of the surface. Spiraling thirty feet through the air, the eighteen-hundred-pound shark crashed onto the crowded pier. Spectators scattered as the shark rolled across the pier, snapping its jaws at those nearby, while blood spewed from its missing tail.

At the stern of his boat, John stood motionless, staring at the spectacle before him.

Beneath the churning waters at the end of the pier, swirling clouds of blood rose from the tangled giant. Another thrash sent more of the net clear from the vast body, but the rear paddle fins remained snared. In a violent spasm, the pliosaur rolled in a final attempt to free itself. A rear paddle fin broke free.

Then, like a wounded bison covered by a pack of wolves, the pliosaur slowly swam out from beneath the pier while frenzied sharks gorged on its flesh from all sides.

The giant frill disappeared beneath the waves. In an awesome display of power, the great creature catapulted from the surface, thrashing in midair. Clinging sharks were thrown clear of the giant's back as it rolled, then plunged beneath the surface, sending an enormous wave over the speedboat, over everything.

Incredible.

With its bleeding back clear of sharks, the pliosaur headed back into the sea, away from beneath the pier. John reached for the throttle, watching as the tremendous creature drew closer. "What I wouldn't give for one more depth charge!"

"Wait," Kate said. "I don't think you'll need it." A streak of spray kicked up from a passing fin. Another gray blur flashed from beneath the hull and headed toward the pier. Two more, three more fins sliced through the water as sharks swarmed back in on the wounded giant from all directions.

The colossal head lifted, swaying above the sea. It twisted in mid-air and slammed down across the backs of two white sharks. Another shark zeroed in on the pliosaur's submerged head. As the creature approached, the giant thrust its snout upward, rammed the shark beneath its jaws, and hurled it toward the surface.

John, Kate, and the photographer ducked as the great white burst from the sea. Flipping thirty feet into the air like a dolphin, the shark crashed down beside the speedboat, showering them with water.

The pliosaur handled the first few easy enough–but they just kept coming.

John moved his hand off the throttle, unable to take his eyes from the spectacle before him. Seagulls swooped down in front of the boat, circling above the turbulent waters as fifty tons of muscle thrashed beneath the surface.

Like fireworks, cameras flashed from the pier, silhouetting the great head as it rose above the waves again. The vast mouth hung in the air, streaks of red-stained water cascading down from its giant, spiked teeth.

The jaws stretched wider.

John felt the vibration before he heard the sound. A haunting groan swelled from within the beast. It rose until a primal roar muted the thrashing waves, echoing out across an ocean the creature once ruled without mercy.

And then silence.

The sounds of ravenous seagulls and churning water again filled the air.

The head slipped lower. A wall of gray, striped skin descended into the sea. The surface swept into the closing mouth, quickly rising above soulless eyes incapable of emotion. Then one by one, the circling fins disappeared into the expanding red cloud.

Exhausted, John eased down onto the gunwale. He closed his eyes, catching his breath and–*wham!* He was knocked onto the deck as Kate threw her arms around him and gave him a long hard kiss. When she finally pulled away, her eyes were moist. "Just now," she gasped. "When you were in the water, I thought you were–"

"Oh that." John gave a modest grin. "I knew the sharks were after the creature the whole time."

Kate smiled. She didn't seem to buy it for a minute, and John didn't mind. Then his smile grew guarded, his eyes narrowed. "It is dead, right . . . still there?"

Kate eased up onto the gunwale, craning her neck. Suddenly, her eyes flew open. She stood fully, a nervous finger pointing at the water.

Then as John got up, Kate's open mouth widened into an 'I got ya' smile.

"You are so wrong!" With that, John wrapped his arms around her. Closing his eyes, he rested his cheek against her forehead and squeezed as tight as he possibly could. He didn't plan to ever let go again. Gazing over Kate's shoulder, he watched as the violent water slowly transformed into mere ripples on the surface.

The sea again fell silent.

The red stain extended from the boat to the pier, curling around a tangle of net and buoys. Writhing gray bodies crisscrossed just below the waterline. As the last flickering tail vanished beneath the surface, John grinned toward the sea. "Who would have thought?"

"Thought what?" Kate followed his gaze.

"The great white. The most highly feared and misunderstood creatures known to man, actually turned out to be his savior."

Chapter 20
TWENTY MOONS LATER

As the sun slowly faded behind the island, evenly spaced torches marked the perimeter of the lagoon. A pulsating drumbeat drifted on the ocean wind. A small tribesman stood alone at the edge of the dock area looking out over the sea. Beside him, the enormous gated doors were spread open, reaching into the abyss.

Across from Onue, on the opposite side of the doorway, two men continued to shake hoop rattles from the dock, chopping the water's surface. They had worked in shifts, night and day, never letting the vibrations cease.

With great honor, Onue followed the instructions Kota had left with him before leaving for the mainland. After twenty moons had passed, and Kota still had not returned, he knew it was time to begin. For the last three days, he had slaughtered a cow every evening and left the carcass in the shallows. He would continue this ritual until his vow to Kota was fulfilled.

In the center of the lagoon, he saw a growing number of small fins crisscross through the torch-lit surface.

He raised his gaze. Beyond the open gates, the red trail stretched as far as his eyes could see, blending in with the setting sun. Slowly, the alluring scent rolled farther out with the tide, reaching through the depths, beckoning to whatever may lurk within the deep, dark reaches of the Indian Ocean.

ACKNOWLEDGMENTS

My special thanks to my editor, Janet Fix with thewordverve, for her keen eye, and enthusiasm for the project.
Also thanks to my friend Steve and his encouragement for this project from the very beginning, which helped push me through the challenging times.

ABOUT RUSS ELLIOTT

Growing up in a small town near Lynchburg, Virginia, one of Russ's earliest memories is standing at the front of his first-grade class with his vast collection of dinosaur figures. One by one, he would explain in great detail the various characteristics of each creature to the class. The seven-year-old's prehistoric presentation was so compelling that his teacher would then send him off to repeat it to every grade in the elementary school.

A move to Tampa, Florida, and nearly three decades later, Russ became an award-winning art director at a Palm Harbor advertising agency. Collecting over a dozen ADDY Awards for creative excellence (advertising's equivalent to the Grammy), Russ later became intrigued with fiction writing. An accomplished painter and sculptor, he found that writing offered something new. It was a medium that could be easily shared. A good sculpture, for example, could only be truly appreciated when viewed in person, where one could walk around it and experience it in its world of light and shadows—an experience that could not be captured in a photograph, therefore not easily shared. But writing offered him something more; it allowed him to sculpt an image in the reader's mind. Someone on the other side of the globe could read a scene and experience the images just as the artist had intended. Russ still considers himself a sculptor, though…only now, instead of clay and plaster, he uses words.

So nearly a decade ago, when one of the original "dinosaur kids" decided to pen his first set of novels, it was no surprise that his subject matter would be the greatest prehistoric predator that ever lived.

Other past and present hobbies include motocross and flat track racing, performance cars and competitive bodybuilding. In addition, Russ has two patents to his name. He created the art for his book covers and most of the images on his book's website: www.VengeancefromtheDeep.com.

He now resides in Tampa, Florida, with his wife Danielle and his Doberman.

CHECK OUT OTHER GREAT DEEP SEA THRILLERS

MEGATOOTH
by Viktor Zarkov

When the death rate of sperm whales rises dramatically, a well-respected environmental activist puts together a ragtag team to hit the high seas to investigate the matter. They suspect that the deaths are due to poachers and they are all driven by a need for justice.

Elsewhere, an experimental government vessel is enhancing deep sea mining equipment. They see one of these dead whales up close and personal...and are fairly certain that it wasn't poachers that killed it.

Both of these teams are about to discover that poachers are the least of their worries. There is something hunting the whales...

Something big
Something prehistoric.
Something terrifying.
MEGATOOTH!

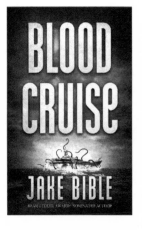

BLOOD CRUISE
by Jake Bible

Ben Clow's plans are set. Drop off kids, pick up girlfriend, head to the marina, and hop on best friend's cruiser for a weekend of fun at sea. But Ben's happy plans are about to be changed by a tentacled horror that lurks beneath the waves.

International crime lords! Deep cover black ops agents! A ravenous, bloodsucking monster! A storm of evil and danger conspire to turn Ben Clow's vacation from a fun ocean getaway into a nightmare of a Blood Cruise!

CHECK OUT OTHER GREAT DEEP SEA THRILLERS

SEA RAPTOR
by John J. Rust

From terrorist hunter to monster hunter! Jack Rastun was a decorated U.S. Army Ranger, until an unfortunate incident forced him out of the service. He is soon hired by the Foundation for Undocumented Biological Investigation and given a new mission, to search for cryptids, creatures whose existence has not been proven by mainstream science. Teaming up with the daring and beautiful wildlife photographer Karen Thatcher, they must stop a sea monster's deadly rampage along the Jersey Shore. But that's not the only danger Rastun faces. A group of murderous animal smugglers also want the creature. Rastun must utilize every skill learned from years of fighting, otherwise, his first mission for the FUBI might very well be his last.

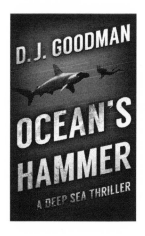

OCEAN'S HAMMER
by D.J. Goodman

Something strange is happening in the Sea of Cortez. Whales are beaching for no apparent reason and the local hammerhead shark population, previously believed to be fished to extinction, has suddenly reappeared. Marine biologists Maria Quintero and Kevin Hoyt have come to investigate with a television producer in tow, hoping to get footage that will land them a reality TV show. The plan is to have a stand-off against a notorious illegal shark-fishing captain and then go home.

Things are not going according to plan.

There is something new in the waters of the Sea of Cortez. Something smart. Something huge. Something that has its own plans for Quintero and Hoyt.

CHECK OUT OTHER GREAT DEEP SEA THRILLERS

THEY RISE
by Hunter Shea

Some call them ghost sharks, the oldest and strangest looking creatures in the sea.

Marine biologist Brad Whitley has studied chimaera fish all his life. He thought he knew everything about them. He was wrong. Warming ocean temperatures free legions of prehistoric chimaera fish from their methane ice suspended animation. Now, in a corner of the Bermuda Triangle, the ocean waters run red. The 400 million year old massive killing machines know no mercy, destroying everything in their path. It will take Whitley, his climatologist ex-wife and the entire US Navy to stop them in the bloodiest battle ever seen on the high seas.

SERPENTINE
by Barry Napier

Clarkton Lake is a picturesque vacation spot located in rural Virginia, great for fishing, skiing, and wasting summer days away.

But this summer, something is different. When butchered bodies are discovered in the water and along the muddy banks of Clarkton Lake, what starts out as a typical summer on the lake quickly turns into a nightmare.

This summer, something new lives in the lake...something that was born in the darkest depths of the ocean and accidentally brought to these typically peaceful waters.

It's getting bigger, it's getting smarter...and it's always hungry.

Made in the USA
Monee, IL
21 September 2020